THE SONS OF WANT

The SONS OF WANT

by

HARRY WILLIAM WILLIAMS

Illustrated by the author

EGON PUBLISHERS LTD

First published in 1997
by Egon Publishers Ltd.
Royston Road, Baldock, Herts SG7 6NW

Copyright © Harry W. Williams

ISBN 1 899998 22 5

Illustrations by the author

Printed in England by
Streets Printers
Royston Road, Baldock, Herts SG7 6NW

To Esther and Alice

By the same author

Non-fiction
The Miracle of Medicine Hill
Booth-Tucker, William Booth's first gentleman
I couldn't call my life my own

Fiction
The General has decided

'Blessings abound where e'er He reigns,
The prisoner leaps to lose his chains;
The weary find eternal rest,
And all the sons of want are blest.'

ISAAC WATTS

'To work for love, is to set a proper example
and if happiness is the profit,
then the example is worth our scrutiny.'

ERIC LINKLATER
'A year of space'

Chapter One
AMBROSE JONES COLLEGE

Brother and sister surveyed the beauty spot

'Ek anna memsahib,' challenged the Lahore urchin – longhaired, brighteyed and barefoot.

'Siraf ek anna.' Only one anna, he repeated in more wheedling tone.

'Do paisa,' responded fairheaded, neatly knickered Jonathan Lindsey, at eight a stout defender of his widowed mother, Jane, and already an experienced bargainer.

'Chup raho,' Jane admonished the boy in his tattered shirt, with broad wicker basket at the ready on his hip, impatient to carry her purchases as she moved along the open-fronted shops of the Anarkali bazaar.

'Tin paisa main deta hun.' She split the difference and terminated the argument.

Alim Salim, the Muslim shopkeeper perched high above the piled trays and open sacks of foodstuffs, cocked an experienced eye on this familiar scene and waited for the Englishwoman's order.

1

'Can we have some dates Mum?' pleaded Jonathan, as he saw the bania break open a wooden case to reveal the solid block of tightly compressed fruit. His sister Mary watched with hope.

'Alright – half a seer', Jane smiled at the expectant salesman who, alert for the decision, had already plied his steel, offering dates to each of the baba-log. Jonathan, though nearly two years younger than his sister, was usually in the van when action was called for. They both loved these bazaar trips; it was part of the real India that they rediscovered when they came down from school for the Christmas holiday. They'd been at the hill schools in Naini Tal for just six months and since Jonathan had been only two when they had left Moradabad, his birthplace, he had few personal memories. But some tales had been told so often that they seemed to the children like personal recollections. At school it was an expurgated India that penetrated the grounds of the American missionary establishments. Here in the Anarkali, 300 years of spilt spices and the endless passage of buffaloes and donkeys had impregnated the bricks and cobbles, to give the authentic aroma of India. The basket-boy had watched the bania's largesse with envious eyes. His deference was wearing thin.

'Mujhe do', he wheedled, as he watched Alim Salim clinching the sale with more dates for the children. Jonathan handed one over.

Soon Jane had her crude brown sugar in rough cakes, her atta-or wholemeal flour, lentils and beans. The quartet moved to the colourful array of vegetables and fruit at the next shop. It made the mouth water to run the eye over the neat pyramids of guavas, loquats, limes and mangoes.

There were even apples from Kashmir, highly polished on the bania's dhoti to a deep claret colour. Mary eyed them.

'They haven't the flavour of the Kulu ones,' she volunteered.

'Or even the ones we get in Naini Tal,' from Jonathan. Eventually the long list in Jane's neat hand had been ticked off. Brushing aside the cloth merchant's pleas to buy a dress-length of printed cotton or Chinese silk, the little group headed back through Shah Jehan's lofty arch, with its intricately carved brickwork. In a patch of shade under a gnarled shisham tree their tonga waited; the horse contentedly munching in his nosebag, the syce smoking an acrid bidi cupped in his hands.

The only vehicle in the Salvation Army establishment was a perk of the Territorial Commander, Colonel Renard. It was a large black tonga that outclassed the ordinary man's taxi in Lahore. Its steed was larger and fitter. Jonathan perched high on the back seat, basked in the envious stares of tonga-wallahs sitting sideways on the shafts of their tatty vehicles. The horse, from long experience of such jaunts, knew the way as he trotted home, clip-clopping along the Mall past Falletti's. Here rich sahibs dined and mahjong ladies entertained their partners to tea and the petit-fours, for which the restaurant was famous. The horse slowed at the parting of the ways, where Queen Victoria, frozen in white marble, surveyed the traffic from her throne. They turned right into Queen's Road, for the headquarters and the girls' boarding school. Jane was mother to 80 Indian girls.

For Jonathan, the exciting point of the trip came soon after leaving the Anarkali. They passed to the left of an ornate Persian cannon, raised on a plinth, in the middle of the road. It stood outside the museum, of which Kipling's father had been curator. Kipling had immortalised the gun as Kim's. Jonathan could see the mercurial Anglo-Indian boy perched on it as he contemplated his next escapade. Of course the whole city had been Kipling's, as a cub-reporter. He had been as familiar with the bhistis, as with the more exclusive society of the Raj.

The horse slowed to a crawl as the tonga passed between the lofty brick pillars of the school compound. They were home. With a small tip to the syce, Jane hoisted the big basket and skipped up the verandah steps and through the heavy teak doors into the gol-kamra, her sitting room. Half-a-dozen doors opened from this large central hall, with its polished cement floor covered by faded cotton dhurries. Jonathan made for the one to his bedroom, small but personal. Here he could display his treasures, a welcome contrast to a school dormitory. There was an alcove in one wall, fitted with white shelves that held his books, his embryo geology collection and a few Indian figures carved in ivory or rosewood. He sat on the bed for a few minutes, accommodating to the cool dimness after the heat and glare of the streets.

It was winter. Punjab nights were cold, but the rising sun slowly wakened the coolies huddled in their coarse blankets. They had to compete for labour on empty stomachs. In the gardens of Government House roses bloomed in profusion. Even in Jane's simple garden beyond the rough lawn, massed shrubs climbed to the top of the perimeter wall – a blaze of colour. Those that had no flowers made their contribution in leaf, even the desiccated crotons.

It would soon be a year since Jane had returned to India with Mary and Jonathan. Life hadn't altered much in the six years she had been away. From the conversation of their parents, it was a life familiar to the children. They had settled in very quickly. Jonathan's lively imagination found ample fuel. He lingered on his bed, thinking of Kim; of the Anarkali where he had wandered and found adventure.

3

The Anarkali not only smelt of India, its sounds were equally evocative. The buzz of Urdu, the twang of cheap barjas and the more refined plaint of the sitar, were accompanied by the high-pitched crooning of women, and always to the rhythm of the drumming of nimble fingers on the black rim of a tabla. He never watched the swaying drummer, with his double-jointed fingers, without seeing his father improvising on a tambourine in Harwich. He had only seen his father between long intervals at the war, but they were halcyon days when he came on leave; days by the sea in Norfolk. Sitting on the pebble bank at Cley, or on the quay at Blakeney, Stephen had conjured up India for his son. It was his tragic death, whilst on a relief mission to Yugoslavia, that had projected the family back to India. Jonathan had always been able to fill out the story from an ever willing Jane, when father had to return to duty. Mum was a natural story teller and this was her own romance. She was only 34 and her 12 years with Stephen were still vivid. She was easy to persuade.

Jonathan came out of his bedroom and launched immediately into a memory of a visit to his father's birthplace.

'I remember the long train journey to Scotland. Dad was very excited.'

'I think you were even more excited. Do you remember the fun you had with Grandpa and Grandma Lindsey in Melrose?'

He could remember his grandmother for her scones and her delight in him. He wasn't so sure about his grandfather. Truth to tell he had been afraid of him; he was so old and stern. But his mother was now launched; she was full of her own questions.

'Do you remember your uncle Alistair teaching you to tickle a trout? You promptly fell into the Tweed,' she laughed. What Jonathan would not forget was being carried up the lane over his father's shoulder, dripping water and feeling very cold.

'I remember Grandma giving me bread and milk with a lot of sugar and carrying me up to bed. Father was born in that house wasn't he?' An amusing thought crossed his mind.

'But the Lindseys aren't Army are they?' His mother caught the smile that crossed his face.

'You were trying to catch a picture of your grandfather with a cornet under his arm – weren't you? Your father came to The Salvation Army when he was an undergraduate in Edinburgh. It was years later that he became an officer and was posted to India.' She paused, remembering that dreadful summer when she was taken to Simla as a very sick young woman.

'I'm glad he did' she said, and fell silent. With the empathy that was so evident in their relationship, Jonathan questioned,

4

'Where did you meet him?'

'We met in Simla and I fell in love with him. You remember what good fun he was. He not only found enjoyment in all life but had a great ability in sharing it. I loved him so much.' she said simply, checked by the intensity of feeling that she had aroused. Jonathan put his arms around her neck. He never felt shy with his mother.

In the six years that Jane had been away from India, her thoughts had been firmly anchored in the hectic life of Europe at war. French had ousted Urdu. But from the moment that she had unpacked her box, she had felt at home again, although this was her first experience of the Punjab. They had arrived in March, Jane less than three months a widow. After a fortnight to settle in, the trio set off on the 500-mile journey to Naini Tal, high above the plains in the United Provinces of Agra and Oudh. Jane had memories of it and could recall the girls' school amongst the trees on the slopes rising on the lefthand side of the lake. It was suddenly glimpsed as the bus turned the last bend in the road and slowed to a halt at the terminus, by the gesticulating crowd of coolies. She did not see the boys' boarding school, until the sad morning when she said goodbye to Jonathan. It was on the opposite side of the lake, so high that she felt quite dizzy as she looked out over the plains, 7000 ft below. Perhaps it was the devastating sense of loss at leaving the children, more than the precipitate drop before her, which caused this. She was a little hurt that Jonathan did not appear to share her feeling. Buoyed up with the excitement of a new experience, he had managed a smile when they parted. She was near to tears all the way down to the train. But she recovered. Her faith was of the simple kind, common amongst Salvationists; a profound trust in Christ, her Lord, to whom she spoke intimately and often. She had never doubted his promise to be with his disciples to the end of time. So she took hold of herself as the slow, metre-gauge train chugged on towards Bareilly. She looked out on the endless green fields, within a month of harvest, giving Mary and Jonathan consciously to her Lord's care.

Colonel Renard had not met the Lindseys until they steamed into Lahore on the Frontier Mail. He warmed to Jane immediately.

'Plucky little woman,' he told his wife, 'coming straight out after losing her husband so tragically. She's not a bit sorry for herself. The girls in boarding will eat her, as well as her two lively children.'

It was not surprising that when the issue of reopening 'The Gables', as the holiday home for the missionary officers, appeared on the agenda for his weekly business meeting with his Chief Secretary, Renard pre-empted any discussion on whom to appoint as matron by suggesting,

'I think we'll appoint Major Lindsey; it will give her a chance to have her children with her for three months.'

So on the first week in June, Jane peered out of her compartment window on the Calcutta Mail as it pulled into Moradabad station. Yes, there were white uniforms on the platform. The doctor's wife and one of the Canadian nurses from the hospital were glancing along the coaches. Then in the background she spotted the beaming face of Ghulam Nabi, the Muslim servant she had taught to cook. How long ago was it? Yes it must be all of nine years. Still beaming, he salaamed her as he took charge of the luggage, whilst her friends had time to greet her.

Moradabad was an important railway junction and administrative headquarters, so the station merited a European dining room. But the prices were beyond Salvation Army purses, so Jane was ushered into the zenana waiting room where Esther Snow and Hannah Winters opened their picnic basket. There was nutty homemade bread, papaya and a chatti of cool, sweet nimbu pani. Nothing was so refreshing as lime-juice.

'The war has made great changes already, but I assure you that you are not forgotten here. Of course we miss the towering personality of Dr. Sikander', said Esther Snow, 'but the hospital keeps busy.'

They chatted on until the little train on the metre-gauge branch line to Kashipur and Kathgodam, hooted its readiness to depart.

Jane was helped into a 3rd-class compartment.

'No need for a zenana compartment for so short a journey', volunteered Hannah, and they all agreed: zenana accommodation was always overfilled with mothers, babes and luggage.

They had not mentioned Stephen, but he was back with her as they chugged leisurely through the Terai, the dense jungle that was only three feet from the windows on either side of this single track. It was used principally for transporting the heavy hardwood logs to the saw-mills.

'This was where Stephen was often offered a tiger-shoot by zemindar patients or the sircar-log', she mused. 'I always saw tigers as I looked out from this train.' There was the remembered fight over her luggage as she transhipped from train to bus at the foothills' terminus. It was then sheer bliss to sit back on her wooden seat beside the driver, as they climbed higher and higher, cooler and cooler, until she felt cold enough to forage for a cardigan in her bag. The last half-a-dozen miles of the road was like a shelf on the steep cliffs facing the plains they had left. Then a sharp right turn through a gully, and the panting bus changed gear with what sounded like audible relief. The lake was before them.

Her joy was full as she saw not only the turbanned figure of Mohan

Das, but Mary and Jonathan, their faces beaming, although they made no rush for her as she alighted. What changes boarding school made in one's children, she mused. But their arms went round her neck, as Mohan Das dealt with the coolies and checked her luggage.

'Some of it is for the home', she laughed as the children looked unbelievingly, as three trunks were hoisted down from the roof of the bus onto the coolies' heads. It was Saturday and the children chorused 'We've got exeats for the whole weekend Mum.'

The Gables was a cheap imitation of an English country house, with whitewashed plaster walls and a corrugated iron roof, tailored to a line of dormer windows on the third floor. The roof was a pillarbox red, already dulled by two monsoons. The house was a hundred and fifty feet up from the lake on a steep incline, so that the bottom line of bedrooms was built into the slope below the broad verandah, with its wrought-iron balustrade. The children explored the house and chose their own bedroom with a view over the lake. It was only a partitioned room with colourwashed hardboard, but to know that Mum was downstairs was great. The house smelled musty and damp. Neglected for nine months, yet in a week or two it would be crowded. Jane would have the little room off the kitchen and stores. She would be up early to get the day organised before her guests appeared. There were always the eager ones she remembered, for whom a run around the lake before breakfast was de rigueur. Brother and sister stood at the window of their room and surveyed the beauty-spot.

'That's my dormitory,' Mary pointed to a long two-storey block in the cluster of school buildings, on the hillside across the lake.

They spent the whole evening in the sitting-room, with a log-fire and the douce light of an oil-lamp, its polished brass adding to its own gleam. Mother was an eager listener as they described life in a boarding school, vying with each other in embroidering their tale. Next morning chappatti and gur had never tasted so good as, with mother presiding, endless cups of tea were poured. Mohan had chanced his arm and bought apples. He knew they were too expensive, even if available, on the plains. The children munched contentedly as plans for the day were discussed. It was Sunday; quite early they heard the tolling of the single bell in the corrugated iron steeple of the lakeside church below them.

'Can we go to the Methodist church by the bus-stand?'

'Why so eager Jonathan?' asked Jane.

'Well, we go there from school on Sunday mornings and I'd like to see John Grundy and Arthur Chalmers.' He didn't divulge his real reason, which was that his friends might meet his mother. He had an immense pride in her. When he had told Tom Bennett of his exeat, his friend had said,

'Your mum has real guts to come back so soon after your father was killed.'

Jonathan held his peace, but he had a very clear recollection of the morning that his mother had told them of her acceptance of the appointment to Lahore.

'Your father loved India and would want us to continue to serve her people.' And then very simply, but so sincerely, that the three of them were in tears, 'I'll never be nearer to him than in India.'

Jane brought Jonathan back to the present by referring to Mary.

'Is that alright with you?'

'Yes – we go there on Sunday mornings too but I can't say that I'm desperate to see my friends when we've got you.'

Down on the level, coolies were ready for the early bus from Kathgodam. Outside the church quite a few horses were tethered, pawing the ground as their syces held the bridles. The organ was playing a Methodist favourite, 'Sagina' and there was a decorous humming of the tune in the pews.

'You'll like old Dosti', he whispered to his mother as he led her into a pew.

'He's the school chaplain; an old boy himself!'

'Why do you call him "Dosti"? Because it means friend?'

'You must ask his father' sniggered the boy. 'His name is Dosti.'

Jane was soon lost in her own thoughts as the minister preached a sermon geared to the outlook of his young audience. It was a long while since she had been in a Methodist church and she was in the mood for daydreaming. The little chapel of the 'Prims' in Upper Sheringham came into focus. Their lusty singing could be heard in the quiet parts of the liturgy, as she sat in the parish church long ago. There were special pews reserved for the Upcher retainers. Cousin Alice who had married the groom, Timothy, would still be there. Dear Alice had taught the ropes to a very young kitchen-maid. The contrast with her own adventures was great. Her story moved before her like a film. She recaptured the Dickensian London she'd experienced at first-hand, in the lanes off Whitechapel Road. The scene moved on to Kaira in Gujerat, with famine children, emaciated and listless. Then she remembered her own dire bouts of malaria, which had taken her to Simla as a pale, thin wreck. It was a good thing that she had three weeks to recover before Stephen walked into the dining room at Portmore, and into her life. Inconsequentially she brought to mind a paragraph in an English magazine, which spoke of a son of the last Earl

8

of Portmore, who had built a house for himself and his three Muslim wives when he retired from the army. Could it be…? but her reverie was broken by the organ which pealed out the introit to 'And can it be?'.

As they came down the steps of the church, she was greeted by young Bennett.

'Hullo Mrs Lindsey, Father says that you are still remembered in Moradabad with affection. Mum would like you to visit.'

'How is the weaving faring?'

'There are new patterns but still the same looms that you put in. There are still many of the same settlers plying them.'

'You must come to tea at The Gables some time. I suppose that it is too short notice to suggest this afternoon?'

The boy was all eagerness.

'I'll waylay Mrs Braun as she comes out of the choir-room. I'm sure she'll be a good sport.' He sped off.

Jane was still debating with herself. Should she go up to the schools on Monday morning after the children had returned? It would be lovely to have them with her for the next three months. She gave it further thought whilst she was with them for a sedate Sunday afternoon walk. For once it seemed strange to her that the Indians were out shopping. She decided that it would be wise not to disturb the boarding pattern so soon after enrolment. So she sent them back with chits; she would visit the schools but content herself with their company each weekend.

So it was that she met Miss Sherriff, Mary's headmistress, and Talbot Braun, the principal at Ambrose Jones School. This time she found the situation of the boys' school superb, with its wide views and the sensation of being on top of the world. In the days that followed she would sometimes stand on the verandah and stare across the lake looking for her daughter amongst the school buildings. One morning it was a netball match that caught her eye, and she recognised Mary as she leapt into the air to score a goal.

It was a month later that Jonathan had his first adventure of a picnic on Cheena Peak. The house was full of tired but cheerful men and women, from a dozen different stations in the U.P. or the Punjab. The middle-aged couples from Bareilly, Kanth, Sheikapura or Ludhiana, were happy to spend their first days in the wicker chairs that stretched the length of the verandah. The yacht-racing season had commenced and there was always plenty to watch. Away to their right, at the end of the tal, where the boat-house and pavilion could be seen, were the 'Flats' with the bandstand. Beyond, on the slope that grew ever steeper as it climbed towards the summit ridge, were the English church and the Government Secretariat buildings, profusely landscaped with trees. To the right of these decorous marks of foreign rule, was a gully redolent of India. When they had acquired their hill legs, the men would enjoy a stroll through the bazaar. Holidays were an opportunity to find a bargain length of Chinese dress material, as a surprise for the wife.

But high above soared the peak. It was first to get the morning sun and a magnet for a communal outing, with a 2000 ft climb to prove they were still young. Robert and Florence Grace, from the Training Home for Indian Officers in Lahore, were friends of Jane. When she brought them a tray of coffee and biscuits, they turned from watching the yachts to greet her.

'You're thoroughly at home here now Jane.'

'Yes, it's a welcome change from eighty chattering girls,' she laughed.

'To have the children at weekends is a delightful bonus.'

'Has there been a picnic to Cheena yet?' asked Bob.

'No, why are you thinking of organising one?'

'What's a holiday in Naini Tal without the mountain-top experience,' he countered.

'If you'd like to organise one for Saturday when the children are out, I'll gladly see to the food.'

'You're on!'

And so it was that on Friday evening, Jonathan and Mary arrived to an excited house. The expedition would set out the next morning at dawn. Robert Grace had made his bandoblast with the ponymen who were standing with their patient horses, as they listened to the regimental band from Delhi, on the Flats. They were playing excerpts from Gilbert and Sullivan. Bob, who was himself a euphonium player, reported at lunchtime. Tom Bennett was with him so they conferred.

'How many mounts shall we need?' asked Bob.

'How many infirm have we?' laughed Tom.

'Well I make it five elderly ladies, but there are two younger ones who are convalescent from malaria.'

'And I suppose John Woolmer, the Chief Secretary, is near enough to retirement to warrant one.'

'That's eight then,' concluded Bennett and they made their deal with the syce.

With the first hint of dawn over the plains to the east, lights were on in The Gables, whilst on the bridlepath horses were neighing vigorously. Two coolies had turned up on a tip from the ponymen; they were quickly engaged to carry the packs of food and utensils which the servants were busily preparing.

Jane's pair were not the only children; young Tom Bennett and Ivor and Violet Grace were there too. They ran ahead up the steep bridlepath. The men, having helped the ladies to mount, brought up the rear. None was an experienced rider but there was little chance of the horses galloping on these steep, narrow paths. And as usual the canny owners kept close to their beasts.

Slowly light filtered into the dark bowl, until the still waters of the lake began to mirror the peak and pearl-green sky. One by one the town's lights were extinguished. The cavalcade reached the rim of hills on the east, where a path went off to Snowview. This spot, with is unsurpassed panorama of Himalayan peaks, would keep for another day; they would start even earlier for that experience.

By the time that they reached the tiny camping-site at the summit, the sun was already high. Balls of mist were forming in the valleys and rolling up to obscure the distant view; none in the party was an experienced climber but all knew the exhilaration of Himalayan vistas. The cook knew the ropes and so did Bennett and Grace. They were old hands at having fun at little expense. The children ran off foraging for brushwood; it was de rigueur to fry the sausages on an open fire. But the cook had left nothing to chance, he already had a sigaree of glowing charcoal and an outsize aluminium kettle boiling for tea. There would be a demand for innumerable mugs and comments on the wonderful aroma of high-grown tea. They weren't planters or affluent, but they knew good tea when they smelled it.

Jonathan, wandering in search of firewood, discovered that the pony-men had tied up their horses to the stunted rhododendron trees that grew at this height. The men were sitting on the grass in pairs, absorbed in the task of shaving each other. To Jonathan they had a dangerous nonchalance. One held a naked Gillette blade between forefinger and thumb, removing his neighbour's stubble adroitly without the aid of lather.

'Ajao chokra,' they shouted to the boy. 'Dekko itna asan hai.' Jonathan drew near as bidden, but could hardly agree that it was simple.

'Char mangta?' he asked them for something to say.

'Ji han,' they chorused, each producing a brass drinking vessel from the folds of their homespun woollen clothes. So the lad had to beg his mother to put on another kettle of water.

By now the sausages were sizzling, and everyone lent a hand to the toasting of thick slices of bread to serve as plates.

'Better than the usual hazri,' laughed Joan Smith, one of the nurses from Moradabad, as she spread the very soft butter. Jane had not forgotten holiday appetites from her own childhood, and for once the children were replete as they sprawled on the coarse grass, munching apples with contentment. By the time that they commenced the descent the sun was high and the day hot, but they still had enough energy to collect posies or to forage for pieces of quartz or mica.

The monsoon came in with a rush, torrential rain causing landslides, with delays on the road into the hill-station. In the dense forest of Himalayan oak, moss, tree-ferns and orchids became florid. Every tree dripped for days on end. Soon the holiday season closed. Government officials returned to Lucknow, whilst Jane packed everything away at The Gables and said goodbye to her pair, comforting them with
'It won't be long before you come down for Christmas.'
Jonathan soon recovered from the parting. He was beginning to enjoy this school. He was not new to discipline and learning was a pleasure.
'You're like your father,' was Jane's inevitable comment. On the whole the staff taught with conviction and warmed to keen students. The school had been started by American missionaries for their own children. By 1920 Americans of all persuasions were being educated at the newer school along the hills to the west. In contemporary style, this new school was co-ed. Ambrose Jones still had its sister school, Butlers, across the lake. Both schools were geared to prepare students for the Cambridge examinations, so they were suitable for English, Indian and Anglo-Indian children. But Ambrose Jones retained an American Principal, Talbot Braun, whose wife, Juanita, taught music. Talbot Braun became Jonathan's role-model as a principal. He was tall and his manner was equally lofty. His M.A., Ph.D. sat him well. He taught history to the senior classes, but remained an Olympian figure, only seen by juniors at morning assembly, or on the special functions that dotted the school year. The Braun's house must have been the original house built on the Sher ka Duandha hill. It was covered in bougainvillaea; at the altitude of seven thousand feet, this was quite a triumph. There were other staff houses on the same level.
The Vice-Principal was Richard Nutt, an Edinburgh M.A. – 'like my father,' Jonathan told Tom. Jonathan fell for his wife, Eleanor, who taught art with rare enthusiasm, in his first year. She in turn found the boy's application and skill commendable, and he became one of her firm favourites. Richard was an evangelical who chose to be secretary of the Crusaders, so the weekly meeting on Friday evening was held in the

Nutt's quarters. It seemed that all the married staff were involved in teaching. The head of maths was an Anglo-Indian with a Lucknow degree. He had met his wife when she was an arts student in the American College for Women. She also taught maths to the junior forms. There were two other English staff members, both celibate. James Hardcastle, with a Cambridge degree and teaching diploma, and Owen Rhys, with an honours degree from London. He taught both Latin and French.

The boys, sooner or later had more intimate contact with Jean Buchan, the matron, and her assistant Chandibai, who had trained in the Nursing School of the American hospital in Rampur, between Moradabad and Bareilly on the main line. Miss Buchan was a graduate of the London Hospital Nursing School, and Jonathan said it was worth going sick to listen to her stories of the hospital in Whitechapel, with a nurse's romantic stories of handsome medical students.

It was a great asset to the new boy, to have Tom Bennett as a cheerful contemporary. He had received all his education in Naini, but until he was eight he was at the junior house at Butler's. They were both entitled to passes to visit their sisters and picnic in the school grounds. They were adept at finding secluded spots which their imaginations could furnish with all manner of exciting possibilities.

They always had a lot of personal news to share. One Friday Mary could hardly wait until the bag of buns was opened to speak of the legendary shikari, Jim Corbett.

'He came to talk to us on Wednesday evening. He had no slides but he made the wildlife of these hills so real. He knows all the birdcalls and can even imitate the monkeys and deer. At the end of his lecture, all the lights were put out and it really sounded as though there were tigers in the room. He had me frightened; it was so real, I was in the forest, not the school hall!'

'I've heard of him, of course; his family goes back a long way. Thompson says that his mother survived the Mutiny, and his father was an apothecary in the East India Company's army.'

'It's strange to think that he's now a sedate member of the Municipal Council.'

'Except that Thompson says that all the coolies know him. His house is at Kalachungi, in the Terai. He walks all the way to council meetings.'

'That's the way to know all the sounds of the jungle.'

'He was a Lt. Colonel in the Indian Army during the war; I wonder whether he ever met Dad?'

With all his holidays in Lahore with Indian girls, Jonathan not only

13

learned Urdu in a colloquial way, but was accustomed to Indian games and foibles. He quickly found friends across communal boundaries. Ram Singh was Hindu; his father taught in a mission school on the plains. Jehangir Cabwallah, a Parsee, hailed from Bombay and was knowledgeable about the wide world. His father had an import/export business and could do favours. Two more of Jonathan's friends were from Moradabad – Ibrahim Allah-ud-din and Arthur Chalmers. Ibrahim's father was a brass merchant, whilst Arthur's was in the East Indian Railway divisional office. Arthur was Anglo-Indian, as was John Thompson. Jonathan soon discovered that John had a fascinating story. His grandfather had come to India as a Salvation Army officer in the 1880s, with the instruction to 'get into the Indian skin'. He promptly married a delightful but low-caste convert in Ahmedabad. He eventually resigned when the practice of mixed marriages was discouraged. An ardent evangelist, he set off to found his own mission amongst the staunch Hindu villagers in the Himalayas, one hundred miles from Naini Tal.

'My Dad says that his father gave him all his education, including Latin and Greek in that remote spot. I'm the first Thompson to come to a boarding school.'

Jonathan found him a refreshing companion. You never knew exactly what attitude he would take in their discussions, though you could be sure that he would be pro-Indian.

Finally there were the two Russians, Peter Drosky and Paul Ustinov. They also fitted none of the regular clans, for their parents had fled from Moscow in 1918, with their terrified children and little else. They had reached India by the arduous caravan route through the Karakorum mountains. The boys had an endless fund of hair-raising stories, told in the ghostly dormitory after lights-out.

On Sunday afternoons there were bible-classes held in the homes of the married staff. They were officially optional but no-one missed attending for there was always an invitation to stay to tea, which meant home-baking in place of the usual stacks of bread and butter. Jonathan was in Mrs Braun's class. She was from the Middle-West, heartland of Methodism. She had the easy smiling hallmark of her church. At forty-five with no children of her own, she welcomed her class of twenty, eagerly. From teaching music she knew the boys well. She had already discovered that Jonathan's father had been a competent pianist as well as a trumpeter. The boy was already familiar with crochets and quavers, and capable of playing simple minuets – rather than Czerny's exercises.

Unbeknown to the children, Jane had smoothed the way for them whilst at The Gables. Following her initial visits some of the staff-wives took to calling at 'The Gables', on trips to the bazaar. It was halfway-house and Jane brewed good coffee.

'She's an original thinker,' Juanita said to her husband on the morning she had found herself unburdening to Jane. 'I wonder what her background is?'

For her part, Jane learned that whilst all boarding schools were a breach of family life and a weakening of parental discipline, these Naini schools were not social factories, designed to turn out standard English ladies and gentlemen. The core of the staff had a true sense of Christian vocation and a love for their pupils. They were not exactly her mould – but they were not so different.

So Jonathan and Mary settled into a life which swung between Lahore and Naini Tal. Theirs' was a kindly world, in which all missionary women of their acquaintance were 'aunties'. They could be trusted implicitly.

From the Olympian heights of Territorial Headquarters, Colonel Renard watched the 'children of the regiment', as he called them to his wife. He continued to send Jane to run the holiday home, year by year. What had started as compassion, continued from sound judgement.

'We've never had a matron as competent, or as well liked by the officers.' Mrs Renard stated when the subject of summer breaks surfaced on the agenda, as it did every Spring.

Jonathan stood on the hillside high above the school, filled with a strange emotion. He'd stood at this point on many occasions, but this morning it looked totally different. The sun was still veiled in eastern mist, which also hid the distant plain of the Ganges, although he knew that its fields and huddled villages of mud houses would soon materialise. This morning he looked on a world of enchantment that he had never glimpsed before. He knew that they said he had a sunny disposition, and he realised it was true that he had an imagination that had peopled his world since he was a toddler. But this was other; as though he were a different person.

Autumn at seven thousand feet in the Himalayas is cold. But when the mist has cleared the sunlight produces a fairyland of changing vistas, from the ethereal to the most gorgeous pageant of colour. The cloud was already moving in the light breeze. It was rolling up the gullies, rustling the evergreens and lifting orange and red leaves from the beeches, maples, oaks and the towering alders. An early-riser, he loved these dawns, awakening the slumbering hill-town. Periodically a school party would set off even earlier than this, to be at Snowview before the long line of peaks was obscured by cloud. As the sun rose, chattering ceased, and awe gripped the most stolid. The whole horizon gleamed with peaks, from Kamet to Kanchenjunga. But the exaltation of spirit he felt this morning was unique. It was as though he was seeing the world anew. He was awed but at peace. With all the romantic poets they had been studying, he agreed that God was in his world this morning.

At eleven Jonathan was at ease with the school and his fellows. He saw them very clearly and detachedly in this exalted mood. They were a mixed bunch in nationality and culture and had been moulded by a gregarious lifestyle. He fitted because of his parents' vocation.

He surveyed the familiar landscape that he was seeing with new eyes. It wasn't difficult to accept the story that he was standing on the rim of an extinct volcano. He looked down to the lake, dedicated to a goddess. At this hour it was a mirror for the town and its dark heights. Its depths, he was told, had never been plumbed. Inconsequentially he spotted the small restaurant on the flats, where they bought a plate of chips and doused them liberally with free ketchup. He picked out the tower of the English church. He had read the brass memorial in the nave, which told of the Victorian tragedy, when a huge landslide had denuded Cheena and buried the children, English and Indian with their nannies.

He was reasoning with extraordinary clarity. Ideas and feelings which had previously been disparate were coming together. As the breeze ruffled his hair, he saw the biblical scene described by the apostle John, when a member of the Jewish Sanhedrin came to Christ after dark, seeking enlightenment on the daring new teaching he had heard at second-hand. How could a man of mature years start again?

'The wind blows without human control; you don't know where it is coming from or where it is going. So is everyone born of the Spirit.'

This was it. In his inspired mood he reinterpreted an old testament story. Jacob, going to bed with a stone for his pillow, had a dream which seemed to resolve his dilemma. When he woke up, the dream was still with him.

'Surely God is in this place.' he had said.

He had to fit this experience into the framework of the spiritual teaching he had received at home and in school. 'Is this what they call conversion? Is God speaking to me through the beauty of the world?' he asked himself.

He'd had his moments of high seriousness, usually in the school chapel. Talbot Braun could be most dignified and persuasive. He came from New England – Longfellow country. 'Life is real and life is earnest, and the grave is not its goal', had companioned him through his career. He had certainly moved the spirit of this young Salvationist, but nothing had ever clicked until this morning. One thing his upbringing had impressed on him; spiritual resolve must have a practical expression. He certainly wanted to be like his parents, with a clear sense of duty. Inconsequentially he recalled his father returning from the trenches with a pack on his back. Jonathan had dived into it whilst his father was obsessed with his mother. He had found what his laughing father had called 'hard tack' and commenced to munch the little square ration biscuits. 'I'm going to help the poor nobodies as my Dad did' he decided.

'Lost in wonder love and praise?' shouted Ghulam Masih from the terrace below him. It brought Jonathan back to the present in some embarrassment, but he quickly recovered to call back.

'Who wouldn't be on a morning like this?' Ghulam was a good fellow.

'I'll join you in a few minutes.' He wanted to continue his reverie for a little longer.

The silence of the mountains, hardly yet awake, was broken by the sound of music. Clear on the frosty air came the skirl of the pipes. The Gurkhas were having their morning parade at the depot on the other side of the lake, high above Mary's school. Another ordinary day had begun. He glanced around the summit of Sher ka Duandha on which he stood. It had been levelled to provide pitches for hockey and football. From the terrace below Ghulam Masih again called to him.

'Come on Jonathan; the breakfast bell will be going any minute.'

Jonathan ran down the steps to the next level on which the main classrooms were situated. Ghulam Masih was the son of the Anglican Archdeacon of Lahore. His mother, Aminabai, often invited Jane to tea. He'd been once. In place of cakes there had been tasty morsels of vegetable in batter, hot to the table from the boiling fat. As he slipped his arm through Ghulam's, he felt that India was his home. He certainly prized those pakoras and hot Punjabi curry above other dishes.

The school had been built on the steep hillside, by excavating levels, then using the excavated rock to build retaining walls for the next. Before they reached the third terrace, with the Assembly Hall, Library and Dining Hall, the breakfast bell rang out. They were hungry; they could smell the toasting bread as they broke into a trot past the library. The cooks produced mountains of it, on a huge iron-plate, 'looted from a battleship's armour plating', said one of the wags. There would be soft

17

butter which contrasted ill with the hard variety he remembered from England. But there would also be homemade jam or marmalade. The staff wives had periodic frenzies of turning hill fruit into conserve. It was usually on a Saturday; a delicious aroma clung to the dining-room all day. Seated at long benches and refectory tables, like monks, they were called to order for grace. A prefect pronounced this with due dignity before chatter resumed. Meals were always noisy, but despite the laughter, the food disappeared at an alarming rate.

For once Jonathan had been silent, he really wanted more time to think things out. He had half-an-hour before the first class, so he disappeared amongst the trees and sat on a boulder. Below him were the dormitories and below them the staff houses. If Jane were here he could talk to her. She was the utterly dependable figure on which he had built his understanding of life. She'd be up already – probably in the kitchen watching the khansamah and his assistants as their prepared the girls' chapattis. He could almost smell the spicy sauce heating up as a delectable garnish for the plain diet. He could hear the high-pitched chatter of eighty girls, awakening to a cold world of bare shisham trees and wintry sunshine. He'd be going down the hill for Christmas in a few weeks. He'd talk to Jane then about his new resolve.

He'd be in the first party for Kathgodam with Ghulam. It was still a perilous trip for the over-loaded buses; local carpenters' bodies on Ford chassis. The older boys could remember the days when they either walked by the much shorter but steep bridle-path, or when accompanied by mother and trunks, by horse-drawn tongas. Little had changed for a century until the world war. That had produced sweeping changes, not only in lifestyle but in political expectations. There was now a definite impatience with foreign rule. Indian soldiers had fought side by side with British comrades in the trenches at Flanders. They had used the same hospitals and brothels. The British were off their pedestal. There had been rioting and death in the Punjab shortly before the Lindseys' return.

But this morning as Jonathan set out for the classroom, he was conscious only of himself. He had grown up.

1926 was a momentous year for the Lindsey family. At its close, Mary would sit the Senior Cambridge exam; by the following Spring she would be off to England with her mother. Jane was enjoying her daughter, now old enough to share impressions and debate the news. They were of an equal height and definitely companionable. In taking

Mary home, it was possible that she herself would not return. The thought made her savour the choice memories of the past six years. It was a sharp fragrance that distilled, for the Lahore family had shared sorrows as well as joys. The girls were mostly from farming communities and with eighty of them, bereavements, bad harvests and cattle diseases were as common as new babies. There had even been an influenza epidemic which had invaded the hostel itself. Jane had grieved for those who had died, as if they were her own daughters.

That summer Jane had been at The Gables as usual. It marked the commencement of a new friendship. One August morning she had seen the children off to school after their usual exeats, had completed the hisab – the daily account with the cook – and with a wry smile turned towards her room for a few moments quiet. She had listened to the khansamah's recital of his day's purchases. He was a good cook but could also cook the accounts. She had to be vigilant to keep his excesses to a minimum. He reeled off the vegetables, spices and dhals, bought at his regular daily visit to the bazaar. Her orders for meat, milk, eggs and bread were delivered and paid for direct. There was a weekly visit to the fruit market. She enjoyed the opportunity to choose, in an area where monotony was all too common. There were always surprises, as when strawberries or lychees turned up. She also valued contact with the ruddy-cheeked hill-women who trudged into the town at dawn, with huge baskets of produce on their heads. They made minimal profit on their wares but seemed so content with their hard lot. They sat laughing with their neighbours over private village jokes, or parting their bodices to suckle the latest baby. They spoke pahari – a hill dialect, which isolated them from the mass of Urdu speakers. She had tried to limit the cook's daily visits to market but quickly learned that he not only made a few annas a day out of her, sufficient to pay for his own requirements, but collected a little sweetener from the stall-holders he chose to patronise; a turnip here and a few chillies there. For these, she discovered, he carried a separate hessian bag, which went into a corner before he unloaded his purchases for the house. No doubt a few more vegetables went into it before he left for home. No wonder they prefer to work for a memsahib, she thought; they would find it less profitable in an Indian establishment.

Preoccupied with their thoughts, she overlooked the fact that in these hill houses, the door frames were not sunk to floor level, so that there was a lintel. She caught her foot on it as she entered her room. She stumbled and then fell heavily against the bedside chair, which toppled with a clatter. She picked herself up quickly; Mohan Das might have heard and come rushing to help her. She closed the door and slipped the bolt. Taking off her overall, she unbuttoned her blouse. She had hit her right breast and it was painful. She sat on the bed and eased the breast out of the bra, she only wore in the hills. Running her finger over the painful spot she discovered a small lump well behind the nipple. She felt sure it was new. With a woman's fear of cancer, the lump dispelled the pain of the accident. She swung her feet onto the bed and relaxed to make a more thorough examination.

She lay for a moment daydreaming. Stephen was beside her, tenderly caressing her breast. As she cupped it herself, a vast sadness swept over her. It must be nine years since that last carefree holiday in Norfolk, before he had set out for Serbia. She longed for that touch again.

'Dear Lord help me', she prayed, 'help me to make a better job of today, because of the wonderful memories that I have.' The pain had eased. Slipping on her bra and blouse, she sat up. 'What do I do now?' she pondered. The Civil Surgeon was an Indian Civil Service Major, whom she had met informally at a school prize-day. She had been munching a sandwich from one hand and sipping fruit-punch, from one of Juanita Braun's best glasses, in the other. They had eyed each other for a few seconds before speaking. He saw a healthy blonde, whom he quickly put into a mid-thirties bracket. She compared him with doctors in the service that she had already met. She knew that Naini Tal was a prize appointment, for it entailed care of the top 'Brass' throughout the summer. She liked what she saw and was glad that there was medical help, if any of her guests had need.

Now she needed it herself, so she sought an appointment with Major Palgrave at the Ramsay Hospital. It was a small hospital for European patients not far above The Gables. Jonathan had told her that it was really a large house, built by one of the 19th century nabobs, who had done well out of the annexation of the Punjab.

'Cecil Bough, who started our school, found it empty and was able to rent it for his first class,' Jonathan had said. 'It soon became too small and he had to move to the present site.' Since her first meeting with the surgeon, Jane had chaperoned several visiting women officers who needed advice, not obtainable in their lonely appointments. She had noted and appreciated his pleasant manner but was most impressed by his brisk style and quick judgement.

Palgrave was a bachelor of 45, a veteran of the war. He had entered Jerusalem with Allenby, in the first ambulance of his Casualty Clearing Station. As a fellow of the Royal College of Surgeons of Edinburgh, plus twenty years of service to his credit, he wouldn't have been surprised if his next appointment were to a medical college as a

Professor of Surgery. He'd never analysed why he remained a bachelor. He wasn't a philanderer nor did he dislike feminine company. He supposed that it was that Indian batmen were always available and highly efficient. And there was a plethora of service clubs when he felt gregarious. So he'd never spent time or money on a home.

When Jane stepped into his consulting room, he instantly recognised her and smiled. Her face, her movements and her voice were so alive. He had pigeon-holed her as a 'religious', but utterly different from the convent type. He'd also learnt that her husband had seen service in the war, though he had not died in the trenches of France.

The English matron, a very dignified Miss Peabody, chaperoned the doctor as Jane undressed behind the screen, on the window side of the room. This was probably the nabob's morning-room, she'd have to tell Jon. Palgrave put her hand on her hip and asked her to press hard, as he ran his flattened hand over the full breasts. He concentrated on the small nodule he had confirmed, checking that there was no fixation to nipple or the underlying muscle. Finally he probed the axilla with a grunt of satisfaction. He could feel no enlarged glands. 'So far, so good, Mrs Lindsey. Clinically it seems a benign tumour; though I'd still advise you to have it out and a biopsy done.'

Jane's feelings were mixed but under control.

'I'm in your hands doctor,' she assured him.

'Well if matron will arrange your admission, I'll do it on my list on Friday. The sooner it is out the better. Do you say "amen" to that?' he laughed.

The news was shared with the children.

'Is he going to cut you?' asked an apprehensive Jonathan.

His sister, with feminine intuition, merely gripped her mother's hand.

'It won't hurt,' she reassured them, 'for I will be under an anaesthetic.' The worst thing will be waiting for the pathology report from Kasauli laboratory, she thought, but kept this to herself.

But she would always remember the stifling mask held over her face. She recalled that Stephen had said, 'Queen Victoria tried out chloroform for one of her confinements.' Miss Peabody dripped it on at a slow but steady pace. The last thing that she remembered, was being told to count up to ten. She hadn't got very far.

Jane was busy at The Gables, so the days went by very quickly; once again she was back in Palgrave's consulting room. This time he was smiling with obvious pleasure.

'As I thought, the verdict is an adenoma, so you can forget the episode.' Their eyes met. In Jane's there were tears of relief. 'Sister says the stitches came out cleanly, and since I used one of the new circumferential incisions under the breast, you will not even notice a scar.' He knew that most women set great store by this; whether the religious were any different, he hadn't a clue.

Another chapter closed, thought Jane as she came down the path. 'I'm skipping', she realised. In the event, it was the beginning of a friendship that was to prove rewarding. She invited the Major to tea. When the last of the guests had gone, he lingered. They sat on the verandah watching the last of the yachts racing, chatting companionably. The shots from the starter's gun reverberated in the crater, but they were unaware of it.

'I suppose you will soon be packing up,' a smile played around his lips, 'The Government will be moving down to Lucknow for the winter. But you're not going to get rid of me. I'm going to be a neighbour of yours in Lahore.'

'Oh!' she ejaculated involuntarily.

'In their wisdom, "the powers-that-be" are appointing me Professor of Surgery, at the Mayo College Hospital.'

'That's going to be very nice for me, though I don't want any more little lumps, however benign.' She beamed at him and turning the conversation off herself, asked, 'I suppose you'll have a buggy rather than a horse?'

'I'm thinking of being more radical than that, by investing in a car.'

'Really!'

'I shall miss the informality of what is essentially here, a country life. So maybe with a car I'll be able to get out of the city sometimes. I hope you'll join me on occasion.'

She left it there without comment.

A month or so after his mother had returned to her girls, Jonathan was again on the hockey pitch before breakfast. This time it was Tom Bennett that found him.

'You're a dreamer!'

'I wasn't far away. I was just thinking that hockey is the poor man's polo, and then saw the gorgeous gilded watercolours in the Victoria and Albert Museum in London. They are of Mogul princes on beautiful Arab steeds.'

Tom was looking down at the lake and saw a cavalcade of sahibs riding up the path below the Secretariat.

'I wonder who they are? I thought they had gone down to Lucknow long ago. There are some good horses for you.'

'I'd love a horse of my own. I think the Raj was built on the horse.'

'It's true that all the Imperial Services have riding schools. We have a good one in Moradabad for the Police.'

'I've seen Deputy Commissioners setting out on their winter tours with a string of mounts.'

'I get no further than one of Behari Lal's sorry nags when I'm in funds for my birthday. But even then I feel like a prince for an hour. It's pretty easy to throw off Behari Lal and have a canter. You're on a higher plane than mere pedestrians when you're in the saddle.'

'Let's change the subject' laughed Tom. 'It'll soon be time for the Christmas hols.'

'Whoopee!'

'And you will be calculating that by this time next year you will be off to England with the Senior Cambridge under your belt. Don't you think you should explore your birthplace before you do that?'

'Now that's an idea.'

'What are you going to do when you go home?'

'I don't know. I'm sure my mother would like me to become an officer. The idea doesn't grab me.'

'Mum says I must invite you to spend a week with us before you go on to Lahore for Christmas. What about it?'

'Accepted on the spot. I know mother won't mind; Mary has to stay for he Senior Cambridge, so she won't get down until later. I might well arrange to meet up with her as she comes through.'

The Criminal Tribe's tonga was at Moradabad station. They bowled along the cankah road, which circled the city outside its ancient walls; shaken all too frequently by potholes in the soft limestone surface. The trunks jolted ominously. Skirting the Badaun gate they turned west towards the Civil lines. They passed the Police Training School, lost in its dense screen of trees. On the left was the rambling thatched house of the Deputy Commissioner; a left-over from pre-mutiny days. It was in a large, uncultivated compound. Jonathan could see an armed police guard, standing at ease outside his box. There was another thatched bungalow amongst distant trees.

'Whose is that?' questioned Jonathan, pointing.

'That belongs to a retired Anglo-Indian P.W.D. engineer. He's one of the very experienced oldies, trained by the Royal Engineers at Roorkee. He says that the present young men, straight out from English colleges, have no feel for the country. Do you think that he may have a point?'

'He sounds pure Kipling. I suppose he helped to build some of the railway bridges, with bricks kilned on the river bank.'

23

'I like him. He used to get some of his masons making carvings, in the long evenings in camp. You'd love them. Most of his masons were Hindus, with gods and particularly goddesses in their fingertips. It amused them and gave an extra rupee or two.'

Then it was the house of the Sessions Judge, from the drawing-boards of more recent engineers. It had a Pimlico look, with its sweep of steps leading up to a pillared portico. Jonathan had yet to recognise Pimlico, but he could label the judge's house Victorian.

'None of these houses has a second storey,' he commented.

'That's true, but all the newer ones have flat roofs, which are ideal for summer sleeping.'

As they neared the long elegant front of the hospital, Tom pointed to a modern bungalow in a beautifully landscaped garden. Incongruously its gate was manned by a turbanned policeman, his rifle at the ready.

'That's the police superintendent's. Dad is down here quite often, for the work comes under that department officially.'

The road degenerated to a broad, sandy track at the chungi. This was just a lockup hut, where the revenue officer collected octroi; the tax that kept the municipality going. As they neared it, an altercation broke out between an irate bullock-cart driver and the all-powerful babu. Behind him was a tailback of similar carts, piled high with merchandise. Jonathan noted some higher box-like vehicles drawn by camels.

'What are those?' he wanted to know. Tom pointed along the sandy tree-lined route.

'It's thirty miles to Badaun and these clumsy carriages carry passengers, who sleep through the night, waking fresh for bargaining when they reach the bazaar.'

It was at this spot that the private road took off for the settlement. It was neatly lined by oleanders. Beyond were fields of ripening pulses. Tom intercepted an appraising glance.

'Those oleanders have red and white flowers all through the winter. The crop is munh-ki-dhal, it sells better than the other pulses, for all the local doctors prescribe it for convalescent patients. At least that is what Dad says.'

The twelve-foot high walls of the settlement looked bleak. There were no windows on the outside, only the name painted in black letters, so large that the name could be read from trains on the main-line. 'Fazalpur – Village of grace', it said.

Before the tonga reached this pacific fortress, it entered a square lined by lofty gum-trees. On the right was a long line of shed-type buildings from which came the clacking of many looms. On the open-ground in front, a talkative bunch of gypsy women squatted. They were embroidering a variety of cloth. They were deft, the patterns obviously familiar from many previous pieces. On the opposite side of the square, two redbrick buildings were pointed out by Tom as 'the office and the dispensary that your father built.' The tonga pulled up at the far side of the square, at a long, one-storey terrace of quarters, with a broad brick-arched verandah.

Mrs Bennett was out to meet them. Tom gave her a hug and Jonathan a shy handshake, before she ushered them through the mosquito-net doors to the waiting table. In a trice she produced an enamel teapot, with a plate of 'what Americans call cookies', said Tom. There was no air-conditioning in these simple dwellings, but it was well known that evaporating water produced coolness. So the brick-flagged floor was wet. There was even more vigorous evaporation on the verandah outside, for a long line of big earthen pots of ferns, zinnias and balsam, were being enthusiastically doused by a barefoot mali.

'Did you like what you saw of the hospital as you passed?' Mrs Bennett had turned to Jonathan. 'Your father had to cede the land from the farm for it to be erected, but in return he had a special ward put up for his settlers.'

'Reason for why,' Tom intervened, 'they were such a dirty thieving lot, that no other patient would have stayed, unless they were well out of sight.'

'That's no longer true,' his mother was quick to retort, 'though townsfolk are still a little scared of them, and quick to blame them for every theft that occurs.'

'What a tale', Jonathan was a little embarrassed.

'And that's not all,' Tom was now in full flood. 'From what father tells me, Dr Andrews had bags of charisma, building a hospital twice the size that headquarters planned. The rich merchants lined up with donations, as long as he gave them a brass plate over a door somewhere.'

'Well it all went for patients,' his mother was quick to intervene. 'He didn't manage to build a house for himself.'

'Then what is that nice detached block at this end of the hospital frontage?' Tom said, 'Dr Snow lives there.'

'That is actually the same place that Dr and Mrs Andrews occupied, but it was built as the Maternity Block.' She paused and a smile spread over her face as she added, 'there is a marble floored room at the front where you were born.'

'I haven't heard that before,' laughed Tom, patting his friend's shoulder.

'What happened to the doctor? From what you've said I'm not surprised that he took Alexander-the-Great's Persian name. He was known as "Sikander", wasn't he?'

'It's a fascinating story,' said Mrs Bennett. 'In the World War whilst your father served in France, Indian casualties were nursed here, with Dr Sikander as O.C. By the end of that war, fighting flared up on the North West frontier; the captain was transferred there. He was killed whilst bringing in casualties.'

'Didn't you know that he was awarded the Victoria Cross?' asked Mrs Bennett.

'Father knew him quite well,' added Tom, 'and his wife Gemma who had to go to Buckingham Palace to receive the medal.'

Jonathan sat silent, thinking of the medal the King of Serbia had awarded to his father. That had come to his mother, unspectacularly through the ordinary post. Mrs Bennett saw the fleeting sadness on the boy's face and quickly changed the subject.

'Come and help me make the scones; I intended to have them ready by the time that you arrived.' Both boys were taller than she was, but Tom threw his arms around her neck, as he had done since childhood. She quickly hoisted her floury hands aloft and dismissed him with a smiling,

'Get along with you.'

It was the next night that Tom woke him.

'Jonathan, Jonathan, there's an emergency at the hospital. Father has been called. He didn't want to disturb you, but I said that if Dr Snow would play ball, I guessed that you would like to be there.'

Jonathan was already throwing off the bedclothes as Tom continued, 'Dr Snow has taught father to give an anaesthetic and wants his help with this one.'

Even before he could reply, Jonathan heard the banging of the mosquito-door to the next room. The light from a storm lantern shewed under their own door. Both the boys were now grabbing the clothes that they had thrown over the chairs, in their haste to get to bed.

'You know you didn't need to ask.' Jonathan already had his arms in the jacket lifted above his head.

Major Bennett had taken the only cycle, so they would have to walk. They chose to run in case they missed anything. Jonathan was out of breath but his mind was busy. This would be something to tell his mother. She had once said to him,

'I'm sure your father would have liked to be a doctor in that hospital.' She was telling the usual bedtime story, only this time it was a true one; the pageantry of the visit of the Governor of the United Provinces, to open the hospital.

It was 1 a.m., the sky was lit only by stars. Along the frontage of the hospital were a few small electric lights; at the centre brilliant light streamed from the outsize window of the operating room.

The patient was a boy of ten, mauled by a tiger in the Terai – out Kashipur way. Two of his uncles had jogged twenty-five miles, with an improvised stretcher slung from a pole across their shoulders. The local hakim, or barber surgeon, had covered the vicious wounds with his usual poultice of leaves and herbs. Neighbours had donated some old rag to tie over. It looked none too clean. In the village, they had sat around the whimpering boy for twenty-four hours of endless discussion before they came to the decision that they must go to hospital. They had a premonition that he was dying. Perhaps the distant Christian hospital could work a miracle. Several of the villagers had jogged with the uncles. In the jungle, life was ruled by events and moods, rather than by clock and calendar.

The little group of worried and bemused yokels, crouched on the cold marble floor of the out-patient hall.

'Kiya hua?' Tom asked them. But before they answered his request to know what had happened, they countered with their own urgent question.

'Will he live?'

Without hesitation, Tom comforted them.

'Umed hai. Doctor-sahib laiq hai.' There was always hope with a clever doctor he assured them.

An Indian nurse ushered the two boys through the outer door from the hall, leaving them at the theatre door with a cautionary finger to her lips. From a foot-square glass panel in one of the heavy swing-doors, a privacy flap on the inside had been raised; they could watch proceedings.

'You first Jonathan; it's your show.'

The boy on the table was partially hidden under green sheets: an extension table clamped at one side, supported the mangled arm on a rubber sheet. The figures moving smoothly and silently, were all draped in the same green; only eyes were visible above masks. Jonathan noted that Dr Snow had bushy black eyebrows. Major Bennett was the only one of the four seated. Beside him was a trolley, with a few instruments, and several brown bottles.

'They haven't started yet, but they must have given the boy an anaesthetic injection; he seems right out,' Jon whispered to Tom. Bennett lifted the head and tilted it back, opened the slack mouth, slipped a ventilation tube over the tongue, then closed the mouth and held the jaw firmly. With the other hand he slipped the mask over, commencing a very slow drip-drip of chloroform from the first of the brown bottles. As he switched to the second the pace quickened. Meanwhile a gowned and masked 'dirty nurse' had removed the

27

poultices from hand and chest. To judge from the nurse's eyes, it was a smelly job. She gently bathed the wounds in antiseptic then saline. The chest was soon dealt with; the arm was more difficult. The wounds were deep and bone was protruding. The nurse finished her cleansing. Holding the mangled hand up by one finger, she deftly folded the soiled linen and swept it off the table and into a waiting bucket. Sister Murfitt, with gloved hands and sterile forceps, spread a clean towel, then taking another wrapped it around the arm above the wounds. Jonathan's nose was flattened against the glass; he could see that the doctor was speaking to the sister, but the whole drama was dumb-show outside the teak door. The sister handed across an instrument with which the doctor probed the gaping flesh but after a minute he laid it down and used his gloved finger instead. Jonathan was so intent on watching the skilled partnership between doctor and nurse, that he failed to hear Tom's whisper. So Tom tried again, only this time he accompanied his words with a poke in the ribs.

'Isn't it time to change places?'

Only when he stepped back did Jonathan realise that he needed the support of the tiled wall. He wondered how different all this was from twenty years ago. He knew that great strides had been made in surgery during the war. Father must have seen much worse wounds in France, he mused. A fleeting picture from childhood flashed on his mind. He was at that quiet mansion in Norfolk when his father had been invalided home. He could see other patients playing croquet. They were all in pale blue uniforms.

It seemed no time at all before Tom was saying 'It's all yours. I'll leave you to it.' Truth to tell, he'd had enough. Jonathan was in time to see the doctor strip off his gloves and soiled gown, not manipulating the fracture until the arm had been bandaged. Then sister was able to apply a wet slab of plaster-of-Paris and bandage it firmly with a wet cotton bandage. The arm now looked normal to Jonathan's eyes.

'Muaf kijiye!' The nurse spoke quietly as she asked him to let her pass, but he was startled. He rubbed his nose in embarrassment. The nurse smiled as she opened one leaf of the theatre door. She commenced to help her colleague in cleaning up. She must have told Dr Snow that he was there, for she returned.

'It's Jonathan Lindsey, isn't it?' She opened the door and handed him a mask.

'I wouldn't come too far, the floor is pretty mucky; but Dr Snow wants a word with you. Don't touch anything,' was her parting shot.

Jonathan had heard quite a lot about the doctor from Tom. 'He's not

28

a Salvationist, in fact I think he is a Plymouth Brother. The townsfolk like him, though I find him a dry old stick. He's certainly a boring preacher.'

The doctor greeted him in a friendly fashion, though he didn't smile. 'Jonathan Lindsey, you've had a pretty nasty baptism of fire. Would you like to know more about it?' He didn't wait for an answer but hurried on.

'Sister will have tea for us in the office, if you care to join us before you get back to bed.'

'I'll have to tell Tom,' thought Jonathan. The doctor had actually smiled!

The cheerful nurse who had first spoken to him, led him across the out-patient hall, to the consulting room. They were waylaid by the patient's relatives, desperate for reassurance. She was very gentle with them. To judge from their faces, she must have been hopeful too.

Jonathan was excited, but he had ten minutes to wait before the doctor arrived. Dr Snow walked in, clad in the pyjamas and dressing gown in which he had arrived an hour earlier. Sister Murfitt and Major Bennett were with him, so there was soon a buzz of conversation around the desk. Jonathan observed them silently. The sister was fully clothed, hair trim and fly-away nurse's cap in place. By contrast the men had obviously been aroused from bed. Bennett was a laughing extrovert like his son, whilst Snow was serious, almost morose, as he assessed his patient's chance of survival.

'The wounds are already infected and that means osteomyelitis, I'm afraid. With that bone infection, he's going to have a stormy convalescence.'

Sister Murfitt was not young, Jonathan had observed, but she was a 'bonny Scot' as Bennett described her.

'We'll nurse him through, never fear doctor.'

They sipped their tea and drew Jonathan into the conversation. 'Is this your first operation?' the doctor enquired, but went straight on with, 'How did you react?'

Jonathan was realising how intently he had concentrated on the theatre drama. He felt drained. He contented himself with 'I was fascinated.'

He returned to Fazalpur on the pillion of Bennett's bike, so full of the experience that he hardly noticed his sore bottom.

In his final year, Jonathan became eligible to join the school's Cadet

Corps. To his peers it was part of the curriculum. It was also a subtle mark of seniority. Jane had told him that one of Palgrave's extra responsibilities was that of medical officer to the local unit of the Defence Corps. Apparently all British subjects domiciled in India, were expected to belong. 'It's a Territorial Army or Militia, if you wish; for use in case of emergency,' Palgrave had explained to her. Jonathan's comment had been, 'I expect it was born of painful memories of the Mutiny.'

When the issue of joining confronted him, he was reluctant to sign the application form. He had no yen to fire a cannon, or even a musket. Whilst the discipline seemed little more than that of a scout troop, uniform had little attraction. He tried to analyse his feelings. He had the greatest respect for his mother and her generation of uniform-wearing Christians. Was he reacting against this? Since his experience in Moradabad, he had felt increasingly that he would like to be a surgeon. The British Army corporal who was the O.T.C. instructor held an informal meeting. He gave a pep talk and invited questions. He singled out Jonathan as a likely medic. He must have been primed, was Jonathan's subsequent conclusion.

'This company will need a medical orderly. What about it?' He saw hesitation, so he ploughed on. 'I could get you a crash course over at Ranikhet, if you take it on.'

So Jonathan signed and was issued with a St John Ambulance Brigade textbook, as well as khaki uniform, puttees and boots. He had become a cadet, so now every Friday evening meant a parade on the hockey pitch. Fortunately the junior forms were at prep, so there were no touchline comments on their clumsy efforts as Corporal Fisher of the Royal Radnors barked out his commands. He obviously hoped to become an R.S.M. one day. They grew accustomed to kit-inspections. His stentorian commands and choice comments were echoed around the school throughout the week.

Jonathan had his week's course at the British barracks at Ranikhet. The R.A.M.C. routine was not onerous and he enjoyed the week. The only part of the experience at which he felt ill-at-ease, was in the evenings. It was a beery cameraderie, in which the attitude to all things Indian, was foreign to his own. He wrote to his mother, 'It is a delightful place for the soldiers here but it must be pretty uncomfortable and monotonous on the plains. They are essentially isolated from ordinary Indian life. All they see is the traders who exploit them.'

Then came the fortnight's summer camp at Almora and he loved every minute of it.

They had pitched their tents off the bridle-path that ran down through the deodar trees, towards Baijnath in the valley immediately below Nanda Devi. Never had sausages tasted better than those cooked in their billycans. Nor would tea ever taste better, than after the slog of setting up camp.

'This tea is better than our school brand,' said Ustinov.

'It was bought in Almora bazaar,' the Corporal told him. 'It is probably local grown.'

'Then I think I know the answer,' Tom Bennett bobbed up. 'My Dad says that the first tea grown in India was planted around here by an East India Company General, who was given land rather than a gratuity. He settled down up here with a local wife, having the first bushes brought from China. The East India did a lot of trade with China. They probably sold tea as well as opium.'

'I have certainly seen the tea in bricks, in the Almora depot, and that is the way the Chinese like it, I'm told.'

The Corporal was showing a real interest.

'We had better tell Grundy about this, so that he can include it in the report he's writing for the school mag.'

Under the instructor's baleful eye they were set to carry pieces of shale of suitable shape and size, to construct a stove of a design that permitted a wood fire to heat water, boil a bully-beef stew and heat a portable oven to bake their bread. Jonathan was highly delighted with their achievement, as the smoke curled slowly from the corrugated-iron chimney. He was unabashed by the Corporal's derisory remark.

'I can see you cissies will be expecting apple-tart.'

They awoke the next morning, eager for the first lesson in map-reading. They sprawled on the grass in the little clearing in the high trees. There was only one map between two. Then it was all action, as they spread out, still in pairs but in all directions, with a map reading and a compass.

Jonathan and Ustinov were ploughing through the woods on a carpet of pine-needles. They came on a small stone house built over a small, fast flowing torrent. It was noisy enough to drown out all other sounds, until they had crawled inside and there encountered the greater racket of the fast-turning millstones. They had lighted on a villager's private flour-mill. A wooden spoke in the upper stone, jolted a crude funnel at every turn, trickling a few grains of wheat or barley each time.

'Who wants modern technology when nature does the job without a minder,' asked Paul, as they backed out through the small entrance on all-fours. They had hardly had time to straighten up, when a series of piercing shrieks echoed through the valley. The boys looked around, trying to locate the source. The cries came from what looked like an orchard, behind a cluster of houses below them. The shrieks died down but were replaced by loud shouts, as men came from all directions, staves and mattocks flailing.

The shrieks had provided a rallying-point, more easy to find than the map-reference. Jonathan and Paul were not the first of the platoon to arrive. They came on a scene that they would not forget. Every boy must have described it in his letter home. The woman's face was just a bloody mess; her blouse and wide skirt equally so. The wailing relatives made way for the young soldiers, with the promise of greater competence than a pahari hamlet could muster. Equally the cadets turned to Jonathan for leadership. Even the Corporal stood back. The cause of the attack was immediately apparent, for the whole area was strewn with the branches of the ravaged cherry tree. The woman had rushed uncalculatingly when she saw the bear raiding her one cash-crop. Normally these beasts would shuffle off; taken by surprise it reacted instinctively. It clawed its adversary's face to blind her. He had certainly succeeded.

Every cadet carried a 'first field dressing' in his knapsack. Jonathan collected three or four to make a massive pack to staunch the flow of blood. He was so keyed up that he had no squeamishness. But he was stumped for a minute on how to control pain. He had aspirins in his pack; they were not allowed opium. But her husband had already anticipated the need. He came running with hand outstretched. In the palm were three or four black, crudely rolled pills; the opium obtainable in every bazaar.

'Get a kettle going and brew some tea, he ordered, 'then we'll be able to get those pills in.' He had an obedient platoon and locals pathetically eager to help. He hadn't worked out yet, how he would get at her mouth. Even as he looked at her she seemed to have difficulty in breathing. With his finger he strove to improve her airway, only to find that she was unconscious. She was already beyond the possibility or need of anything by mouth.

'Watch that the tongue of an unconscious patient does not fall back and obstruct the airway.' He could quote the passage from the handbook. So as they lifted her onto the stretcher they had thrown together from boughs and rope, he turned the poor bandaged head to one side.

A crowd quickly gathered as they reached the outskirts of the ancient Gurkha town of Almora, cadets and villagers acting as stretcher-bearers by turn, on the three-mile hike. It was still another half a mile, before the crazy-paved street, lined by two-storeyed houses and shops brought them to the small district hospital. Over its portico it had the same name as the hospital in Naini Tal. The cadets were intrigued, for they knew that Sir Henry Ramsey had been the first Commissioner of Kumaon, at the close of the last Gurkha war. He was a household name to the locals, and he was a legend for his benevolence.

The I.M.S. Captain, the Civil Surgeon, was Indian. He was a Tamil, a long way from Madras. He appeared to take Jonathan as a professional. He complimented him on his primary care, then invited him to assist in the operation room.

'I think that the bear bowled her over, so that she hit her head. She's concussed. I'm going to do a little cleaning-up without anaesthetic, whilst watching her reaction.'

When the bandage was removed, even the hardened professional gasped.

'I haven't seen anything so gruesome since France,' he said. The three-inch claws had virtually pulled the face off the skull. One eye had gone and the other looked damaged. The doctor replaced the ragged flap, securing it with a few strategically placed stitches. Then wringing gauze swabs from a bowl of saline he applied them to remould the contours of the face. A generous pack of cottonwool and a pressure bandage completed the operation. No anaesthetic had been required.

'How it will turn out I don't know, but she is most likely to be blind.' He looked despondent and sounded like it.

'Isn't there anything more that can be done,' pleaded Jonathan.

'You've been reading the textbooks I fancy; what is it that they say? "Replace the blood and the fluid" they say. But here we have no facilities for transfusion. We haven't even a bottle of glucose or saline in the store.' He began peeling off his gloves and mask.

'I've read the account of that New Zealander who made new faces for soldiers at the end of the war. I know one surgeon in Calcutta who tried a facial repair with a pedicle but it was a failure.'

Jonathan hadn't any idea what he was talking about, but he made a valiant attempt to keep up.

'It must be exciting to try new operations.'

'I confess I'd like to try sometimes, when the police bring women whose husbands have mutilated them, claiming infidelity.' Jonathan waited, aghast that such things could happen in the 20th century.

'Of course the police have the husband in jail, but the people of these hills nurture the old Rajput ideals of the virtuous wife, and of summary justice. I suspect that the men have a good deal of sympathy.'

There must be quite a lot of hankering for the old-time attitudes and methods still in India. Jonathan had heard of a recent case of suttee in a remote village. The British had stopped that a century ago. Despite the desire for independence, there was little, he was sure, for social justice. This Civil Surgeon was typical. Western trained in terms of medicine, he was content to do the best he could with inadequate resources, psychologically accustomed to a high mortality in an overcrowded land.

Grundy made a good job of writing up the whole adventure in the School Journal and the headmaster included a letter of appreciation from the Station Commander in Ranikhet.

When the magazine reached Lahore, Jane sent it straight off to Grandpa Lindsey.

Jane had returned from England in the Autumn, having much to report. When Jonathan reached home he was just in time to hear the girls' laughter as they fixed up the Christmas bunting they had spent weeks cutting and pasting. He was nearly six-foot tall now and the girls excitedly welcomed a handsome big brother. They feted him then and again when Grandpa Lindsey's letter arrived with the news that he had a good pass in the Senior Cambridge results. He had, in fact, several distinctions.

'Your grandfather is becoming a happier man in his old age.' Jane reported. 'For one thing he's loosening his purse-strings. He's also long forgotten that your father failed him as his eldest son. Uncle Alistair is running the business efficiently. The gaffer only goes into Galashiels once or twice a week. He's keen as mustard that you should take medicine as a career. He's even offering a modest subsidy!'

The old man had never been a letter-writer; now he wanted to make personal contact with his grandson. So he commissioned Alistair to write for him. He enclosed a cheque for ten pounds 'for extras on the voyage home', plus the news that an account had been opened for him at the Royal Bank of Scotland, with a deposit of £50.

Mother and son hugged each other, more for the sense of family solidarity than for the money. In the immediate situation, Jane was finding it a novel situation to be squired about Lahore, by a son taller than herself. And he was gallant; the years slipped away as they sat by a wood fire in the gol-kamra on cold evenings. There was no generation gap as she told him of his sister. She apparently had no desire to return to India and had already found herself a job as a clerk in the largest booksellers in Sheringham. It all seemed smooth and natural but aeons away from Naini Tal. Jane had herself stayed with the cousin Alice, who had once introduced her to her duties as a parlour-maid. Her husband Timothy still worked for the lord of the manor. Mary herself

34

was living with them, so altogether it had been a refreshing furlough for Jane. Timothy and Alice had remained loyal Salvationists in the fishing village. Mary was already in the swim. Jane had visited her own mother, now a widow, living with her son. He was the tenant of the house in Glandford in which she had lived as a child. As she sat with the old lady who was almost a stranger, Jane looked around the kitchen, remembering her wild excitement when they moved into this new house and she had a bedroom of her own. On a second visit Alice and Timothy had gone with her, for there was now a bus from Cromer to Kings Lynn which stopped at Sheringham. The ambitious scheme for a railway line through Cley and Blakeney had never materialised, although there were spurs to Holt and Wells separately.

She made one more trip with Mary, before packing her trunk to return. This time they went by train to Holt, where Alice's brother Dick met them with his wife Bertha. He was still a porter. Now he was the proud owner of a motorcycle and sidecar. He not only showed it to his sister, but with Mary riding pillion, hair streaming in the strong breeze and the two older ladies in the sidecar, he drove them to Glandford, where the neighbours turned out to admire his equipage. Jane had made a mental note that the machine was a Zenith. Jonathan was sure to ask. The hamlet was unchanged, but Jane had the sad opportunity to attend the funeral of Sir Alfred Jodrell. 'Imagine, he was lord of the manor when I was born' she said to Jon. 'It was the passing of an age.'

The decision having been made that he must become a doctor, Jonathan was astonished to find that everything began to fall into place.

A letter came from uncle Alistair.

> 'Dear Jane,
> Pa is delighted that Jonathan is set on a medical career. My nephew writes easily and well. Pa has quite a vivid picture of India. It's the first time that I have ever known him to be interested in anything outside of Galashiels! He takes it for granted that the study will be in Edinburgh; he's equally sure that the boy will make his home at "Riverview". He's written off to Edinburgh for details of the M.B.,B.Ch. course and the cost.
>
> Alistair.'

But Jonathan found that Mr Hardcastle, who had taught him physics, had other ideas. As a Cambridge graduate, he was anxious to pass on his brightest student to his alma mater. He'd obtained word of a scholarship to his own college, Emmanuel, and even secured the concession that Jonathan could sit the examination in Delhi. It was arranged for January 1929.

The trip to Delhi was a first for Jonathan. He stayed with Captain and Mrs Elliott at the Naval and Military hostel, in the new capital built by the Raj. From this pied-a-terre he explored the Mogul city.

He didn't find the examination difficult and he felt that he had done quite well. So he wrote off to his sister in high spirits.

> A Rajah's Palace,
> New Delhi.
> January 9th 1929.

'Dear Mary,

I feel quite a nabob myself, for I've been given a bed in a domed tower of the hostel. From it I can look over all the new buildings in red sandstone, and on to the Red Fort, with Shah Jehan's mosque, the Jama Masjid. A hostel sounds humble enough, but I learn that this was a Maharajah's town house. I'd like to see Fatehpur Sikhri, Akbar's deserted city before I leave, as well as the Taj by moonlight, but I doubt whether I'll make either of them this time. I certainly haven't got the money. They've booked a passage for me on the S.S.Cairo. Think of me with awful dilemmas, as I face the vast choice on reading the menus. I'll probably put on a stone before I reach Tilbury.

Lots of love,
Jonathan.'

Before he left Lahore he had a reply from his sister, in which she wrote:

'You know how little we saw of the Army whilst we were in school. What we did see of it was its good works for the poor and needy. Living here I get a different picture. I've had to debate my allegiance. Our Naini experience of a more cosy Methodism, makes the Sheringham scene – the band leading open-air meetings on the beach three times on a Sunday – blatant evangelism for which I was not ready. You know I share your faith in Christ, perhaps also that sense which permeates all that Mother does, to wit that all life is spiritual, even though lived out at a most

36

practical level. So I've had a battle. Uncle and aunt, keen though they are, have been patient with me.

WELL I'VE JUMPED THE HURDLE – I'm now a uniformed soldier of the Sheringham corps.'

He knew quite definitely that he was not ready to jump that hurdle for himself.

Chapter Two

A TOSS UP

He was a role-model for young surgeons

Jonathan leaned over the taffrail of S.S.Cairo as it steamed across the Indian Ocean. They had sailed from Bombay that morning; Jane was the last figure that he had picked out, waving him off from the Ballard Pier. Trim as ever at 42, she was becoming more and more a companion to her tall son, mature in manner, if a boy in all else. He knew where he was going; she was content with that.

Night had fallen and the ship's lights spread over its wash. The light caught the gulls, never tired of circling in search of the food thrown out from the galley. The voyage wasn't new to Jonathan, but going it alone was. He had much to think out, but there was no hurry. It would be three days before they anchored off Aden. He spent most of his time on the Tourist Class deck. He was in a four-berth cabin down at sea-level, the occasional high wave splashing over the porthole. The three men who shared the cabin were older than he; a varied group but all unattached and determined on a romantic cruise. Already he had been asked to keep out of the cabin during the afternoon. Some were fast movers!

He was glad of this pause, after several months of intense activity. He found the ship's library attractive; a range of books quite different from the school ones. He had the place to himself this evening, as he found a corner with an armchair. Very distantly he could hear the ship's band playing a waltz-tune; the dance had started and his cabin-mates would be in the swing.

When anchored off Aden, they were soon engulfed by launches with eager shouting salesmen.

'Mrs MacGregor, what about a lovely watch?' or, 'Sir, Sir, here's a flash camera for five pounds!' floated up.

The vendors were in their element. Money was flowing. Jon went ashore. It was a barren dump. Only in the one square, flanked by classy shops, were there any trees. The few shrubs were being assiduously watered by a young Indian, with a feeble hosepipe. After careful viewing in every shop, he bought a wristwatch for a pound. He was saving Grandpa's money for Egypt. He'd longed to do the trip on their last voyage out, but Mum hadn't the money for three of them.

They anchored off Suez as the sun went down; the sea was on fire. That flamboyant sunset filled his dreams that night, a backdrop to history as perverse and frustrating as anything out of Alice in Wonderland. After breakfast the next morning, he was disappointed with the greyness of the Suez waterfront, as he waited for the Thomas Cook launch. He bought his ticket and still had a comforting thickness of notes in his wallet.

It was cold as they sped across the featureless desert, but by the time that they reached Cairo the sun was high. A cool drink at an alfresco restaurant – courtesy of the travel agent – was welcome. They boarded a bus for the pyramids. He sat next to an Australian nurse who took his arm and said

'Let's do this together.' It was said in a way that brooked no refusal. Daphne Gough had only just been admitted to the State register; she was confident that she could work her passage round the globe before settling down. She knew her qualification was a marketable one wherever the Union Jack flew. She was very sure of herself. Jonathan, though nearly six-foot tall was still short of his seventeenth birthday, and gauche with younger women. Daphne Gough literally took him in hand.

'It'll be more fun together.' The smile on her freckled face melted his shyness, so when she added, 'My name's Daphne and I've heard you called Jonathan – is it a go?'. He took the plunge.

'Why not? You must tell me where you are from. Is it Australia or New Zealand?'

'Pure Sydney accent,' she laughed. 'The New Zealander has a more Pommy one and wouldn't want to be confused.' So he handed her into the window-seat, as the bus honked its way through the crowded suburbs.

They were deposited at the foot of a long sandy slope. At the top, the Great Pyramid filled the sky. Eager camelmen in their long brown robes and fezzes, urged the experience of a lifetime. Daphne was excited and soon beguiled. As the camel crouched in the sand for her to mount, Jonathan cocked his old camera and took a shot. He walked beside her as she swayed in the saddle.

'You should have joined me, Jonathan. You may be tall, but you can't see as much as I can up her. Why I believe that must be the Sphinx down there on the left.' She leant far out in the saddle to point. It was the afternoon tour of the Cairo Museum that held the most excitement for Jonathan. Daphne was all 'Oohs and Aahs' at the fabulous gold treasures of Tutankhamen, but Jonathan was faraway in memory. It was a bright cool morning and he was eight. The liner was steaming south, with the Sinai Desert on the left. The sun rose above the low cloud, flooding the sand with sudden light, throwing the jagged peaks of distant mountains into sharp relief. They stood on the deck, still and awed. Only Jane spoke.

'That one there,' she was pointing, 'is Mount Horeb, where Moses received the ten commandments from God.' He had no words to describe the realisation that all the stories of Jewish history that had been his Sunday reading for years, were real; not the stuff of fairy tales. With the fabulous wealth of the Pharaoh's court all around him, he was seeing Pharaoh's daughter, who had reared the Israelite foundling, found floating in his basket, whilst she was having fun with her maids in the Nile. Into his mind came the words of the Jewish Christian, which précised the history of his people, sometime in the first century A.D.

'By faith, Moses refused to be called "the son of Pharaoh's daughter", choosing rather to suffer affliction with the people of God, than to enjoy the pleasures of sin for a season.'

'Come back Jonathan you're miles away,' laughed Daphne, 'look at that chariot over there. It's so slight that I can't see a Pharaoh and a charioteer in it together.'

'There's too much to take in at a go. I'm seeing hundreds of chariots like that, racing after the terrified Israelites. I can see them being bowled over by the returning waves, can't you? You know we're very lucky to be seeing all this, for it is only a few years ago that Howard Carter first held a candle to the hole made in the tomb wall. He must have been speechless with what he could see.'

It was night as they drove to the railway station. Lights were reflected on the broad waters of the Nile, as the whole city twinkled. They were tired but wide awake, as the train chugged across the desert to the canal.

'Look Jonathan, ships cruising on the sand!' Daphne was clearly pleased with her remark, and true enough a line of ships – a lofty, brilliantly-lit liner leading them, was moving sedately without a sign of water.

'That must be our ship, which means that we will be in Port Said before it.'

That prediction proved correct, so that they had time to look around Simon Artz's great emporium, before passing the police-post and stepping onto the crocodile-pontoon that wound its way out to the ship.

Even then the night was young. Vendors in small boats were all around the S.S.Cairo, throwing up coils of rope, to be quickly followed by woven baskets. These contained articles requested by passengers leaning dangerously over the rails. On one of the hatches, a 'gully-gully man' was at his tricks. Children were still on deck, so gathered around him, shrieking with laughter as he found his lost chicks up the friend's frock or jersey. They were aghast when they were retrieved from their own.

'Time to turn in Jon. I'm dead beat; but it's been a wonderful day. You've been a sweetie.' She gave him an affectionate kiss and fled down the companionway before he could react. He stood musing.

'She's five or six years older than me. She's been a good sport.'

They docked at Tilbury and a white-haired Salvationist came down to the dining saloon to greet him.

'Though I've never met you, I knew your father and was his great admirer. So it will be a pleasure to help you, if I can.'

He had the luggage through customs before most of the other passengers were off the ship. Jonathan only managed a handshake, pulled into a fleeting kiss by Daphne, before Captain Daly found his reserved seat on the boat-train for Liverpool Street.

'Your sister will be there to meet you, so we've arranged for you to stay at the Highbury Hostel for a couple of days. I gather that you will be going north to your grandfather.'

Mary seemed a masterful young woman as she showed Jonathan

some of the highlights of London. She had money in her pocket, which was all to the good, for they both enjoyed coffee with Danish pastry. Then it was au revoir, for they anticipated many more hours together.

Uncle Alistair had a house in Melrose, quite near to the ruined Abbey. He had a car waiting at the railway station above the town. It was a Morris-Cowley open tourer, which was kept polished and roadworthy by his grandpa's old groom, James, whose duties now swung between the saddle and the oily mysteries under the bonnet. It took only fifteen minutes between the two homes if one used the footbridge, but the car had to take the high stone bridge over the Tweed, on the road to Galashiels; quite a detour. 'You'll find my father has aged since you were here last,' warned Uncle Alistair. 'He only comes to the mill one day a week now, just to show who's boss!'

But Jonathan found that at 73, his grandfather was still vigorous in mind and body. The next morning James had the trap ready, to take them the four miles to Galashiels' Academy.

'I'm taking you to see the Rector, who can remember your father. He is only too happy for you to work in the Science Laboratory with Mr McGrath, until you go to Cambridge. I wish it were Edinburgh – but you will still come here for your holidays, won't you?'

He smiled fondly at the lad.

'He's his father over again,' he told his wife. He'd be happy to have a doctor in the house; he had the bawbees to help him.

The next morning there was a letter propped against the marmalade-pot. Jonathan recognised Jane's handwriting.

'Dr Palgrave called to see me,' she wrote, 'and we talked about you. He's now a Lt Colonel, and a Professor of Surgery. He was delighted to hear of your plans. It turns out that Emmanuel College is his "alma mater" as he puts it. He's written to the Master, recommending you for the scholarship. I hope that you will be able to spend some time with Mary, when you go down to Cambridge for the interview. By the way, the Colonel told me that students are not admitted to the university unless they have Latin or Greek. He says that you have a good pass in Latin, so that you will be spared "Little-go". I expect it makes more sense to you than it does to me.'

The Summer passed all too quickly, but everything had fallen into

42

place. The scholarship was his and he had fallen in love with Cambridge. He had stood on the bridge that approached King's College Chapel from the Backs, watching the ducks sail under the willows. He felt the contrast between the serene calm of this flat Fenland, and the mystery and danger of the Himalayan foothills.

'Emma' was now familiar territory. From the Bursar's office, he obtained a list of students' accommodation in the town. He went straight off on a tour of inspection. It took little time, for he settled for the first house he visited. Mrs Triptree had four rooms for undergraduates, three already booked. So it was the third-floor front of the terrace house in Templeton Street, which became his first retreat from the gregarious life of the university. The allowance from Grandpa had been carefully worked out to cover all but fees. The margin for 'high jinks', as Uncle Alistair put it, was minimal. The canny-Scot mill-owner had a picture of aristocratic rave-ups at these English universities. But even more potent than the financial curb, was the youth's inner integrity.

He screwed up his courage and went along to the Salvation Army in Tennison Road on his first Sunday. His welcome was warm. He soon found that he was not the only undergraduate in the congregation. This influenced his course. Already he had been bombarded with invitations to join a great variety of groups both in and outside of the college. He was cautious, pondering his priorities. A commitment to full-time participation with the Army might well conflict with his studies. These must come first. But the corps became his spiritual home. This was his anchor he assured his mother. He spent much time with the supervisor who had been appointed for him, but even more in the old chapel library, on projects set by the worthy Mr Milton. His main programme was at the Medical School off Downing Street. There he was to learn anatomy and physiology at first-hand. This led to the horrors of medical education. He'd braved operation theatres without alarm or an emotional reaction; now it was the dissection room.

There was an ante-room with coathangers and washbowls; here the odour of the embalmed bodies penetrated. He preferred the astringent smell of antiseptics to that of death. He scrutinised the notice-board to see who was to partner him in this grim exploration.

'Are you Jonathan Lindsey?', a slim figure hailed him. Jonathan studied the face of the student who introduced himself as Joseph Silk. He noted the acquiline nose and black hair.

'I see they have given us the right arm on table 3. Shall we see what he or she looks like?'

Two more students were already at the table, exploring the brachial plexus of nerves entering the opposite arm on the old man's body. Legs, abdomen and head would have been assigned to other pairs, but there never seemed to be more than four of them at one time. Jonathan and Jo Silk, having discovered that they were both from Emmanuel, settled quickly into an easy relationship. For the first time Jonathan was tempted to smoke. He was certainly grateful for the gentle cigar aroma that Jo provided.

'I'm not a smoker normally', he said, 'but I think this demands it.' It partially banished the acridity of formaldehyde, which lingered about the room.

They had an instructor, a junior doctor who was working for a higher qualification in Anatomy. When partners felt ready, the instructor would give them a practical viva, signing up their cards if satisfied. They could then apply for another area on a corpse.

They were an interesting couple to their contemporaries, who dubbed them 'Yo-yo'. They had quickly learned that they were Salvationist and Jew. It was a friendship that would last right through clinical years, and up to final graduation.

Nothing in dissection looked as clearcut as the textbook, they soon discovered. The flesh was a uniform grey; only the main arteries, injected with red-lead, were easy to find. It took them a long while to trace the brachial nerve, and even more patient search to find the branches near the wrist. It proved a recurrent temptation to break off for a 'milk and a dash' in the refectory. On Jonathan's tight budget, he became quite addicted. It was certainly more nutritious than the strong black variety that they brewed in their rooms, to keep them awake through the long evenings before exams. They became inured to the crudities of the flesh. Jonathan was soon laughing as loudly as the rest, at the Professor of Physiology's Rabelasian wit, as he propounded the mysteries of digestion.

Jo Silk's rooms were not so far from Jonathan's. They spent much time together then and even more when, in their second year, they secured rooms next to each other in Emmanuel. Most of the students knew little of Judaism; Jonathan's own knowledge was entirely biblical. He knew little of the saga of the Jews after the Acts of the Apostles. He quickly learned that Jo prided himself on his ancestry, in the Sephardic branch of Jewry. His ancestors had for long periods been the leaders in Spanish erudition.

If Emma's tradition was from the Puritan wing of the Anglican church, in Elizabethan and Stuart reigns, Jonathan soon discovered that Jo's patron saint was Oliver Cromwell.

'He was the first English ruler to permit Jewish immigration on humanitarian grounds. It had been the financial skill of our race that had been the over-riding attraction to earlier kings. When they couldn't repay their loans, the king usually found good reason for expelling them and his debt.' Jo spoke with unusual bitterness.

'I thought you were going to say that you liked him for his Cambridge background.'

'Isn't it strange too, that our tutor is a namesake of the Milton who also belonged to the Puritan group in the university.'

Jonathan became a regular participant at morning chapel; occasionally also in the evening. Atmosphere had played a prominent part in his spiritual development. Cambridge immersed him in a sensuous bath, to which he instinctively responded. The first impressions weren't particularly spiritual but rather architectural. Some were mediaeval but most were classical. Lofty pillars from the Renaissance contrasted with Gothic curlicues and flamboyant Perpendicular glass. They were blended by ancient trees and cropped lawns. Jonathan found these tailored gardens, glimpsed through every gatehouse, an invitation to quiet reflection. The courts, of which Emma had four, were patently derived from the cloister, with the meditative tread of hooded monks, easy to imagine. They were still ambulatories for students but the folded hands and faraway looks, were now more likely to be romantic than spiritual. But the dominance of the college chapel was still there. In Naini Tal he had not been aware of his own spiritual pedigree as odd. He had worshipped with Methodists, whose style had not been dissimilar to his home pattern. Now he felt an outcast in the Anglican world. It was essentially the Anglican order of the Restoration, upper-class and sure of itself. However, he had been drawn to Emmanuel because of its history. It was one of the colleges built in the reign of Elizabeth I, by reformers who sensed a dichotomy in the state church. They wanted their pastors to be of their own persuasion. When the tension with the Laudian right-wing crystallised into the Kings' Party in the Civil War, only the Puritan Sidney Sussex and Emmanuel colleges backed Parliament. Now all was reconciled; all comfortably Anglican. Only Jonathan Lindsey remained as a left-wing irritant!

There had been a sizeable group of boys of Salvationist parents in Ambrose Jones. One of the masters had laughingly said,

'You're only lapsed Methodists.'

The eucharist appeared to be a major barrier. He'd shared Communion on occasion in the Methodist setting, though it had never been a specific means of grace. He'd thought about it a bit. Actually he could understand the Roman officials, who, without personal

45

experience had reported that this new sect were alleged to hold cannibalistic rituals. After all, the private worship spoke of eating the flesh and drinking the blood of its Founder. He brought the matter up when on holiday. Jane responded seriously to his bewilderment.

'We were all Anglicans in my village. I grew up with it. I was baptised and confirmed. So the Salvation Army approach was at first strange to me. But I warmed to it. I believe that communion is based on a true discipleship to Christ, which his loving atonement made possible.' So Jonathan had neither been christened nor confirmed.

'Dear Mum,

Here in Emma, Every Sunday morning service is Holy Communion. I have spoken to the Dean and even the Master, who regard me whimsically as an 'odd-bod'.

"We've now got two of you," the Dean said ruefully, the last time I saw him. I've asked Arthur Blow what he thinks of the matter.

"The Dean writes me off as a hopeless case. I've explained that I realise that the sacrament means a lot to many students, but that for myself, I'd rather make a sacrament from Christ's other command at the Last Supper. 'Wash each others' feet' is a regular reminder that we promise to be like him in serving others."

It is such a beautiful chapel that Wren built, so I content myself with the daily prayer-book service. Don't worry about me. I'll survive.

Jon.'

So he settled into a two-tiered pattern of worship. On weekdays it was the sonorous prose of the collects, but on Sundays the ebullience of the warm-hearted enthusiasts at the Tennison Road Citadel. Arthur Blow was his confederate. They had met on Jonathan's first day at the college. Arthur invited him to a cup of coffee in his well-appointed rooms. Arthur was a mathematician and disdained fashion in clothes. Very tall and thin, he tended to bend, as though constantly passing under six-foot doors. He was dark-haired and bespectacled, 'a text-book academic', Jon wrote to his mother. He sat the new boy down in his most comfortable armchair, before introducing himself.

'I hear on the grapevine that your parents were Salvation Army officers.'

'You needn't use that in the past-tense; Mother still is and working in India.'

'Tell me more.'

46

And so Jonathan launched into the saga of his parents' lives; of the romantic marriage and career that ended in Serbia.

'I'm only a year older than you, so I suppose that I must have been nine when my father, who is the bandmaster in my home town, read us the sad story in the "War Cry". I always remember my sister in tears for the little girl and her younger brother, who had lost their father.'

'You say that your father is a band-master. Does that mean that you play a brass instrument too?'

'Yes, I'm one of the cornet players in the Cambridge Band.'

'Do you mean to say that you go out of here in uniform every Sunday?'

'Inevitably.' He was smiling at Jonathan's surprise.

'Well I take my hat off to you. It must take a lot of nerve.'

'I'd thought about it a great deal, before I left home. You see I won a rare National Scholarship, with a special place in mathematics. It somehow puts an extra strain on performance. But I took my father's advice and went to the Army in uniform on the very first Sunday. Like you I was in digs, so found it easy. By the time that I'd moved in here, I'd grown use to the ragging and occasional horse-play. Plunge straight in is my advice.'

Arthur, despite his angular frame, was keen on all the water-sports. Already he had won for himself a place in the trial-eights. Amongst his friends, there were those rich enough to have private sailing dinghies. Jonathan's introduction to the river was not auspicious.

'Whilst we still have some warm days, you must come punting, Jonathan.'

'I've never been on one in my life.' His mind drifted to Naini Tal. When they had any pocket-money, they used to hire rowing-boats, showing off their elegant feathering to any girls who caught their attention.

So he was taken, in his new flannels, on the Cam. It was a Saturday when half the university seemed to have the same idea. Harold Burgess wielded the pole with studied ease, Arthur and Jonathan shared the middle seat, whilst Tom Grainger sat in the prow, fingers trailing loose weed. There were many girls in flowered frocks, rather older than Jonathan's memories of the lake. Their favourite spots to linger were the bridges. They punted as far as Grantchester, then turned and glided for home; it all seemed so effortless. They were nearly home when Burgess called,

'Come on Lindsey, have a go.'

He'd been watching long enough to have become certain that he'd appreciate the opportunity. He took the long pole without rocking the boat, let the pole glide through the water until it met mud, then he

47

urged the boat forward. He soon developed the rhythm, which involved feet and hands. The moment when his body became taut, he pushed the boat away from him. By the time that Trinity appeared on the right, he was feeling pleased with himself.

'Look who's on the Kings' Bridge, Arthur.' Tom called from his seat in the prow. Arthur, watching the tow-path for familiar figures, glanced up to pick out the magnificent white mane of the Regius Professor of History, who was leaning on the parapet and glancing up river.

'It's Trevelyan,' he called. 'I like his style. He makes history enjoyable reading,' Jonathan looked up to the bridge, now only twenty yards away. It proved a fatal loss of concentration, coming when the pole met an unusually glutinous patch of the river-bed. The pole stuck and with incredible speed, the deck sailed on from under him. He was left in an idiotic position, hands and feet twined around a pole that was angling slowly towards the water. He had ample time to appreciate laughter from the bridge, before his final rapid plunge beneath the waters. It wasn't deep, but it was weedy. When he crawled out onto the towpath, he was festooned with long green ribbons. He missed the smothered laughter, instinctive from the other three. He was only aware of their solicitude, as they came running back to him. No one had a coat or a towel, so they hid him in their midst, as they jog-trotted through Kings to Trumpington Street, to the digs that Arthur knew.

He lived it down, and even accepted an invitation to sail at night with Arthur and a friend who owned the boat. They tacked to and fro, as the Cam broadened beyond the town. The contrary wind held, so that they had an easy sail home.

Arthur did his best to persuade him to join the band, but he resisted the pressure, contenting himself with playing the accompaniments when the regular pianist was away. He limited his attendances to Sundays and special occasions. One of these interested him greatly. The visitor was from Travancore, giving Jonathan a glimpse of another India. He projected slides of walloms cruising under coconut palms on the backwaters near Trivandrum; they looked like canal barges with matting roofs like Noah's ark. He registered an intent to take Jane on a holiday in this tropical India, when he started to earn a doctor's salary.

But the pictures shook his comfortable content with academic life. He was reminded of his reason for being here in Cambridge. Though Travancore was a very different India from the Punjab, the slides had shewn the same teeming crowds of poor villagers. There was one of women bathing and washing their clothes.

'The women only have one garment – the sari, but between a pair of them they can wash themselves and their garments, without immodesty.' He had an afterthought, 'though the countryside is always crowded with people.'

Jonathan realised again that poverty and unhappiness were not inevitably yoked together. Every cause for celebration was exploited. Simple pleasures and life's surprises engendered disproportionate enjoyment. Between the lines of the lecturer's story, and more obviously in his pictures, Jonathan glimpsed the toll of disease and mutilation. They suffered stoically but survived apathetically. They hadn't the money for western medicines and equally could not afford convalescence without going hungry. Disaster and old-age seemed to be mitigated by the solidarity of the family and community. Of course much of this was the same in the north of India, but he had to admit to himself that he had never appreciated this so clearly before. As he sat in this attentive audience, he saw the Girls' Home in Lahore. Joel, the cook, had a brother who died, leaving a widow and a string of children for which he must now make provision. Before he slept that night, Jonathan made a resolution to do something about it.

One morning Arthur Blow came into his room, with a warning rap on the door. It was Sunday. He found Jonathan and his Jewish friend, in animated discussion.

'Am I interrupting something?'

'No. You're most welcome. How long have we got before we must set out?'

'A good half hour; in fact I hoped you might offer me a cup of coffee. What's the discussion about?'

'We've a tutorial tomorrow, and have been mugging up for it. I think we've had a surfeit.'

'Hoping that the appetite may sicken and so die?'

Jo ignored the light-hearted crack.

'We've agreed that Freud's rejection of all religion as a disease of the mind, is unacceptable to both Jew and Christian. But we were discussing Jung's perception that there is common ground in the myths of all religions, even in animism and the oriental cults. It's a sort of age-old dream, that au fond, the universe is good, and has a creator that the human spirit seeks to know.'

'I certainly find Jung's judgement more balanced', Arthur chipped in. 'I know that he accepted personality as a combination of reason, feeling, sensation and intuition. All four are involved in reality.'

'Jo was just reminding me that the story of Adam and Eve, presents the problem of good and evil at war in the world and in the human spirit.' said Jonathan. 'He was referring to the Genesis reference to a future salvation through a "second Adam".' Jo came in quickly,

'We differ of course, in interpretation. Does that refer to an historical Jesus of Nazareth, or to a Messiah yet to come?'

Arthur took up the subject.

'It's not a subject that interests the majority of our contemporaries in this place. Most sit on the fence. They may come to chapel, but they keep faith and science in separate compartments.'

'Keep talking to Jo whilst I get that coffee.' Jonathan was off, but soon returned with three cups on a tray. Arthur was still holding the floor.

'I find wisdom in Christ's insistence that by remaining as perceptive and trusting as children, we glimpse reality. It's hardly a universal dogma!' There was a pause. Jo put his coffee down to cool. He was obviously digesting Arthur's statement.

'Well, I agree that children accept all aspects of life easily and relate to nature and animals with ready sympathy and imagination.

'Mother says that she doesn't have to teach the reality of God to Indians. Immanence is part of the culture in which both Hindus and Animists are reared.'

It was Jo who was watching the clock.

'I'll nobly do the washing up, if you'd like to get off, Jonathan.'

They changed into their blue uniforms and peaked caps and set off briskly down St Andrews'. They quickly left the gowns and cycles, the ancient stone and tailored lawns of academia. They were now in a working class area, of respectable terrace houses in long parallel streets. The roads were clean, hedges trim and Sabbath rest prevailed. They passed a cloth-capped milkman, trundling his cart, lined with cans and ladle measures.

'Morning Capn.' he sang out as he deftly turned the brass spigot of his churn.

As they entered the hall, both the building and its congregation were very warm. They were cheerily welcomed from all sides. Arthur sped off to the band-room, leaving Jonathan to find a seat on one of the long wooden benches. He had time to reflect before worship commenced. Arthur was quite an astonishing chap. He was obviously an outstanding mathematician, yet could spend so much time on his band duties, on weekdays as well as Sunday. Of course he was friendly with Hilda Currie, a soprano in the Songsters, who was working for her Teacher's Diploma at Homerton College. It must undoubtedly sweeten duty.

The Captain, an Emrys Jones, had been a miner; he was forthright. Jonathan soon came to appreciate the practicality and clarity of his sermons. It mattered little that he lacked the voice and measured eloquence of the chaplain in the college chapel. It was enough that he found food for mind and spirit in the captain's exposition of scripture, in his earthy diction.

The two students were never allowed to return to college for meals. Their fellow soldiers vied with each other in hospitality which included Hilda. The soldiers were as forthright as their captain.

'If you have a girlfriend, she will be most welcome here.' Bessie Hill smiled conspiratorially, as she invited Jonathan. She was remembering the days when her apprentice-swain had to cycle from a village five miles out. But Jonathan hadn't a girlfriend, though these bonnetted young women were overtly friendly. Even those temperamentally shy seemed to know how to talk. It was basic to their faith, that they be able to analyse experience and express it. But only occasionally did Jonathan hear a truly original statement of faith. In the days when Emmanuel College was young, John Bunyan had described Christian as losing the bundle from his back as he stood before the cross. This picture was still norm to most.

Jonathan tried to analyse the paradox of this branch of the Church.

On the one hand it seemed to be the ultimate in spiritual democracy, every 'saint' expressing his own conviction, with strong discipline always apparent. But it was a society full of odd characters; yet there was a definite family likeness. It was a very human society, in which young people were expected to fall in love, where children were enjoyed, and there was a healthy interest in good food and social intercourse. Special events such as Harvest celebrations, were entered into with great gusto. They spoke of Jesus with reverence but also familiarity. Divine help had a warm, brotherly reality. Though theological niceties had no attraction for them, they could be painstaking in bible-study, to learn how to live. If he analysed his comrades, they also evaluated him.

'Jonathan Lindsey can be a bit distant, can't he?' Songster Lilian Brague turned to 18-year-old Florence Timms who sat next to her on the soprano row.

'He's not exactly cuddly, I agree; but he's nice all the same.'

Jonathan began to enjoy feminine company but formed no close attachment. All this intrigued Jane, who tried to read between the lines in her son's letters. As the months and years went by, she came to believe that he was immune to feminine attractions. She wasn't altogether pleased with this conclusion. It was sad to be so far away from her children.

The Salvation Army was highly organised, but despite its global involvement, relatively small. Word reached headquarters in London of an officer's son studying medicine in Cambridge. There came a letter from the Chief Medical Officer, Colonel Dr Martin.

'Dear Bro. Lindsey,
I am delighted to hear of your studies. It was 35 years ago, when I was a medical student in London, that I met the Army. I still remember the furore that I created, for I went the whole hog, wearing an Army guernsey to hospital! I have a personal reason to be interested in you, for your parents came to India a few years after my wife and I were appointed to Travancore. I am sorry that we never met – we were 1500 miles apart! But I heard of their exploits from the War Cry.
If you have a reason to visit London, do let me know. We'll have a meal together.
Yours sincerely,
Theodore Martin'

Jonathan noted that the private address was 'Travancore'.
A year passed and the finals of the Natural Sciences Tripos loomed up. Jonathan had to decide where to continue his studies in clinical medicine. The university had no medical college hospital, which meant that all Cambridge students went elsewhere, mainly to London.
The subject had been exhaustively discussed in Common Rooms, dissection sessions and physiology labs. Jonathan opted for The London Hospital; it had a variety of attractions. Jo had a lot to do with the decision.
'It has the largest number of beds, hence the greater experience of patients. It's in the poorest part of the metropolis. I have to admit that for me it has yet another attraction. It is in the Jewish quarter of London; it even has an endowment by the Rothschilds for my people.'
When Jonathan wrote to Jane on his decision, she proved enthusiastic.
'I worked in those slums when I was a very young officer. I can still remember some of the characters that I met there. I would be working for them still, if famine in India had not produced orphan children. They wrung my heart and altered my course.'
There was a final advantage that clinched Jonathan's programme.

They had decided on a recce. Borrowing a motor-cycle, they roared up the A10 to the capital.

Colonel Martin, interested in them both, took them out to tea. His conversation fascinated them, for he conjured up the Victorian medical scene. His father had been an apothecary and sent him to Barts.

'I was a young doctor when the Prince of Wales had an appendicitis and was operated on by the famous surgeon of the London Hospital. It was an unknown diagnosis, when Sir Frederick Treves operated. In fact little was known about any abdominal condition. When I was a medical student I remember operation lists that read, "Laparotomy – laparotomy – laparotomy", which you know simply means cutting open the abdomen.' Jo interposed brightly,

'I've read that inflammation of the appendix was first called "perityphlitis". Is that correct?'

'Yes, I remember that diagnosis. But enough of the past. I want to make a suggestion to Jon. Why not apply to the "World Medical Alliance" for membership? If accepted, the Alliance has a long-standing relationship with the London, which likes their applicants... with very good reason. And of course you would then be able to live in their hostel, which would have its advantages.'

'I'm going to the London for another reason,' said Jo. 'My uncle is one of the Governors, so it's virtually a family tradition.'

The Colonel was taken by surprise, but after a pause said. 'I didn't know that you are Jewish. I had a wonderful colleague of your race. When we started a Medical School with the Maharajah's backing, he taught surgery and I medicine.'

'How come? Was he from one of those Jewish families who had a synagogue in Cochin, before ever the Portuguese turned up?'

'No, he was an Englishman, whose family lived in the West End and sent him to Tommy's. He told me that he fell in love with one of the Nightingale probationers. She was a great character, invaluable since Mrs Martin had started a School of Nursing.'

'That doesn't explain how they came to you in India.'

'It certainly is a tale. He walked past the brightly-lit doors of the Salvation Army in Oxford Street periodically, and one evening went in.' He never wore our uniform but he was a lover of Indians, and was an example to us all in hard work and patience.'

'Where is he now? I'd like to meet him.' Jonathan had stopped eating. But Jo was looking sad, posing his own question before Dr Martin could answer.

'My father gets most disturbed when a Jew changes his religion. Was he from a family like the D'Israelis?'

Martin chose to answer the first question, avoiding a possible argument.

'He was patriotic; joined up in 1914 and went off to Mesopotamia and was killed in the siege of Kut. Ephraim was a good surgeon. Patients came many miles to consult him.'

His taxi climbed the hill out of Finsbury Park. It slowed into the private drive, fronting a long Victorian terrace, to which a line of lofty plane trees, lent shade and elegance.

Built as the homes of city tycoons, a century had passed and they were shabby; survivors of many 'pea-soup' fogs. No 10 had a well polished brass plate – 'The World Medical Alliance'.

He rang the bell and the door was opened by a uniformed maid, who took his name, asking him to wait in the hall. It had a wide staircase, its mahogany handrail curling up towards a lantern-light four storeys higher. At the foot was a wall telephone, a framed notice beside it. He studied it. It looked like a list of names, each with a morse-code signal. The maid came out of a doorway on the left, holding it open for him.

'Dr Holmes will see you now sir.'

As he entered the room, the doctor stood up behind a very large desk. It suited him for he must have been six foot four and broad to match. He was silhouetted against the window, which stretched from floor to ceiling. Jonathan's first impression was of a heavy bony face and balding head. He was wearing a lounge-suit as negligently as a farmer. He smiled his welcome; then his booming voice, fitting his frame, said

'Mr Lindsey, we are happy that you are joining us.' So was Jonathan, for there had been a number of hurdles. He remembered a questionnaire on his faith and interests, as well as three interviews with committee members. Two of these had been local general practitioners, with genteel waiting rooms as shabby as the exteriors. The third had been different. He reminded Jonathan of his grandfather, prickly and opinionated. He proved to be the secretary of a missionary society that had its headquarters in the vicinity. But he brought his mind back to the present and shook the proffered hand.

'Mrs Holmes has tea about now. Does that suit you?'

'Very well thank you. It's several hours since I left Cambridge.'

Holmes led the way, through a dining room that extended the whole width of the house. It had a very long, polished mahogany table. At a glance, Jonathan could seat 20 to 30 around it. At one corner there was a door through which they passed into a private sitting room. There was an air of elegance in its furnishing. Colours in carpet and upholstery, reflected feminine taste and care.

Mrs Holmes was petite alongside her massive husband. She surveyed Jonathan through gold-rimmed spectacles. Her eyes twinkled reassuringly.

'Dost thou like China tea, Jonathan?' She was already pouring.

'It's a foreign variety for me, for my background is entirely Indian. I can recollect a small tea-garden in the Himalayas, where I was told the first British planters had started.'

'Bushes from China no doubt,' boomed Holmes.

'You can see that we are old China hands,' smiled his wife.

Through the open window to the rear of the house, Jonathan could see a very large garden. That lawn must belong to three houses. The boundary was screened by mature elms. Beneath their shade he noted the Victorian stables but also a fives court.

'Tell us about your family. Is your mother still in India?'

And so the pattern of a relationship was set. It developed into respect and friendship over the next three years.

'I expect that you would like to see your room. Your boxes have arrived and if I know anything about students you'll be thoroughly settled in by dinnertime. It's at six. I think Jim Schofield is in. I'll call him, for he is the elected Senior Student and can show you round.'

The doctor found Jim and retired to his office. Led by the little lady, they climbed to the third storey. She unlocked the door and handed him the key.

'It's all yours.'

Jim grinned as they looked out of the window overlooking the garden.

'I expect you'll bag a better one, when a senior leaves.'

He introduced Jonathan to the common-room on the first floor. It was once the elegant drawing-room of the city merchant. Its three windows started from floor level. He could see the wrought-iron balustrades outside. The rear half of the room, big enough for dancing, had long been divided. There was a backroom, with a window on the garden. It had a table littered with papers and human bones.

'It's silence in these rooms after dinner. You may choose to study in your own room. But in the winter you will probably find it warmer in here, without having to keep plugging shillings into the gas-meter. Do you play rugger? I know that you are coming to the London and there's room for you in one of the fifteens.'

'It was very much my father's game, for he came from Melrose. Growing up in India, hockey's my game. Is there an eleven?'

55

'I'm sure that you will be welcomed with enthusiasm, for there are few who play. I'll leave you now. The bell goes at six for dinner and the Holmes expect us to be prompt.'

Jonathan took stock of his room; worn carpet, old heavy furniture which included a handsome bookcase. There was a made-up bed against the window. Sure enough there was an old gas-fire. It had a trivet, so tea would be easy. He soon learnt that the kitchen maid gave generous hunks of bread and outsize pats of butter for twopence.

For three years the house-party at no 10 provided him with a liberal education. It was smaller and closer-knit than Emma. Though the twenty students belonged to different churches and hospitals, they had a common allegiance. Nominally, at any rate, they were committed to missionary hospitals in any part of the world. They mirrored Christianity in England in the 30s. Anglicans, Presbyterians, Congregationalists, Methodists, Baptists and Plymouth Brethren. Salvationists were the end of the line; there hadn't been one for several years, so Jonathan was ribbed unmercifully in those first months. They shared more than religion. Though not all had been at public schools, most had been at boarding schools; many like Jonathan, overseas. Their lifestyle was that of their class. Most were sportsmen and all had abundant animal spirits. High-jinks were common. They were a practical lot.

One day in his first week at the hostel, he returned in the afternoon to find Harold Casson and Jim Schofield busy in the common-room. On the previous evening there had been a rag. Jonathan hadn't been involved but had heard the noise including that of shattered glass. Those tall sash windows were highly vulnerable. The two students were busy with repair, working up the putty in oily hands. 'We're trying to put things shipshape before Holmes looks in. Take a good look,' said Jim, 'master the technique. You'll need it before many moons.'

Harold wrapped up the putty in greaseproof paper, wiping his hands on the towel Jim had already brought from the stove-rail in the basement. They were all in the same year at hospital and usually cycled together. They'd evolved a most labyrinthine route, revealing the shabby poverty in Islington, Hoxton and Whitechapel. It took Jonathan some weeks to become accustomed to the soot-grimed brickwork, peeling paint and broken fences or walls.

At hospital, students were young doctors to the patients in the long wards. They were expected to be properly dressed, which meant collar

56

and tie. So if the weather was inclement, bikes were left in the shed and it was the Tube to Whitechapel. It made a dent in the week's budget; on two pounds a week every penny counted.

Despite the tight budgets, they were all fascinated by cars. Jonathan was quickly involved in a deal. There was a pool of knowledge in the house and a chain of backstreet workshops, where ancient models and secondhand parts could be bargained for.

They invested £10 in an old Ford. They parked it in the service lane behind the converted stables, where the doctor kept his two big cars. These were both expensive second-hand models, bought very cheaply because the road tax was high. The doctor was very generous with them. Jonathan had driven the Invicta in his first week in the hostel. The students were soon made aware that it was not wise to park in the front of the terrace. This was not for snobbish reasons, rather the reverse. Policemen on the beat were most interested in parked cars and liable to ring the front doorbell, pointing derisive fingers at smooth worn tyres, or illegal windscreen glass. Jonathan watched the pantomime from the common-room window. Dr Holmes had been summoned by a flustered maid and was assuring the Law that the offending tyres would be replaced at once.

Jonathan wondered how he had been inveigled into the deal. The car was only of use to him at weekends or on holidays. However Harold had a home in Hertfordshire, so they occasionally went together. They spent hours with their heads together under the bonnet, or separately stretched full-length under the transmission. It was part of that liberal education. Come winter and they were glad of the car for the Saturday afternoon at the hospital sportsground in Essex. It was not easy to reach. However there was always a carful to share the cost of petrol – and the oil, which 'Bluebird' drank freely. After two hours of exhausting exercise and the exquisite bath in a communal hot pool, they relished the thought of unlimited tea and toast in each other's rooms. Hilda, the kitchenmaid, always ensured that there was plenty of bread and butter in the larder at the weekend. The hospitality was rich. Harold was always stocked with home-made jams, whilst Eric, with a father in the highlands of Ceylon surrounded by hundreds of acres of tea-bushes, could provide the best of tea. There were always apples in Kenneth's store. His room was always fragrant with the smell. His home was in the Malvern hills. Punctuality at dinner was never a problem. They were always hungry, waiting for the bell. But breakfast was another matter. Jonathan's habituation to the Indian practice of early-rising, meant a commitment to a 'waking-up round' – a thankless task, ripping the bedclothes off students who had been working till past midnight.

He was surprised that one or two wore no pyjamas. But Holmes was always in place at the head of the table, big bible open at the ready. Slinking into the last seats was always noted.

The hostel had been established in the heyday of Victorian charity. Long before even Lloyd George's limited health service, a chain of dispensaries developed in the poorest quarters of London. In the main they were staffed by volunteers. Dr Holmes was the Medical Officer at two of them. Students took it in turn to help out. They made up mixtures with the pharmacist, dressed varicose ulcers with Unna's paste and applied iodine and bandages to innumerable household wounds. On Sunday afternoons, weekday waiting rooms became meeting-halls and again students handed round the hymn-books and afterwards the cups of tea. Jonathan was a surprise to his peers. They took it as read that every Salvationist could preach. He wasn't good at it.

At the beginning of each term, the Senior Student called a meeting and hands volunteered as roles were outlined. It all worked out most amicably. He certainly became familiar with the vagaries of the poor. He found it easy to feel with them.

In the hospital, the pattern of apprentice-style education persisted from the 18th century, when the hospital had been built in the fields on the main road to the east. Jonathan would have four six-month appointments as assistant to a consultant, either physician or surgeon. Both were doctors but somehow they were of different temperament. Gone were the long vacations of Cambridge. He would now have two weeks' holiday by applying for it at the Registrar's office.

He first applied for a posting as a dresser to the famous surgeon, Sir John Hammond.

'He's a great chief,' volunteered one of the students who was just finishing his stint. 'He took a team to Belgium in 1914, before any British troops were dispatched.'

'He's quite an artist too,' said another. 'Have a look at the map of the district painted on the wall of the midder-boys room.'

'And above all, he's generous to all in his team,' commented a third. Jonathan was to be painfully aware of the truth of this in his first fortnight on the firm.

The anaesthetic room was a narrow one alongside the main theatre. Sir William Rawnsley was the senior in his speciality; elderly and genial. Someone had gossiped to him that the student with this patient was destined for India. Thirty years before he had visited the sub-continent with Treves. He retained a memory of a mysterious country, 'very primitive'.

'I'll show you how to put your patient to sleep when your chloroform has run out... you've only got ether... you see. You have to sneak the ether in gently, for it is irritant. If you are not very skilful you will soon have your patient coughing.'

'So that is why we usually induce with chloroform, is it Sir?'

'Yes, really ether is only possible when the cough-reflex has been suppressed.' He suited action to his words as the patient commenced to breathe deeply. He checked the level of anaesthesia by raising the patient's eyelid to examine the pupil's reaction. Satisfied, he removed the mask and substituted the rubber one connected to the Boyle's machine. Once linked up, the patient's trolley was moved into the theatre, the anaesthetic machine with its battery of heavy gas-cylinders trailing behind. It was time for Jonathan to scrub up. The last time had been years ago, it seemed. Almora was a long way away too.

Now he was definitely the least in the team. But he was the one that the patient knew best. Thomas Walker was a middle-aged shipwright from Canning Town. He was one of eight patients assigned to Jonathan as dresser. The ancient title still kept its meaning. Though the Chief and the house-surgeon arranged everything, he had shaved the man and would tend his wound in convalescence. The man was apprehensive. As Jonathan had shaved, washed and applied the sterile towel, he had poured out his fears.

'I won't know anything about it. Will I? You will be with me won't you doctor?' He felt he knew him and could rest his cause. Jonathan had not found it difficult to be gentle with him and to encourage him to talk about his life on the river.

'Do you think I'll get better?' was a facer. Jonathan honestly didn't know. He knew that the diagnosis was cancer of the rectum and his textbooks didn't give all that much hope. So he countered, 'You couldn't have a better surgeon. I'd ask for him if I needed an operation.' He spoke with the absolute confidence of two weeks' observation.

It wasn't a very large theatre and it seemed crowded with trolleys and people. The theatre-man was the lynchpin, handling instruments and unobtrusively directing all the minor actors in this daily drama. Ward Sister was there of course and one of her probationers of Jonathan's age. She caught his eye and smiled apprehensively as he slipped into gloves and joined the houseman opposite Sir John.

'Just do what you are told to do and nothing else,' had been Sister's advice. So he watched the instrument-man offering the exact silver-plated tool at each stage; whilst Sir John taught, as his fingers moved in the pattern of years. He was supremely confident and competent.

'First we have to isolate the area to be dissected, by diverting the

59

intestinal contents. We divide the gut just before the small intestine joins the large.'

He picked up a loop of bowel, clamped it with rubber-covered instruments, then one by one tied off the blood-vessels that entered it. Jonathan was tense as he retained tight hold of the retractor he had been given to hold. The surgeon had carefully inserted it over a large wet swab to keep abdominal contents out of the way. The theatre-man kept wringing large cotton swabs from a bowl of hot saline. The house-surgeon wielded the scissors, and removed bloodstained swabs, which were dropped on a sheet spread on the floor. Jonathan was to remember the small brass discs tied to each like a nameplate. Sir John closed the abdomen and stood back as the staff altered the table, hoisting the patients' legs over stirrups to expose the perineum. It wasn't a pleasant part of the procedure; there was a lot of blood. The Chief spoke quietly to the sister.

'I think that we had better have a pint of blood.'

Jonathan had already learned that this meant phoning a voluntary agency, requesting that a donor of the right blood group be sent. It took time and was a rare event. Before the operation was complete, the blood collected in the next room, was brought in by a nurse and immediately hung up, replacing the bottle of glucose and saline already dripping into an arm-vein.

Only the next morning, did the houseman greet Jonathan with the news,

'One of your mates didn't count the swabs correctly. Because sister had a doubt, the patient was x-rayed and the disc spotted. Sir John is a real gent – came in the moment that I phoned him and retrieved the swab. I doubt whether he will ever mention it. But I am! Don't let's have any more sloppy counting.'

Jonathan won a new friend over this, the ward-sister. He estimated that she must be about 50, which was ancient to the student. She was certainly an old-timer, not only in the masses of goffered lace in her cap, which trailed to her waist, but in her aristocratic bearing. When he discovered that her honorarium was pin-money, he realised that she must have a family income. For her part, she warmed to the student who was so faithful in attending to his patients' daily dressing. Many of his peers neglected this chore, knowing that sister would see that a nurse did it. So Sister Gurney helped the young man, showing him how to lay up a dressing-trolley. For several days she turned up to help him, as he pulled the screens around the bed. It was a huge wound filled with vaseline gauze and gamgee packs. There was an infection around, hence the wound must be allowed to 'granulate' – to heal slowly itself.

The shipwright was stoical and very patient with his trusted 'doctor'. He was aware of the young man's solicitude.

Weeks went into months, then slowly, despite the efforts of the staff, he went downhill.

'I'm dying doctor, I know it. I'm not afraid – in fact it will be a relief to go. Thank you for being so kind.'

The young hate to be impotent; this tragedy lived with Jonathan for a very long while.

He found hospital duties fascinating, but they were time-consuming. He had to keep up with lectures, as well as the digesting of heavy tomes recommended by the First Assistant. This junior surgeon acted as tutor, piloting their studies; oft despatching them on private investigations in the museum. The textbooks weighed a ton and cost a fortune. Jonathan was relieved when he found that it was possible to borrow an agreed number at a time, by a subscription at Lewis' in Gower Street. He could have hired a microscope but his grandfather insisted on buying this. He wasn't a night-bird by inclination, but he was often still at it at midnight. He had a board of stained and varnished whitewood, long enough to rest on the arms of the adjustable wooden armchair. Uncle Alistair had given him an angle-poise stand lamp.

He looked up occasionally from the pool of light, aware of the vast silence in the room. It was an exciting time to be studying medicine. New specialities were opening up. Every keen student could afford to give a little time to one or the other. Brain-surgery was one of the pioneering fields. The students tip-toed past the theatre where operations were known to go on for hours. But Jonathan was attracted to a humbler department. 'Septic Surgery' was mucky no doubt, but likely to be his lot if he returned to India. There were many children in these wards. Some came in comatose with high fever. In a bone somewhere, a virulent infection was brewing. It often took days to reveal its location. These poor youngsters had a white-haired little lady as their guardian. Jonathan quickly found that she was another of the old guard, caring little about off-duty. Like the others she had a neat little sitting-room off the ward. Here she entertained the surgeon after his round.

One morning Mr Townley had just dashed off to an emergency in Harley Street, when sister called Jonathan in.

'I've got something interesting to show you. Mr Townley only got this packet from Germany this morning. Has he told you about it?'

She would have ploughed on, but Jonathan was also excited,

'It's Prontosil I bet!'

61

'You're right. I hope and pray that it will conquer the infections that kill so many little boys and girls.'

Before Jonathan was to finish all his appointments in Britain, English chemists were not only manufacturing Sulphanilamide, but had produced a new wonder drug, that was to control 'the old man's friend' – pneumonia. They called it simply by its research label, M&B 693.

Each four days, the surgical firms took turns in handling emergencies. The dressers were given rooms in the staff quarters and were liable to be called at night. It was exhausting, but the cameraderie was superb. The sister on the theatres – there was a whole floor of them – had a screen across the end of the long corridor. It was private to full-duty staff; here she dispensed not only tea, but generously buttered slices of new bread with the invitation,

'As much as you can eat for fourpence!'

Contact with probationer nurses was never cosier than in the shaded pool of light around the duty-desk, in the long Victorian wards with 50 beds – in darkness.

Jonathan's last spell of full-duty was at Christmas. A majority of the students were the sons of practising doctors; not only familiar with the ropes, but with some money jingling in their pockets. They could finance theatricals requiring props and hired costumes. Patients well enough to be able to enjoy the show had a wonderful time. On Christmas Day, sisters and their staff went to town with decorations and food, not to mention carols with sister at the portable organ. But on Boxing Day the students took over with more ebullient entertainment. All the porters were in it, dragging the heavy trolleys on which they normally distributed drugs and dressings. Today they were laden with the material for a troupe, including their private crates of beer. Music hall was not Jonathan's relaxation but he became familiar with all the popular hits that Christmas. New words were set to old tunes; were excellently sung and wildly applauded. By December 27th there were casualties. One of his peers was desperately ill in Howard Ward. He was vomiting blood copiously.

'This is the inevitable result of drinking too many glasses of whisky on an empty stomach, my lads,' commented the physician, to any students within earshot.

Clinical appointments completed, Jonathan faced his Cambridge finals.

'I'm not a brilliant brain like Jo,' he wrote to his mother, 'so I just have to swot, swot, swot.'

Now those loose-leaf notebooks, with his personal distillation of the wisdom of the 'grand-old-men', and their equally weighty textbooks, came into their own. Some who had not made this initial effort were anxious to borrow – or even buy. He was beginning to feel jaded.

He was not only jaded, but unsure of himself. Sunday morning found him unhappy about his normal programme. He usually worshipped morning and evening at The Salvation Army in Oxford Street, and then spent the afternoon at the Bloomsbury Dispensary. He phoned Les and Betty Kingswood, with whom he usually had meals at their Marylebone High Street flat. He cried off for the day despite Betty's protests. He took the Tube to Hampstead, walked up the High Street and out onto the heath. It was early; a cool Sunday morning, with the first wild-flowers and gorse in great golden swathes. Soon the rolling hillsides would be alive with young couples, or even their sedate elders, walking to church or coffee with their friends. But for the moment it was all his.

All the certainties of the last six years were no longer immutable. He was not even sure of God's presence. He sat on the massive trunk of a felled oak and looked out over the hazy spires of London. Somewhere near here, it was said that Dick Whittington had done the same, but with a sense of destiny calling – a bright one. Jonathan had no sense of his future now. A breeze rustled the leaves above him; the voice of wisdom said, 'Slow down – live in this stillness and let God restore your faith.' The minutes ticked away and slowly the peace of this quiet morning crept over him. There was no elation; he felt very tired, and he was still uncertain about his future.

Even the next day, Jo noted his friend's loss of èlan. He put it down to normal causes – the looming exams.

They were in the Senate House beyond Kings. The two friends stood together in the long line, gowned and waiting to be presented to the Vice-chancellor, in the Bursar's best Latin. Jonathan seemed quite happy; he was certainly talkative. But as congratulations began to pour in, he felt a fraud, in talking to his W.M.A. friends. He had not lost his faith but felt quite certain that he could not pursue the calling of a Salvation Army officer. India still lured; he could think no further than that. So he held his peace, saying goodbye to Dr and Mrs Holmes without hint of defection.

For the nonce he was off on holiday with Uncle Alistair. He could leave a decision until this was over. An answer presented on the first evening with his uncle.

'Your Aunt has arranged a party to celebrate your graduation. Folk will want to know what next. They'll probably rib you that Dr Goodrich in Melrose is waxing old and needs a partner, who will be prepared to take over. What about it? Are you still set on the East?' The flood of questions had to be halted somehow.

'Well, for the immediate I'll apply for house jobs. Would you like me to try my luck in Edinburgh?'

'We'd certainly be glad to see a bit more of you. Anyway Edinburgh is tops in Medicine.' He threw this out with a smirk at his obstinately Sassenach nephew.

'I doubt whether you will see much more of an overworked houseman.'

He applied to the Royal Infirmary. His excellent Cambridge result and good testimonials from the 'London' did the trick. He was interviewed by the Superintendent of the historic hospital, that had produced both Symes and Lister. Jonathan had learned that its administration differed from that of the English hospitals, with which he was familiar. The Superintendent was always a very senior doctor. Since Indian Medical Service doctors retired at 55, they were favourites for the post.

'I see from your curriculum vitae, that you were educated in India. Were you born there?' Jonathan told him of Moradabad.

'I was Civil Surgeon in both Agra and Lucknow so I know it well. I hope you will accept an invitation to tea with us when convenient. We'll have lots to talk about. It's not very often that we have a 'Koi-hai' around!'

Jonathan set about making the one spacious room which would be home for the next year, his own. As he put a pair of rosewood elephants on the mantel, he pondered the Superintendent's welcome. India certainly got into the blood, if it could bridge an age-gap of 35 years. Undoubtedly Uncle Alistair would say 'It's merely a matter of being amang yer ain folk.'

His first six-month appointment was with Dr William Wilton, a Scot with his native history at his finger-tips.

'The Superintendent tells me that your father was an Edinburgh graduate but you deserted us for Cambridge.' He saw that Jonathan was about to answer, so forestalled him.

'All is forgiven since you've come back to the home of Medicine. Do you have any family here?'

'My grandfather and uncle still have the family business in Gala and live in the same house that my father was born in.'

'You won't have much free time, but it is good to know that you will have somewhere to go if you do.'

Every houseman is elated at being a doctor, able to sign prescriptions, and welcomes questions from patients and friends. He treasures the deference of visiting relatives. He is conscious of clothes for the first time. Jonathan bought himself a Homberg hat and walked down Princes Street, seeing himself approvingly in plate-glass windows. He was even gratified when he was told that he looked like Sir Anthony Eden. But Wilton was right, it was a hard grind. True he had a registrar, to whom he could refer, but many decisions needed to be made on the spot. There were many minor crises when only he was available. It was surprising how many were in the night. Again it was the long dark wards of the Nightingale era, with pools of light over screened beds with Sister and the duty-nurse standing by, holding an instrument tray. He had knowledge, knew the big tomes to consult when necessary, but most importantly he was finding the confidence, without which a doctor is a broken reed to his patients. He soon noted that patients and relatives had antennae out, eyes and ears alert to detect, 'Does he really know?'

The corridors were even longer than the wards. He walked many miles in the course of a week. Looking young, he was the first to be accosted by lost students, with all manner of questions.

The weeks came and went and the six months soon passed. Dr Wilton thanked him after the last round, and offered him a glass of sherry. He closed for a cup of tea in Sister's sanctum. Then it was the train, the thirty miles to Galashiels and trout-fishing with Uncle. His six months on the surgical firm went equally quickly. It was memorable for the amount of time he spent in Casualty, when Mr Falconer's firm was on call. More than ever it was quick decisions that were called for. He decided that surgeons must be temperamentally unfitted to deal with the slow-witted. He came to appreciate how the intense concentration of an operation brought all his powers to their peak. He felt fine-tuned like an athlete. In later years, he was to reflect that this was his finest hour. The years brought competence, patterns of detection that made him a good diagnostician, and he certainly developed a comforting skill in execution. But never were his powers better focused than at the Royal Infirmary.

He made no sudden decision about specialisation, but the realisation was rapidly growing that he was born to be a surgeon. When the choice had to be made, he had no hesitation in settling for Edinburgh. An invitation to tea came from Mrs Wilson, the wife of the Superintendent, towards the end of the surgical appointment. Lt. Colonel Wilson had a house in Corstorphine, a western suburb. Mrs Wilson was proud of her garden for she had created it herself.

'Very different from Lucknow,' she told him, 'there I had two good malis.'

'The Moguls certainly left a fine legacy of gardens for the Raj,' commented the Colonel.

'They themselves acquired it from a civilised Persia, didn't they?'

'No gardeners have such green fingers as the Indian mali...' Her words were cut short by the roar of a tiger which startled Jonathan. The Colonel laughed.

'We should have warned you, we have the zoo just along the road.'

'What are you going to do when your present post finishes?' Mrs Wilson enquired.

'I want to take the post-graduate course in surgery. I'll be looking for a flat that I can afford, whilst I attempt the Fellowship.'

'May I make a suggestion?' asked the Colonel.

'I'd welcome any advice.'

'Do you know the Royal Infirmary Annexe along the road from here?' Jonathan smiled,

'You've kept me so busy that this is my first visit to Corstorphine. However I've sent convalescent patients to it, of course.'

'The resident post for a Surgical Officer comes up next month. It's a light post that goes well with study. There's a comfortable quarters and the princely salary of a pound a week. What about it?'

He saw Jonathan's eager reaction, so continued.

'The appointment will be made next week, so I'll give you an application form tomorrow morning.'

On weekdays he took the rattling double-decker tram to St John's Church, at the western end of Princes' Street. From there it was a stiff climb to Nicholson Square and the Royal College of Surgeons. He spent hours in the pathology museum, or reading in the library, though most of the lectures were in the Medical School along the road from the Infirmary. To be a lecturer on the course was an honour. So Jonathan grew accustomed to famous names in the flesh. His fellow-students included many bright young men, intent on a lifetime in surgery. But more than half were older men, returning after service overseas. Some were foreign nationals. There were even two women, in saris that trailed in the wet streets of winter. It was stimulating company.

He had a study on the first floor of the Annexe and as the winter moved into the Spring, he opened the windows to the scent of flowers and the occasional jungle-noises from the zoo.

One evening there was a tap on the study door, and the duty-nurse walked in. He'd known her now for a month, a raven-haired beauty with an assured manner. The patients vied with each other for her attention. Jonathan had seen a few boxes of chocolates handed over on departure. Nurse Caddy was popular.

'What can I do for you nurse?' he asked.

'I'm afraid it's rather personal, doctor,' she opened, her intent smile belying anxiety. 'I'm worried about my heart. It races sometimes in an alarming way. It could be paroxsymal tachycardia,' she trailed off brightly, offering her wrist, presumably to prove her point. Innocently enough he felt her pulse, which rapidly quickened under his finger. It felt otherwise normal. Even as he was intent on evaluation, Rose Caddy had dropped the bib of her apron and unfastened her dress invitingly. She wore no bra. Jonathan's own pulse had begun to race, as a full white breast was revealed. It was a flagrant invitation to an amorous interlude.

He was out of his depth. He had never fought or even been brusque with a woman, but he had no intention of being lured into action that breached his whole understanding of sexual relations.

'I'm sorry Rose, I've no stethoscope here, so button up. Your pulse suggests nothing more than excitement, so I advise you to forget about tachycardia.' He stood up.

'I'll let you compose yourself before going back on the ward.'

As he walked towards the door, Rose scowled after him, and took her time before following him. Jonathan didn't know what to expect when he met her on the ward the next day. Nurse Caddy smiled sweetly and said with overt innuendo,

'Did you have enjoyable dreams doctor?'

The course finished, he had about a month for final revision before the marathon of examinations. Edinburgh basked in an unusually warm Autumn. Sunshine lured him from the study to the steep grassy hillside behind the hospital. He climbed to the summit, crowned with gorse. Behind his screen of bushes he heard the conversation of golfers on the links. It was obviously not the time for serious tournaments, they were all too cheerful.

He came through the gruelling round of papers, vivas and practical examinations. Results were not long delayed.

'You've made it,' telephoned a friend at Nicholson Square. So a highly elated grandfather welcomed him to Riverside with unusual abandon. 'Hail Fellow of the Royal College of Surgeons of Edinburgh.'

He threw a party. The long extended table in the dining room was laden for a buffet meal. It was a warm evening and tables and chairs were scattered around the lawn.

'This is father's occasion you can see,' Alistair was highly amused, 'You're only the excuse, Jonathan.'

It was true that in the main, the guests were the old man's neighbours and his Galashiels' associates.

'It doesn't worry me Uncle, and to be fair, he's spent a good deal of money on me.'

To see the stern old face relaxed in genuine pleasure, added to Jonathan's own elation.

'He's a real Scot now,' he heard the voice of his Grandfather, talking to Mr McGrath, who had coached him in zoology aeons ago.

'You can be proud of him.' He pumped his friend's hand.

He'd already decided on his next move. It was good to have the imprimatur of the Royal College, but he would need experience before he could be recognised as a surgeon.

'There have been great advances in the treatment of fractures during my years as an undergraduate,' he told his uncle.

'I think I'll apply for a Registrar's post in Orthopaedics.'

He searched through the posts advertised in the British Medical Journal. He found what he was looking for, at the famous specialist hospital in the West End of London. He was still relaxing in golden days of trout fishing in the Tweed, when the foolscap envelope arrived informing that he had secured the Junior Registrar place. His Chief would be Sir Christopher Raymond, doyen of orthopaedic surgeons. There was a salary of 500 pounds a year, and a flat adjoining the hospital.

Sir Christopher still wore frock-coat and pin-striped trousers for his weekly round, but to Jonathan, his manner was friendly from the start. Before long there was an invitation from Lady Raymond. They had a spacious flat overlooking Regent's Park.

'I'm near a Zoo again,' he wrote to his mother.

He wasn't as tied as he had been in junior appointments but he found that Sir Christopher expected his team to produce some original research each year. His long-term interest was in tuberculosis.

'It's a pity that sulphanilamide does not appear to have any antipathy to the tubercle bacillus, but the chemists are producing newer products. I'd like you to undertake experiments with one of these, which they are willing to supply to us. I'll see that the lab is alerted and has an adequate supply of mice and guinea-pigs. The latter are particularly susceptible to tuberculosis and should be useful.'

So Jonathan grew familiar with the smell of mice-cages as well as the refined scents of Georgian Terraces.

He was drifting pleasantly in terms of a career. This year taught him two things. The first was the attraction of a professional career in England. Sir Christopher was an Oxford don; a cultured man and a world figure. He travelled, entertained many foreign visitors and when he lectured, the journals gave full reports. He was a churchman, with a simple but definite faith that coloured his views and his practice. Somehow this challenged the automatic link, that Jonathan's upbringing had forged between Christian faith and the self-sacrificing service of men. Sir Christopher certainly gave himself to his patients. Some would say that his fees from Harley Street and the London Clinic, gave him ample opportunity to do this. He was a role-model for young surgeons.

The other factor concerned his research project. Raymond knew that the road to fame must include published papers in a man's early professional years. So he also took a special interest in the sad complication of tuberculosis of the spine, paraplegia. Raymond had dozens of patients in plaster-beds, both in town and at the windy branch hospital in Hertfordshire. Some recovered, but as in the main chest hospital, where Jonathan spent one or two days, many young women were dying of the disease. He had every reason to work at his research. God could be served in more ways than one.

It was an absorbing life but even Jonathan could not blot out world events. It was 1939. The previous year war-clouds had gathered. Even in hospitals, sand-bagging had commenced at panic speed. Then Chamberlain had come back from Munich, waving a piece of paper that was to ensure peace.

It was not to be. Now all stops were out. Britain was preparing to fight. Jonathan hadn't had a proper holiday for years. He had money in his pockets. He'd spend a few months with his mother in India.

Chapter Three
ENGULFED BY WAR

They used local labour and materials

Lahore engulfed him as though he had never been away. His mother's image had been kept alive by a racy correspondence. She had remained his confidante. They were quickly back in an easy, intimate relationship. He told her about life in Edinburgh, with a freedom difficult in letters. She laughed girlishly over his account of Rose Caddy.

'How many more girls hung-up their hats Jonathan?'

'She's so gay,' thought Jonathan, 'but she's past fifty!'

'Sister Foxglove, who was matron at Corstorphine, was the daughter of a Gurkha Colonel, with regimental depot at Bakloh. She remembered dances in Lahore and schooldays in Simla.'

'Did you get to the Army in Edinburgh?' she asked him, making no mention of his defection from the ambition to become a Salvation Army officer. He knew that she must be deeply disappointed.

'I tried to link up with the corps where father joined the ranks. It's housed in an old theatre, quite near the Royal College of Surgeons. However, I was very irregular as a houseman and when I got to the Annexe, the Superintendent made his weekly round on Sunday. He suddenly remembered the official Church of Scotland chaplain, who came for a Sunday afternoon service.

'Dr Somerville told me something very interesting. Do you remember I told you about him in one of my letters?'

'Yes, I remember the impressive figure with the long white hair! I saw the long black coat and heard the "refined Scot's accent!"' she laughed.

'Yes, he'd been an educationalist in Calcutta and was an eminent Sanskrit scholar. But this is the interesting bit. You'll recall the boy who was at school with me, whose grandfather had resigned from he Army and set up his own mission in the mountains...?'

'That would be John Thompson.'

'The Church of Scotland still sends an annual donation to his work. "A fine piece of pioneering work," is what he called it.'

Jane turned the conversation back to Lahore and the present.

'There are only a few girls here who can remember you.'

'That's hardly surprising – they must have been infants when I left.'

He turned the spotlight on his mother. Looking up from his chappatti and gur, he asked with a twinkle,

'Is that old friend of yours, Major Palgrave, still at the Mayo, Mum?'

'Major indeed! He's now a full Colonel and Surgeon-General to the Punjab government. We must go and see him. He'll be very proud of you. He's followed your education with the greatest interest.'

'I bet he's given plenty of advice too. I remember one or two gentle nudges in your letters.'

It was September. Britain at last came off the fence, declaring war on Hitler and the Third Reich. The Viceroy had not been slow to commit India to Britain's cause. The Civil and Military Gazette had front-page pictures of the Commander-in-Chief, in conference with Lord Linlithgow. The columns spoke of a massive expansion of the Indian Army. Jane hastened to write to Colonel Palgrave, giving her chitti to the H.Q. peon to be delivered to the Secretariat. By return he replied. Jonathan, browsing on the verandah, looked up to see a government chaprussi, in his brilliant scarlet and gold livery. He called his mother. The chaprussi stood to attention as she slit the envelope, with the brass

71

letter-opener that Stephen had bought her in Simla on their honeymoon.

'Tori der-men main jawab dunga.' Jonathan told him to wait whilst his mother wrote a reply to the Surgeon-General's dinner invitation, Jonathan chatted to the servant. He was elated that his Hindustani was coming back so easily. He had found that the chaprussi, his elegant turban bowed to the seated sahib, was enjoying a chat with one who was not of the Sircar.

It was a new experience for Jonathan to dine with a Burra-Sahib. The mahogany table and the silver-plate gleamed in the candle-light, whilst a bearer stood behind the host's chair. His mother was in a Salvation Army sari, an off-duty one in deep-blue. She was completely at ease with her friend of many years. Jonathan felt sure that the Colonel had wanted marriage.

'I wonder whether he got as far as proposing?' he mused. He realised how little he knew of his mother's private thoughts and feelings. He had an instant realisation of his own private isolation. In John Donne's words he was 'an island'. He had an overwhelming desire to experience the emotion of 'falling in love'. He'd watched the transforming magic of the experience on the faces of others.

'You're day-dreaming Jonathan,' smiled Jane.

'Are you wondering what your next step must be?' Palgrave asked.

'I'm applying for a commission in the Indian Medical Service.' It was Jonathan's turn to smile. Palgrave took his time, wiping his lips on the enormous napkin.

'That gives me great pleasure. I've followed your education with the greatest of interest.'

'As though I were the son you haven't had', thought Jonathan.

He looked again at his mother, seeing her in the role of chatelaine of a house like this. She'd do it very well. But she'd never give up her love for poor Indians. The Colonel was looking at him intently. 'He's reading my thoughts.' Jonathan was sure he was blushing.

'I know your family's devotion to the simple folk of this land, but I maintain that no service has a better track-record than the Indian Medical Service in this respect.'

'It was an I.M.S. Major who brought you into the world.' said Jane. 'He proved to be a great friend of the Criminal Tribesmen. He was a mine of information as Stephen developed the dispensary for them.

'I've more than a sneaking idea that he would have liked to be a doctor himself.' Jane and Palgrave exchanged glances, Palgrave continuing,

'I hope you won't mind if I write my own introduction to the Director

72

of Medical Services in Delhi. He's an old colleague of mine...' He left it in mid-air, offering the fruit bowl to Jane to forestall further comment. She took an Alfonso mango and cut it expertly. Beside each plate, the bearer had placed a small, engraved brass bowl of water, fragrant with floating rose-petals. She dipped her juicy fingers. The meal was following the leisurely, time-honoured pattern of a sahib's life. They had started with an hors d'oeuvre of anchovies on toast, followed by soup, fish and the main course of roast duck.

'Shot on a jhil up country only yesterday,' Palgrave had informed them. They moved on to caramel-custard, before the fruit, nuts and then, with coffee, a bowl of Cadbury's tinned chocolates. It was even more luxurious than the top-table at a Cambridge college.

'It would be pleasurable to us both,' said the Colonel, including Jane, 'if you were to be posted to the Punjab, after your training. But I imagine that is unlikely with a temporary commission, which is all that they are issuing, with war declared.'

They sat out on the lawn, the size of a field, sipping iced drinks. The thick fringe of oleanders, topped by mature shisham trees, screened out all other buildings. It was quiet but for the occasional shouts of tennis enthusiasts, enjoying the cool of the September evening, on floodlit courts at the club. Soon after ten, they were driven home by the Surgeon-General's chauffeur.

Wartime fever had not yet reached the top circles of the services. Jonathan had a relaxed half-hour with a Colonel, who argued the superiority of Glasgow over Edinburgh in a light-hearted fashion. He was then escorted upstairs to the sanctum of the Major General himself. This august soldier, only one-up from Palgrave, was friendly, no doubt in response to his erstwhile colleague's letter.

The war was already changing New Delhi. The sedate garden-city was disappearing under masses of temporary office-blocks. Connaught Circus was crowded not with tourists but with armies of Indian babus in white shirts and pants. He sought out the naval and military hostel, where he had stayed on his first visit to the city as a boy. It was now labelled 'The Red-Shield Hostel'. Eggs and chips were being served, with hefty portions of apple pie, to ravenous service-men off-duty.

He'd been back in Lahore for less than a week, when the long O.H.M.S. envelope arrived. He was now a Lieutenant, instructed to proceed 'forthwith' to the I.M.S. Depot at Lucknow. A travel-warrant was enclosed.

'I'm going up in the world,' he called out to Jane, busy as usual with the cook in the hostel-kitchen.

'Oh', she responded with a question in her voice.

73

'This warrant is for first-class travel.'

'You'll come down with a bump in a few months, when this war is over.' She shared the optimism, that the war would not last long, which she read in the press.

He walked along the Lahore platform, eyeing the reservation slips beside the doors of the Calcutta Mail. He was not to be a lone traveller – every berth was taken. The coolie put his bedding roll on an upper-bunk, but before he could unroll it, the two young men sitting on the berth below jumped up to greet him.

'I say, you're not going to the I.M.S. Depot by any chance are you?'

'Right first time', responded Jonathan, stretching out his hand, 'Jonathan Lindsey.'

'Rhys Morgan', he grasped the proffered hand and then introduced Stuart McMillan. He had an Edinburgh accent, which Jonathan immediately recognised.

'We're out of the same stable', he laughed.

'If you're thinking of Edinburgh you're wrong. Aberdeen is my stable.'

'Well, at least I can claim to have been taught by one of your "grand old men", for George Smythe was my first medical chief. He had me doing lumbar punctures, from my first week on his firm!'

The fourth berth was claimed by a Sikh, who introduced himself as Inderjit Singh. Rhys Morgan pumped his hand and asked where his home might be.

'My family owns land near Amritsar, but my father is a vakil, practising in Lahore.'

'With a father who's a barrister', said Jonathan, 'I can see you as a medico-legal buff. I am taking for granted that you're also bound for the depot in Lucknow.'

For McMillan and Morgan it was a first time in India, although Morgan had an uncle who was a tea-planter in the Nilgiris.

'I just came for a holiday; now I'm hooked.' He didn't look at all rueful. They were full of questions, regarding Jonathan as the authority on the country.

'I'm mystified', he said to them both. 'If this is your first visit to India, why are you coming from Lahore?'

'Explain yourself Mac,' laughed Morgan.

'I've been staying with an uncle also. He's Commissioner in Peshawar. He's convinced that the I.M.S. is a much more interesting outfit than the R.A.M.C.'

'That's interesting', Morgan chipped in. 'I've been holidaying in Kashmir, that's why I'm on this train. I met a knowledgeable chap up in Pahlgam who has just had a book published on the "Romance of

74

Disease".' The flood of laughter halted him momentarily. 'Yes I know it sounds barmy, but he was telling me the tale of a Major Ross, who worked out the transmission of malaria, with nothing more than a bathroom in his bungalow as laboratory.'

'It has the attraction for me, that it is versatile.' Jonathan gave the reason for his decision. 'It serves the Army but also civilians and even provides the senior teaching staff for India's medical colleges; to say nothing of the total Public Health Dept.'

'That explains me', laughed Inderjit. 'I was brought up to believe that it must run the medical services in England too!'

They rolled out their bedding rolls and settled down for the night. On the few main-line stations where they stopped, the newcomers awoke to enjoy the colourful nightlife of the food vendors, who never gave up. Dawn came early; a crisp sunlight that made every village and every copse of trees, stand out from the vast Gangetic plain; endless ploughed fields, with the occasional green break of sugarcane. Inderjit wanted his chhota hazri, introducing them to tea brewed in the carriage, with boiling water from the engine.

'Mail trains normally have an Anglo-Indian driver. I usually find them cheerfully co-operative, especially if I go back with a cup.'

Jonathan was more eager to go on to Moradabad. This would be the first visit on which he could afford a pukka breakfast in the station dining room. His mouth was already watering at the prospect of bacon and eggs. As they sat in the station restaurant, Stuart, listening to Jonathan's exchanges in Urdu with the bearers and manager, said

'You seem to know them all here.'

'I don't know them personally, but I do know the set-up.' He paused then threw in, 'I was born in this town.'

This astonishing information rattled the teacups.

'Well I'm dashed' was all that Rhys could muster. The other ejaculations mirrored his surprise. When they recovered, they were curious.

'What was your father doing in such a place?' Inderjit was their spokesman.

'My parents ran a settlement with a thousand Criminal Tribesmen.'

'I've read that they are the descendants of the Thugs, is that so?' asked Rhys.

Before he could receive an answer from Jonathan, Inderjit plunged in rather angrily,

'Yes, but they are no longer distinguishable from any other gypsies. It is high time that they were freed from this British stigma.' He paused, but throwing caution to the wind continued, 'I'm

75

sure it is one of the first things that an independent Indian government will do!'

They were taken by surprise at this outburst. More in amusement than in anger, Stuart asked,

'Are you a Congressman?'

'No, I keep clear of politics.' He had recovered his easy manner again. 'You don't think I would be joining the armed forces if I were a member of the Congress Party. You know it is very displeased with the Viceroy, for drawing India into this European war.'

Jonathan, looking around the restaurant, changed the subject.

'The burra-sahibs used to buy all their stores here – drinks, bacon, biscuits and even chocolates. As a youngster, I remember envying those who could afford boxes of Playbox biscuits for the baba-log.'

'I see that they stock those tins of Cadbury's chocolates,' Stuart was looking along the shelves. Jonathan joined him, picking up a packet of biscuits.

'"Britannia", made in Cawnpore I see. So Huntley and Palmers' have a rival.'

At Lucknow they piled into taxis and enjoyed intriguing glimpses of old mosques and crumbling palaces, as they moved out into the landscaped gardens and tarmac roads of the Raj.

'This was once the capital of the Kings of Oudh.' Inderjit was in his element as guide. 'Now it is more famous for its medical school and factories.'

The I.M.S. Mess was in a peace-time establishment, with dignified buildings and furnishings. Designed for small annual intake, it was now adapting to war-time needs with tented accommodation in the grounds. At first each doctor had his own tent with a flapped annexe, equipped with 'thunder-box', washbowl and bath in webbed canvas on portable frames. Already the newcomers were reduced to sharing four to a larger tent, with a line of hutted latrines and showers. The programme was tough too. Every morning for the first week, there was a route-march, usually on a surfaced road out of Lucknow. It was late autumn and Jonathan was grateful for the Mogul transport system that decreed wide roads and shade trees. Even so, the return march was hot. They kept in step for three miles or fifty minutes, with a stentorian British sergeant, like a sheepdog moving up and down the line. The ten-minute break was a mercy, only then could they relax and take a swig from their water-bottles. They were warned not to try to splice their drink. A previous group had been too clever, landing themselves in hospital with antimony poisoning, from the mass-produced war-time containers, with poor enamel finish. By the time that they reached base, heavy boots and coarse woollen socks had played havoc with peace-time feet.

Before lunch there was a lecture on public health and two more in the afternoon on tropical diseases and military organisation. Jonathan quickly learned the ranks of the Indian Army, with its strata of Viceroy's Commissioned officers, Subedar-Major, Subedar, Havildar, Naik and Lance-naik. The last, with such a mixture of English and Urdu amused him. The jargon of the Indian Army was a fascination. The average sentence consisted of an Urdu frame with a generous interlarding of English nouns. The nouns were commonly turned into verbs on the parade ground. 'Halt-karo!' was the most staccato.

In the second week, the timetable became more interesting. Route-marches gave way to cross-country runs with the most intriguing terrain, which led to questions in the Mess after dinner.

'Does anyone know anything about Claude Martin? We ran across the grounds of a "La Martinière school", this morning.'

Jonathan had heard of the Frenchman, who had modernised the Nawab of Oudh's army in the 18th century. He had settled down in a princely style but used some of his wealth for the benefit of Eurasian children. But he held his peace, for there was a babble of comment and ribald laughter.

'He had several beautiful Muslim wives, I've heard,' volunteered Stuart.

'And so many children that he needed a private school,' shouted another.

'The Lucknow school is not his only benefaction,' Inderjit interjected. 'He had another built in Calcutta and another in his homeland, near Lyons.'

They ran through the grounds again the next morning, giving Jonathan time to take stock of the impressive stucco palace. It was crowned by arched stairways that met at a central platform with a flagstaff. He could imagine the flamboyant ceremony for the Nawab's birthday, whilst in more recent times there must have been similar junkets in honour of the Queen-Empress. After their work-out, they showered communally. Stuart next to Jonathan asked,

'Have you had any opportunity to explore the old city?'

'No, but I'm going to. I remembered this morning that the boys of La Martinière, shouldered muskets and marched to the defence of the British Residency in the Mutiny.'

'Now that is one of the historic buildings that my uncle said I must see. He says that it is preserved just as it was when Sir Colin Campbell relieved it.'

'Not quite,' he laughed, 'I believe it is in a most attractive park. Let's go in our off-duty on Saturday.'

So amongst the lawns and winter flower-beds, they explored the shattered home of Sir Henry Lawrance. They were silent for a while, each recapturing a scene that had been painted for them in childhood. They read inscriptions on gravestones, predominantly of women and children.

'I always thought of the defenders as British, but it's obvious that there were more Indian than British inside.'

'Forget the cannon-balls and bullets, imagine the heat through that long summer, limited water and little effective in the way of medicine – it's astonishing that so many survived.'

'I suppose that there were religious animosities even then?' Stuart asked.

'You probably know the usual explanation of the cause of the rebellion. New rifles had been issued, for which there were cartridges that had a cardboard end – it had to be bitten off before loading. Agitators passed around the word that the cartridges had been deliberately smeared with lard. Since the sepoys were recruited largely from Bengali Brahmins, this would force them to break caste rules.' Jonathan told him.

'About the level of Adolf Hitler and his claim that Sudetan Germans were being humiliated by the Czechs,' McMillan recalled.

The lasting memory that they carried away from the visit, was of the huge open basement of the Residency, running the whole length of the building. It was cool; its only light slanting down from the barred ventilators near the ceiling.

'Men, women and children of both Indian and British race died together down here, for this was the hospital.'

Jonathan had an invitation to dinner on two occasions during this Lucknow training. Jane had written to an American contemporary from her Moradabad days, who was now very senior – the principal of the women's college that was part of Lucknow University. Jonathan, resplendent in starched shirt, barathea uniform and Sam Browne, was shown into a spacious tiled lounge. Heavy, slowly revolving ceiling fans, creaked their age, as he glanced around at the chintz-covered settees and the carved occasional tables, littered with American bric-a-brac.

'It's a pleasure to have you, Lieutenant Lindsey,' Miss Schultz held his hand, as she sized him up. 'I'm sorry that your mother is not able to come too.'

After dinner they walked slowly around the well-watered and landscaped grounds. It must be a cool retreat from the city in the summer. The city was only a distant glow in the night-sky. Here the stars reigned. Periodically during the next five years, Jonathan was to be acutely aware of the tension between the pleasures of peace in such oases and the arid, coarse and brutal life of a world at war. But for tonight there was no tension, as he discovered what good cooks these ladies from the Middle-West were.

From Lucknow, Jonathan's training continued with a posting to Kirkee. Kirkee was a cantonment on the edge of the plateau, 2000 ft above Bombay and not far from Poona. The small military hospital was considered inadequate for the expanding Army, so a British barracks was swallowed up. His formal training was to continue, but he was to assist Major Rushden, one of the surgeons, from an R.A.M.C. stable. He wrote to Alistair.

'Dear Uncle,

They're still trying to make a soldier of me, but the situation has the saving grace of giving me half my time with patients. They aren't battle casualties yet, so the wards look little different from the Royal Infirmary, until you note the Indian orderlies instead of charming probationers. Of course the long line of creaking fans reminds you of the tropical climate, even though this is regarded as a semi-hillstation. They say there are already 50,000 troops around Poona. Only a few are regulars. Many are recruits straight from the villages – very thin and bumpkinish. A trickle from the U.K. is beginning to arrive, mostly in technical fields such as R.E.M.E., R.A.S.C. and Signals.'

Alistair, who was reading the letter to his father, paused to comment, 'He'll have to watch his pen; I'm surprised that the censor hasn't scored out all this information.'

'Mm', was all the old man would permit himself. He was proving a staunch admirer of his grandson, who was turning out a capital fellow. So Alistair continued the reading.

'I was called out after midnight last Saturday. A Major from the Signals School brought in a Lieutenant with a lacerated face, from a fall from his bike. There had been a Mess party, and the Lieutenant had not yet learned to hold his drink. A fuddled head and a stony track had produced some deep cuts. There was a strange sequel. It was very quiet in the theatre, just two nurses and the orderly Medical Officer, who gave the anaesthetic. So I agreed the Major's pressing request to stay and watch, on condition that he stayed back near the wall and made no attempt to come to the table. There was a quiet hum of conversation, as the cuts were cleaned and sutured. But the peace was shattered by an almighty crash. The Major had fainted, falling against a line of bowl-stands, ready for Monday's long list. They tipped over in a chain reaction that seemed never ending. He hit his head on the marble floor and already there was blood pouring from a split scalp. The Lieutenant was wheeled out and the Major took his place. He must have felt foolish in explaining his injury when he went to breakfast the next morning.

Love to Aunt, Grandpa and Grandma,

Jon.'

Major Rushden had been a general surgeon, consultant to a provincial hospital.

'Your recent experience in orthopaedics is proving invaluable, Jonathan; I am most impressed by this new concept of the conservation of tissue, avoiding amputations.'

He'd seen his assistant handling the leg of an Indian driver with a crush fracture. Jonathan had thoroughly cleaned the wound, excising every fragment of devitalised flesh, had dusted it with sulphanilamide, packed with a non-adherent dressing, before manipulation and the application of a plaster-cast. After a couple of weeks the plaster looked messy and smelt even worse, but when after another fortnight the plaster was changed, the wound looked clean!

'You'll walk again,' Rushden assured the anxious man. But turning to Jonathan said 'That was due for amputation in my book.'

'Not since the Spanish Civil War, when the Austrian, Bohler's, revolutionary technique was tried out in battle conditions,' was the reply.

'War's a hateful business, but it usually means rapid advances in medicine and surgery,' Rushden concluded.

Jonathan was sorry when the month was up and he was posted to Poona. This was the final British Base Hospital, from which invalids with no military future, could expect a passage on one of the rare hospital ships. To Jonathan it proved to be a sort of military post-graduate school. Leading surgeons, now in khaki, pronounced on the suitability of Captains and Lieutenants to be graded as

Surgical Specialists with promotion to Major. Even in peace-time it had been a plum posting, its cool nights, landscaped bungalows, and abundant social life were coveted. So the O.C. was a senior R.A.M.C. surgeon, whose career had started in France in 1916. Colonel Routledge was bluff but known as a disciplinarian. General Duties Officers like Jonathan took no liberties with him. His weekly ward rounds were feared. His look could be fierce and his tongue sharp. By contrast, the O.C. Surgical Division was a brilliant surgeon who had achieved a professorial chair by the time that he was forty. He was still young enough for the rigours of war. He ran his 500 beds like a medical college hospital, holding weekly case reviews, where his G.D.O.s presented patients, answered questions but left him to pilot the discussion. Col Routledge often came but never made a contribution.

'He's professionally ossified,' said those who suffered under his strictures.

The huge campus was criss-crossed by roads and studded with gnarled trees – planted by Wellington – the wags maintained. Under wartime limitations and in an alien land, they managed to keep civilised. The old regimental theatre staged amateur concerts; there were soprano soloists as well as basses, for to Poona came all the British nurses before they were posted up country. Flutes and even violins appeared from nowhere. To these weekly concerts came service personnel from miles around, their 3 ton lorries parked all up the main avenue. The cheers for encores could be heard in all the wards. Not only nurses with a pip on each shoulder, but soon the first physiotherapists, more young women to add a little spice to the monotonous life of a male organisation.

Dances became frequent and even weddings. There were the inevitable tears when postings shattered budding romances. Mess parties became frequent. Jonathan found himself paying for other men's thirst, for the total cost was levied on every member of the Mess. As a rare teetotaller, he was frequently sought out by worried bearers, who needed assistance to get their masters to bed. He became quite an experienced physician at handling hangovers.

Three months of this almost civilian life passed very quickly. Professional assessments must have reached Command H.Q., for Colonel Routledge, almost smiling, had some postings to hand out. Jonathan could hardly believe his ears.

'Lieutenant Lindsey' – a long pause whilst he adjusted his bifocals, 'You are to proceed to 120 Indian Base General Hospital, stationed at Moradabad in the U.P. It carries the brevet-rank of Major.'

'Good gracious, that's the very hospital in which I was born!' he burst out as soon as they were out of earshot of the Colonel's office.

'Back to the womb, old boy,' said Arthur Phillips, also a new Major. It was hard to tell whether there was envy involved, for his own appointment was to the front line in Persia.

He got a week's leave and knew what to do with it. He'd had a yen to go south, ever since he had seen those slides of Travancore, in Cambridge.

'Go down from Poona on the metre-gauge,' Rushden, in from Kirkee, for a clinical meeting, suggested. 'It's slow and old-India – off the beaten track.'

It certainly was. It was sheer luxury to be given one of the retiring rooms at Mysore station. There were marble floors and ample space with elegant furniture. There was even a princely shower that worked.

'The Maharajah treats us all as his guests,' commented an officer just leaving. In the morning, refreshed and eager, he set out for Ootacamund, using the bus that chugged at leisurely pace through dense jungle. It chugged, because war-time restrictions on petrol meant that it was powered by inefficient producer gas, made in a cumbersome burner erected on a Heath-Robinson platform on the back. It even had to carry a sack of charcoal! They crawled slowly at every suggestion of a gradient. It came to a full-stop at the first hill. Jonathan welcomed the quiet of the forest shade. He sat listening to the birdsong until a smaller, petrol-driven bus arrived. The conductor attempted to get a quart into a pint pot, with fierce arguments from those who could not get in.

They circled slowly upwards through the increasing coolness. It was Naini Tal all over again, with more lush vegetation. But Ooty wasn't. It was higher but more like Gattonside, with rolling grassy slopes. The little town was quiet and sedate; a little bit of Victorian England. Its row of shops sold books, watercolours and cream-teas.

'You'd love this place,' he wrote to Lahore. 'I can't imagine a place where war is more unthinkable.'

It was a wrench to go down the hill again, this time to Coimbatore, with many changes to reach Delhi; then the final hundred miles through sugar-cane and bajri to Moradabad. Fortunately it was winter; it was pleasant to spend a couple of hours wandering around the well-stocked shops on Connaught Circus.

He stepped down from the train to be greeted by a smart salute from an Indian Havildar, with a traffic officer's brassard.

'Major Lindsey Sahib?'

He led him to a staff-car, parked in the spacious station approach.

Jonathan paused to look around. It was ten years since he had last seen it, yet it was little changed. Of course on that last visit it had been the tonga of the Criminal Tribes' settlement which had been waiting for him, not a staff-car with saluting orderly.

He was taken to his quarters, in the block behind the Officer's mess and was nearly unpacked when the orderly returned. He stood at the open door, clicking his heels to attract attention.

'Huzur. The Officer Commanding would like to see you at once, if that is convenient.'

Jonathan had not heard any detail of the take-over of the erstwhile mission hospital. It came as a surprise to find that the Colonel in charge of 120 I.B.G.H. (Indian Troops), was a short wiry Tamil. He was a regular I.M.S. officer of seniority. He was immediately friendly. Initial salutes and introductions over, Colonel Devaraj left his desk, waving Jonathan to a comfortable armchair. There was a small carved table beside it.

'What will you drink?'

'Nimbu-pani if you have it, please.'

'Certainly, and I'll join you. A surprise and a pleasure to find a Britisher who doesn't want alcohol.'

As the Colonel filled his glass, Jonathan looked around the room. It was Dr Snow's consulting room. It was even the same desk at which he had been offered tea, after the emergency operation that had first kindled the thought of a medical career.

'I know a lot about you Major and am glad that you are joining us. When I was a medical student at Madras Medical College, a few of us used to go to the Muktifauj* on Sunday evenings. I'm not Christian, but I enjoyed those meetings and I hope I learned something. I respect the work done here by the Salvation Army and can understand that the locals are upset that we have taken over and denied them a medical service. So if you can find a suitable building, on the periphery of the hospital for the treatment of villagers, you have my blessing. I hope to get to know you socially, but it is war-time and mine is a mess life, I'm afraid.'

Havildar Gulzar Masih introduced himself as clerk to Block 10 with its forty beds, now Jonathan's responsibility. As he followed the havildar along the verandah of the new but temporary ward block, he reflected that the clerk must be a Christian by his name.

'Have you been here long Havildar?' he asked him.

'For quite a few years, sahib, for I was trained here when it was the Muktifauj hospital.'

*Indian title of the Salvation Army

83

'You don't belong to the Muktifauj as well as the Indian Army, do you?'

'Ji han. And so does Sister Burdett who is in charge of the block.' He continued, 'The news has reached the bazaar that the Chota Sahib has come back. People were very fond of your father.'

In Edinburgh Jonathan had received from his mother, copies of the Indian War Cry published in Poona. He remembered reading of the appointment of a Captain Burdett – from New Zealand, if he remembered correctly.

He followed the havildar to a broad hall with offices on either side. They paused outside one which was clearly labelled 'Sister-in-charge'. The clerk knocked, opened the door, clicked his heels, saluted and departed. Rebecca Burdett took a long look at her new boss, before he had time to speak. He was handsome as well as a co-religionist. Things were going better than she had ever expected, when her world had been turned upside down by the invasion of the military.

'Jonathan Lindsey', he offered his hand. 'I'm afraid that we are going to see a lot of each other.'

'No need to be afraid. I for one, am delighted to know that you are here. It will be like old times to have you as a colleague. I have taken it for granted that you are a Salvationist.'

He had been studying her. She was about five foot five, he judged; dark-haired, with what looked like a natural wave, not suppressed by a bun. She was slight in build but unquestionably feminine. He had a question to answer.

'Yes – but not a very active one. I don't drink or smoke, and I'm still paying my cartridge to Edinburgh.' He laughed outright. 'Does that satisfy you?'

'I'm sure we will get on famously', she smiled back.

As the days went by, they learned more of each other, though Jonathan felt that he had talked more about his life and interests, than about hers. They shared many cups of coffee but had little privacy for closer contact. They became conspirators, when the Registrar showed them a building which stood back from the long lines of the main wards.

'Built for isolation, then found to be in the wrong place. Typical military planning', he grinned. 'If you want somewhere for your civilian patients and will be responsible for their nursing care, it's all yours for a trial period. You can get what furnishings you need from the Quartermaster.'

The Quartermaster even fitted up a partition, so that they could admit both sexes. They arranged to hold surgeries two evenings a week, Christian volunteers from the town quickly came forward to staff them.

By the second week, the whole of Moradabad had heard the glad tidings and there was a long line of waiting patients, down to the gate from the Mall. To Jonathan and Rebecca, it was so much a shared baby that they were drawn into ever increasing reliance on each other.

Saturday mornings were special. The O.C. Surgical Division did his round. Sister laid on coffee and bacon sandwiches, for the friendly chat that followed. What a contrast from the wary move from bed to bed of Poona days. It had been a very hot summer and the Medical Division had been overcrowded with dysentery and malaria. It was still a quiet war, with almost a peacetime level of surgical practice. The monsoon came with its blessed coolness for a few hours after each storm, only to be followed by a sticky heat. Even black stormy skies were a welcome sight, after months of unvaried dust-blurred blue. The club was a small provincial one, boasting few amenities; certainly no swimming pool. When Lieutenant Colonel Sen Roy and the General-duties-officer, Lieutenant Hamid, had thanked Sister and gone off to their quarters, Becky turned to Jonathan.

'Do we go for a swim in the Fazalpur dhobi-tank this afternoon?'

'It's getting a little cooler now, so why don't we take our bikes and go down to the river for a picnic?'

'Sounds good to me. I'll see that my saddle-bag has something tasty, if you will see to the flasks.'

They cycled down from the Chungi, along the old cankah road to the maidan. They passed the riding school, where the Risaldar Major was putting police cadets through their paces. Then it was Allah-ud-Din's mango bagh and the old British church, its yellow and white stucco gleaming in the afternoon sunshine. Becky waved an arm towards the expanse of scrub grassland which was the maidan.

'This must have been an impressive parade ground when there were East India Company troops here.'

'And can you see the Victorian ladies getting into their carriages at the church door and processing sedately down the long avenue to the gate?'

'It's a full century that you are looking back, for all that ended at the Mutiny.'

On their left were open fields and the thatched village, where the sweepers lived. These were the lowest of the outcaste people who performed the most menial tasks in every household. Several children called out to them, and even kept running alongside. Sahibs often kept sweets in their pockets; these were not the desi ones made in the bazaar, but English ones, wrapped in paper. The near-naked urchins were not disappointed.

85

They took a path between fields of dhal. After the rains and Autumn sunshine, the narrow track was hard and irregular. Becky feared for the basket on her carrier. It contained what Jonathan called the New Zealand speciality – a Pavlova. They reached a rare clump of trees on the bank of the broad river, flowing smoothly to its confluence with the Ganges. Becky spotting the shade, beamed at him, as she spread the small ground-sheet on the sand.

'That was clever of you.'

'It's a bit early for tea isn't it? I think it is a wonderful opportunity for me to hear all about New Zealand and what brought you to India.'

'The sun will have gone down before you get your tea if you want me to blether. Oh well, be it on your own head.' She rumpled his hair to make her point.

'Be it ever so long, I'll enjoy every chapter of it, if you are in it.' He put his arm round her shoulder and kissed her hair.

'No distractions then,' she laughed up at him. 'Here goes.'

When the first settlers, led by Wakefield, sailed into the choppy waters of the Cook Strait, they sought the marvellous harbour described by the explorer as being near the southern tip of the north island of New Zealand. They sailed between the rocky headlands and made for the opposite shore. Amongst the small party to land on the beach at Petone, were the two Burdett brothers. In a mixed bag of farming types, they were useful craftsmen; one a blacksmith and the other a carpenter. Near the first camp, the Hutt river flowed down from the forested hills to the sea. The Burdetts moved a little way upstream and put down their roots. Their descendants continued to live in the valley, as the forests were felled to be replaced by farms and homesteads. Becky was born at Lower Hutt in 1914. Her father owned a general store which still stocked the ironmongery that his forebears had introduced to the country.

It was a conservative society, still loyal to the village mores of Buckinghamshire. Old family names appeared in every generation. Rebecca's earliest memories were of a kitchen mantelpiece, with a pair of china dogs, that were from one of the trunks hoisted from the cutter on Petone beach in 1841. Neither James nor Victoria Burdett could be called religious, but tradition demanded the blessing of the Anglican Church at the great events of family life. Victoria Clausen, in trailing bridal gown, had proudly, if nervously processioned down the aisle of Hutt Church, on the arm of her father, to blend her Dutch traditions with the stolid Saxon ways of James Burdett. Occasionally, literally on highdays and holidays, Rebecca held her mother's gloved hand as they entered the South porch for Matins. She had been christened in this wooden church. Whenever she met the black-coated Vicar, he patted her dark curls and invited her to join the Sunday school.

Becky was eight when, on reaching school one Monday morning, her friends Emma and Joan rivalled each other in describing an adventure of the previous day. They had gone with other youngsters from their street, to a novel Sunday school, run by a Salvation Army Captain. He had cycled out from Wellington they learned.

'It was great fun', said Joan. 'We acted Noah's ark. There were so many children, that we paired up – a boy and a girl', she giggled, 'and we had to say what animal we were.'

'The Captain was Noah,' Emma took up the story, 'and put on a long beard and dressing gown, and told us all about God.'

Joan managed to get in again here.

'We kept making the noise of our animal.'

'And we all sang; "and the rain came tumbling down".'

So when next Sunday came, Emma and Joan appeared on the Burdett doorstep. Becky's entreaty to be allowed to join them, fell on Victoria's reluctant ear. But James had heard from the parlour, and called out,

'Let the lass go. The Salvos were very good to me in the War. They can't do Becky any harm.'

Rebecca was off like an arrow before her mother had any opportunity to remonstrate. As she fled she heard her father describing the horrors of trench warfare in France and the cups of char the Salvos had specialised in.

The event lived up to her classmates' glowing account.

'The Captain is jolly, but he's shrewd too', she told her father. 'Shrewd' was a word that she had looked up in the dictionary her father had given her the previous week. It was already dated, but Becky was finding it intriguing. She was keen on derivations. 'Shrewd' was given as, 'from Early English shrewen – to curse.' How did that get to mean astute or sagacious? Anyway the captain was astute. He could manage boys and divert their penchant for mischief, into dramatic roles. The bible scene this week had been the Good Samaritan, with parts for robbers, priests and donkeys; all were male castings. Becky put all the pathos her imagination provided in caring for the woe-begone traveller, as maid-servant to the innkeeper.

March came, and Becky ran home from her regular Sunday afternoon engagement, with the announcement that next Sunday was the Harvest Festival with an evening meeting for adults.

87

'Dad, can I have some of your carrots and tomatoes?'

'Sure.'

'And Mum, could I take a jar of your raspberry jam?'

Parents were also invited in the afternoon, to see the display their children had created, as well as to admire their play – 'The Sower'. James in a new bowler hat and Victoria in her flowered straw, were there. They silently assessed their produce against that of their neighbours, glancing around discreetly to see who was there. They were back again at night, and soon in conversation with the Salvationists who had come out from Wellington to provide a musical accompaniment. James discovered that one of the cornet players was the wholesaler who supplied most of his groceries.

'Didn't know that you belonged to the Army.'

'I'll have to start wearing a badge in my lapel.' They shook hands, to cover their initial embarrassment. James quickly recovered with a quip,

'Will I now get a discount on my porridge oats?'

'Now, now,' responded Timothy Bracebridge, 'but there will always be a cup of tea when you're in Wellington. Better still, bring your wife into the morning meeting at the Citadel, joining us for lunch afterwards.'

'I'll pass that invitation to Victoria and let you know, Timothy.'

It was the friendliness of the Salvationists which cemented the Burdett association. Before long, Victoria was a regular at the women's meeting on a Tuesday afternoon.

Lower Hutt was virtually a suburb of Wellington now, although it kept its village culture. It had a tiny hospital, supported by local gifts, mostly in kind. 'Pound-day' was a school event, when pupils vied with each other in gifts importuned from their parents: a blue bag of Burdett's sugar, or a white one of McDougall's flour. Becky could usually cajole a few tins of cocoa or prunes which put her amongst the elite. They were proud of their hospital. Becky ran home breathlessly with the news that one of the assistants of the New Zealand surgeon who had become famous in London for repairing soldiers' faces, had returned and was coming to operate one day a week 'at our hospital'.

'It was Becky who was responsible for the Burdett's first appearance at the hospital. Her tonsils were condemned by the school doctor. The E.N.T. surgeon still followed the traditional technique, so Becky had the simple but frightening experience, afforded by near suffocation with a mask which had been stuffed with cottonwool, doused in a chloroform-ether mixture. Once unconscious the child's glands were guillotined. The child came round very quickly, but she never forgot awakening with blood trickling from her mouth as the nurse swabbed her face. It was an inauspicious introduction to a career, which was to open for her when highschool days were drawing to a close with the Senior Cambridge examination.

By that time Becky and her parents were Salvation Army soldiers of the Lower Hutt corps. The highlight of that year was the Congress, when for four or five days the city of Wellington was invaded by Salvationists of both islands. Becky, as an alto singer, was involved in the Saturday evening programme, with youth bands, choirs and drama groups. There were even gymnasium events, with vaulting horses and pyramids. But it was the climax in a whole Sunday of meetings in the City Hall that she would always remember. At ten thirty in the morning, the Territorial Commander, a tall dignified Englishman, took the salute from the steps of the City Hall, as a dozen bands punctuated the long procession with martial strains. Many of the men were veterans of the N.Z. Expeditionary Force, from the struggle in Europe. They marched well and proudly under another banner.

Each year an outstanding leader from overseas was guest speaker. In 1930 it was Commissioner McDowell, who delighted Becky with racy tales of pioneering in Korea and Japan.

'One can travel for miles in the mountains of Korea, village after village, without a sign of medical care.' He described the village Salvationists' love of their church.

'They are rather like the Jews of the Old Testament. They love scriptural songs and also tithe on the produce of their farms.' He contrasted their poverty, with the relative affluence of his present congregation.

'We are not only richer, but we have excellent healthcare. Shouldn't we be sharing this also? We need doctors and nurses willing to make their homes in an alien culture. I am sure that someone here this morning is waiting to volunteer.' His outstretched arm rotated slowly around that vast audience, stopping Becky was sure at her. In a flash she challenged herself, 'Couldn't I take nurses' training?' Her grades in school finals were good, and backed by her headmistress she was accepted for Wellington Hospital's School of Nursing. But she was only seventeen. She had a year to fill.

'If I were you, I'd go to the Salvation Army hospital and see how the other half lives,' was the advice of the tutor who interviewed her.

'It's not only good at obstetrics but they care for unmarried mothers, some of them very young.'

Four further years were to pass, before she qualified as nurse and midwife. They were years of gloom in New Zealand. Economic depression meant unemployment and hunger. This had minimal effect on the spartan existence of a student nurse. But at home, father reported greatly reduced sales and mounting business problems. It hurt him, but he had to cut staff or go bankrupt. This moral dilemma lived with him more than his increasing workload or bad debts. Even in the first year that Becky had been at Bethesda Hospital, she listened to personal tragedies

'I didn't expect this baby. I wouldn't have let Tom love me, but for the fact that we were to marry very soon. Then he lost his job and went off to Australia. I have never heard of him since.' Annabel cried inconsolably.

Becky's salary increased as she signed on as a staff-nurse at the Wellington Hospital. She also had more regular off-duty and could attend the meetings at the Citadel. It was on the hard benches, that her mind frequently wandered when the captain was preaching.

The idea which had impelled her into nursing waxed and waned. She was part of an ebullient group of young people, in love with their church, but equally in love with life and each other. The young men were all bandsmen, and it seemed to Rebecca that their greatest ambition was to triple-tongue. She did keep her sights on excelling in her profession. She commenced study for a tutor's post. One free afternoon she walked down Cuba Street and saw a sale notice in the window of the Salvation Army bookshop. She went in and browsed. She returned to her flat with a copy of 'The Undauntables', written by a woman who had served in China and in India. As she read of girls of her own age, who had lived as Indians in the villages of southern India, her ambitions faded. In tears she came to prayer. She was set on her original compass course. The next day she was back in Cuba Street, but this time to apply for overseas service.

Jonathan interrupted with an occasional question, but he mostly listened in silence to her surprising story, so different from his own. He could place those pioneers. Those families from Buckinghamshire would be neighbours of his Norfolk forebears. Like them they would be concerned about the price of wheat, or the pig killed for winter bacon. They sat in the village pub most evenings, gossiping about their neighbours.

By the ruins of the picnic-basket, they sat wordlessly at one. The sky was on fire; red, red the river flowed as they embraced. They knew that those two separate courses were now one.

The expatriate grapevine in Moradabad worked quickly.

'I gather that handsome surgeon at the military hospital has taken a shine to his ward-sister.' Inez Pasquale, the youngest of the American teachers at the mission girls' school, just outside the city gates, told her principal, Hope Harwell from Indiana.

'I'm almost envious,' the younger woman sighed.

'I think I'll invite them both to dinner; ask him to find a mutually convenient date.'

'Playing the matrimonial agent, Hope?'

Jonathan had experience of Inez's banter.

'These American miss-sahibs have little respect for their elders,' he had told Becky. Miss Harwell kept a good table. She was famous for her ice-cream and mango tart. She watched her guests discreetly. She was sure that the romance was going well, before they reached the after-dinner mints.

'You two find comfortable seats in the garden, whilst Inez and I look to the coffee and cookies.'

As they sat out under the great trees, Becky said, 'You'll find it hard to resist her cookies. She makes them of cashew nuts!'

'Do you notice that the Americans use servants much less than we do?'

'I wouldn't mind doing a little more myself, if I had all the gadgets that they have.'

They walked their cycles home. Never had the stars twinkled more brightly. The road was empty. Occasionally the silence was broken by the call of a jackal, but they didn't hear it. They paused before they reached the hospital and with one mind turned in an embrace. The cycles clattered down unheeded as the kiss was prolonged.

Until Pearl Harbour and the entrance of America, India, though on a war footing, was not conscious of the horrors of war. There was an ever increasing military build-up with recruits coming from remote villages, for service in Africa and the Middle-East. There were no military camps around Moradabad, so that emergencies were local, or the normal post-operative alarums of a surgical division. It meant that Becky, whenever off-duty in the evening could spend her time with Jonathan. Already social mores were changing. For a nurse to be entertained in an officer's quarters, now aroused little comment. But Mrs Mason was from an older school. As wife of the Principal of the Provincial Police Training College, she had a spacious old bungalow set in acres of land. She gave them a standing invitation to spend their leisure at her home, along the Mall towards the old city.

Virginia had been a patient in Rebecca's care, when the hospital had been a mission one. It had a comfortable private ward, used by quite a number of staff of the Imperial services and their families. Her hysterectomy in '38 had gone smoothly and she had grown very fond of her nurse. Her garden seemed immense and was famous for its herbaceous borders and brilliant canna beds. They were revitalised every year by manure from the riding school.

'Cannas like it raw', she informed Becky. 'The malis have the cannas up every year and shift the soil to the other beds, where the plants are more delicate feeders. The cannas then have the new mixture.'

'Everyone says that you have the best blooms in Moradabad.'

So in the hot season, it was pleasant to sit out as the sun sank. The garden scents were strong, after the gardener's evening watering. Dusk was short and they were quickly enveloped in the Indian night. It had been described as 'velvety', Becky reflected and echoed that sense of softness after the harsh, enervating heat of the tropical day. The air became alive with the buzz of a thousand insects.

They relaxed; their communion could be wordless. As the relationship ripened it brought the future into focus. They decided that marriage must wait until the war was over; surely that would not be long now. Happy in the present, they knew that a vital decision must be made. Either Becky must resign, or Jonathan become a Salvation Army officer. It was back to the old challenge for Jonathan. The war had only left it in abeyance. Daily intercourse with his peers made it clear, that a conventional surgical career could not satisfy him. His original intent in becoming a doctor had been altruistic; the war was allowing him to drift on the current of events. They discussed it one evening when Horace and Virginia Mason had moved indoors with their chhota pegs, leaving them with a jug of iced nimbu-pani and the conventional warning to be good.

'I suppose I've been fortunate,' said Becky, 'I've not had any real doubts about what I should do. I've had many about my ability to stay the course.'

'It's hard to imagine you with any doubts; you spend most of your time dispelling mine.' They fell silent as usual, with the issue unresolved.

Periodically Jonathan needed to discuss the administration of the civilian unit with the registrar, another Tamil regular, Lt. Col. Swami Das.

'Your special local unit is arousing considerable interest amongst those on high!' He told Jonathan. 'It's good publicity and they want your figures regularly.'

'I do the occasional visit in the bazaar; usually to the zenana quarters in a brass merchant's house. Do you want those figures too?' he laughed.

'There's another matter I wanted to raise with you. You are due for a bit of leave. Even if you don't want a month it would be wise to take ten days, whilst we are relatively slack.' He liked this Englishman who obviously loved ordinary Indians. 'Of course he grew up here,' he mused.

'Didn't you go to school in Naini Tal? If you'd like to go up into the hills I could easily fix you up for a few days in the mess at Ranikhet.'

'That's thoughtful of you. I may take you up on it, but for the moment let me sleep on it.' As he left, there was a smile on the Colonel's face. 'It isn't time to sleep on it – he wants to discuss it with that Sister he's keen on, I'll bet.' He was an interested observer of the alien Angrezi attitude to marriage. His own, he reflected, had been arranged for him by his parents, after the usual casting of horoscopes and professional assistance in seeking potential brides, from his own bania caste. He hadn't given it a lot of thought but it had worked well, he concluded. Love came after marriage, not before it.

So that evening Jon broached the subject with Becky.

'Would you be happy to come on a trek with me?'

There was a long pause, whilst Becky's thoughts travelled a record distance. Her upbringing would have vetoed such an intimate adventure before marriage. But times were changing, and her love jumped at the prospect. Anyway she'd trust Jonathan till Kingdom Come. Jonathan surveyed her face, it always betrayed her feelings. It was now revealing indecision. The minutes ticked away; their eyes locked.

She twined her arms about his neck and whispered,

'That would be lovely. I can get leave easily at the moment.'

They alighted from the chhota-line train at Kathgodam, to be beset by a gesticulating mob of coolies, not the regimented redshirts of the main stations, but hillmen in ragged homespun clothes; sturdy men of short stature, earning a few rupees to augment the income from the produce of their terraces. Becky dealt with them competently and cheerfully. She had done it many times before. Jonathan was at the bus-office grille. Twenty years slipped away; he was a schoolboy again. The clerk singled him out for the front seats by the driver, at double fare of course. Their bedding rolls and bags were hoisted on the roof of this utilitarian conveyance. Its wooden body was covered in painted floral arabesques. What the Mogul craftsmen had produced by marble inlay, their descendants conjured up with Britannia paint.

Becky had the outside seat, and whilst the noisy loading was in process, could watch the tousled-haired women seated in the shade, completely absorbed in the task of mutual delousing. Only when every seat had been paid for, did the driver climb in, whilst his mate, a self-important little youngster, cranked with the heavy starting-handle. Then he used his buttocks to force a seat on the already crowded back row.

The first few miles were a foretaste of a delightful holiday as they rattled through the forest, beside a mountain stream flowing over boulders which sparkled where the sun caught them. It was in a hurry to reach the Kosi, which then ran on more sedately to join the mighty Ganges. Here and there were clearings with plantations of bananas or groves of young mangoes. It was a road constructed before the days of reinforced concrete. Local engineers had used local labour and material. Becky watched Jonathan lost in dreamy recollection.

'You're far away Jon.' She pressed his arm affectionately.

'It's incredible that nearly twenty years have slipped away. It's going to be fun rediscovering all this with you. I'm excited at the chance of introducing you to Mum.'

'I'm going to love her: I already admire her.'

The bus pulled into a teashop carved out of the hillside. The passengers, welcoming the relief from the congestion, literally fell out of the vehicle. The driver's mate put a rag over the radiator cap before turning it, jumping back as steam and boiling water burst forth.

'How about a pakora with the tea?' Jonathan was already in the queue. 'I was always so impecunious that I had to give such luxuries the miss. It's going to be fun having the largesse of a Major's salary.'

Becky spontaneously threw her arms around Jane's neck.

'It's going to be lovely to have a mother in India.'

Jonathan took them out to dinner and they toured the bazaar in a leisurely way and expectantly, Jonathan's wallet at the ready. There were rugs from Mirzapur, but also some that had crossed the passes from Turkestan. It was Jonathan's first opportunity to buy an intimate gift for Becky, who discovered a cache of prewar goods from China. Her eyes lit up as she found a flowered Shantung dressing gown and held it against herself questioningly. There were pyjamas to match.

Jane, with a sparsely furnished home in her mind's eye, accepted a circular Mirzapur.

'It will give quite a lift to my gol-kamra; the girls will be full of questions about you. They will want to know what colour your fiancée's hair is, and how tall she is.'

94

They stayed two nights, which meant that he took his mother to the bazaar for her weekly shopping, with the opportunity to talk to her alone. 'I've already taken to Becky, and I'm delighted for you. I'll admit I've been a little concerned that I had a confirmed bachelor on my hands.' Their eyes met. 'May you find marriage as rewarding as I did.'

They were silent for a long while as they walked beside the lake, oblivious of the yachts and the flower-beds.

Jonathan was sorry that he could not introduce Becky to Ambrose Jones school – it was no more. The Americans had sold it. So on Monday morning it was another crowded bus to Ranikhet. The road wound downhill for many miles before it crossed the Kosi on the only major bridge of the whole route. Then it was a long tortuous climb to the cantonment, a thousand feet higher than Naini. It was a totally different setting. The snows looked more intimate and the conifers and gentle greensward that made an 18-hole golf-course possible, contrasted with Naini's steep crater. They were taken further, by the touting driver of a local bus. They were embarked on a visit to the ancient Gurkha capital of Almora, where Jonathan had an indelible memory to share. They still had a three mile hike along a ridge that gave them fleeting glimpses of Nanda Devi.

Despite the altitude, it was hot; though the coolies carrying their baggage made light of it. In a glorious spot, with a view between the deodars of the Trisul massif, the bungalow owned by the American Methodists and named inevitably 'Epworth', had been built by the first Commissioner of Kumaon, the redoubtable Ramsey, as his own home. The Lucknow academics, holidaying nearby, had been well primed by their Moradabad friends and invited the engaged couple to be their guests. They had a feminine curiosity to see the surgeon's girl. Becky was tired but Jonathan called her out to share the sunset. As the last light faded there was still an alpine glow on the snows. They were so close that Nanda Devi seemed to fill the sky. Out of hearing of the Americans, Jonathan informed the New Zealander, 'The highest peak in the British Empire.'

'No wonder that the Hindus see it more reverently as the home of the gods.' The dark night shrouded their long embrace and then it was separate rooms.

'We've two days here, haven't we?' Becky asked at breakfast.

'That's right. This is the end of our exploration.'

'Would you forgive me if I had a really lazy day? I will be happy for you to explore on your own.'

He looked anxiously at her.

'You're not going down with something sinister are you?'

'No there is nothing obscure. I'm just tired out, and will enjoy the rest of the holiday more for a long rest. I've plenty of daydreaming to do.'

He set off immediately. Although it was early, clouds were already obscuring the peaks. He wanted to visit the valley where the bear had given him his first patient.

'I could do that operation better myself now,' he thought. Below him was the infant Kosi, and in a bend of it, the very old temple of Bageshwar. He climbed down rapidly to it and found that at this time of the year, he could cross on massive stepping stones. Years before there had been an earthquake that had ruined the shrine.

There were large mounds of squared stones covered with vegetation like shrouds. He found the heart of the temple largely intact, the squat tower arched to a rounded crown – a lotus flower.

He bowed below the low lintel, a truly massive slab that somehow reminded him of Stonehenge and the Druids. Those ancient British priests had never attracted him. Here the imagery was more human. As his eyes became accustomed to the gloom, he made out the simple altar at its centre. Its huge stone base again reminded him of the Jews, with such a plinth for the ark of the covenant. Here the symbolism was not of an austere code of disciplined living, but an open invitation to erotic indulgence. The erect phallic stone was black from centuries of the oiled caresses of childless women. In the desolation of the earth's tremor, this smooth apex had survived and was still used. It was encircled by many faded garlands and on the plinth were the remnants of the food that had been offered to the gods. It was now prasad – the only devourers, the crows.

The minutes ticked away as Jonathan crouched. He pondered on the obsession of ancient peoples, with the rhythm of conception, birth and death, as a reliable fulfilment – a stable basis of life for man, beast and crops. To them it was a life-force to be worshipped – and to be enjoyed. When that life-force failed and the longed-for babe did not come, it became a cause for heart-searching, pilgrimage and the bringing of gifts to placate a vengeful god.

Jonathan was very hungry by the time that he got back to Epworth. And he was tired. So after a late lunch they sat in companionable silence. Eventually the sun went down and the forest cast a ghostly gloom.

'I feel the better for a quiet day, but I haven't been idle. The ladies have taught me how to make American doughnuts. They are much crisper than the ones that I remember and they have a hole in them. You are going to have them for sweet, after another American dish. Guess – hamburgers!'

It was a cold night, but cosy in his sleeping-bag Jonathan had learned to use his heavy military valise in this way, he drifted from reflexion on the day to profound slumber. His dream took him to the shrine. He was asleep on a pilgrim mat before the lingam. He was stirred by a woman's touch. She was whispering endearments and searching him. The devadasi clamped her mouth on his, offering the delights of the pagan deity. He awoke breathing heavily and slowly made out the walls, not of a temple but his bedroom. He instantly thought of Becky, asleep in the next room. Half awake, his reverie continued. He recollected what he knew of oriental religions. They viewed all life as the merging and fruitfulness of opposites, male and female, light and darknesss, summer and winter were the universal obsession of primitive man. From ying and yang he moved to the Jews' first glimpse of God, the only creator and sustainer, a righteous God who taught men to distinguish between the ultimate opposites of right and wrong.

'I wish you had been in my dream!' he said to Becky as he told his tale over breakfast. She nursed her own thoughts, but said,

'I'm no devadasi, Jonathan. I hope I won't disappoint you!'

Pearl Harbour changed everything. News reached the mess of disturbances in the town, following the Congress party's launching of a campaign of civil disobedience. Jonathan was sad. He could not believe that Gandhi was really saying that India would be better off under the Japs. He found that most of his friends shared his views. Singapore fell, providing thousands upon thousands of prisoners, Indian and British. Slowly tales of atrocities were being whispered in Club and bazaar.

Rioters burned down a part of the railway station, but fled before a police lathi-charge.

'What happened at the American High School, did you hear?' asked Becky.

'There were a lot of smashed windows I understand, but any attempt to fire it must have been forestalled.' The havildar informed her.

He continued, 'they say that Jai Singh, who publishes the local left-wing paper, is behind it and has been arrested.'

Quiet returned to Moradabad, but Japanese victories continued. Burma fell, and the war was now on India's north-east border in Assam – in the tiny frontier towns of Imphal and Kohima; 'very un-Indian names', said Becky when the expatriate women in Moradabad started discussion – what they would do if the Japs broke through and swept on to Delhi?

A long trainload of serious casualties arrived and the whole town was agog with the news. Many had survived the most terrible injuries, and Jonathan spent hours in the operation theatres. They were an astonishingly cheerful lot, despite repeated surgery. Some taxed his skill to its limits. He began to see further areas in specialisation, where he'd like to pioneer.

Jonathan was pleased with the way in which military service was overcoming the old provincial enmities. They were all Indian, proud of the tradition of the regiment. There was only one Gujerati in that first batch from the front.

'He must have been the company clerk,' volunteered Lt Jai Singh, with a martial Sikh pedigree. 'It's mostly banias like Gandhi from there,' he added.

But the Gujarati wasn't a bania, Jonathan discovered. Joginder Patel's father was the hereditary official responsible for land and legal records. They were leaders in their village hierarchy. He was a challenge to Jonathan professionally. A piece of shrapnel had carried away his nose and one cheek. He commenced a series of operations to transfer tissues from the chest to the face.

'I wish we had a McIndoe around,' he said to Becky, 'one of your illustrious countrymen.'

'Everyone has heard of him', she countered, 'for his "guinea-pigs" at East Grinstead.' She had to nurse Patel through the long weeks when he was trussed up with a long pedicle joining chest to face. Most of the staff found an excuse to call in the ward. The patient took it all in good part and made them laugh.

'I must look like Ganesh, the elephant god,' he told them.

Lt Col Sen Roy said 'I've always been proud that the first surgeon to construct a new nose was an Indian, Susruta, in the days of Buddha. He used no stitches, fixing the flap of skin, rotated from the forehead, with clay.'

'I suppose that is why the operation remained a trade secret of the potter-caste for more than two thousand years; it's some story.'

Then came a serious medical emergency that put Becky on temporary transfer. An epidemic of amoebic dysentery broke out sixty miles along the line at Bareilly, where the military hospital was already full with bacillary dysentery and malaria. A convoy transferred many to Ranikhet, where tented accommodation was provided.

The lovers had long known that they could be separated at any time. The most likely event would be Jonathan's posting to a combat unit, on the Burma Front. So they were not greatly concerned, by what most likely would be but a short separation.

'You'll have to see if you can get a little leave and come up to the mountains again,' was Becky's parting shot as he waved her off at the station.

In the event, a fresh convoy of casualties arrived, and Jonathan had little time even to write letters in the next month.

Becky was a more faithful correspondent, but her letters were written in snatched moments too.

'We're very short-staffed, so there is little off-duty for Sister.'

It was a fortnight before another letter came and this time it was not in Becky's familiar hand. Jonathan tore open the official envelope, looked at the heading, I.B.G.H., Ranikhet, and the signature, Ralph Best, Station Commander, before reading the letter. It was short and carefully written.

'Dear Major,
It is my painful duty to give you the sad news that your fiancée, Lt Rebecca Burdett died here yesterday, following a break-in at her quarters. I can tell you little more at the moment, as a police investigation is underway. I would express my heartfelt sympathy. Becky has not only been with us through six weeks of hectic activity, but has warmed all our hearts by her high spirits and her manifest love of her patients. I am not a practising Christian but I know that you are Salvationists. You will know how to handle this disaster better than me.'

Jonathan joined a large crowd that stood at the open grave, in the tiny British cemetery, outside the city walls of Moradabad. It was a crowd mostly Indian. He had never been in this place before. He noticed gravestones that spoke of young wives dying in childbirth, far from home and years ago. There were three near to each other, all Salvation Army officers. They had died in different typhoid epidemics. Floods of thought overwhelmed him. It was impossible to think of the future, yet Becky was warmly with him. 'God is with us all the time', a line from a hymn came to him. In a dim way, he knew that he would find his way; he need not fret. He had learned the futility of questioning events. 'Why me?' never occurred to him.

The Indian servant was quickly apprehended, and charged with murder, Jonathan had no desire for retribution. If he could have influenced the court he would have appealed for clemency.

99

It was some time before his colleagues in the Mess, felt it right to raise the subject, but when they did, they marvelled at a calm that was neither indifferent nor cynical. He was reacting as his faith dictated; it was neither forced nor basically reasoned. By bringing the profound issues of life, to the forefront of his thinking, it was crystallising his intentions for the future.

Chapter Four
JONATHAN TAKES THE PLUNGE

Below them lay Kangra, with its temple

With the dropping of bombs on Japan, September 1945 saw V. J. celebrations in India. Repatriation got under way. Jonathan applied for early release to join a session at the William Booth Memorial College, at Denmark Hill in South London. He arrived there in the following January. His last two years had been spent on the Burma front under the Australian Field Marshall, Slim, as the O.C. surgical division of a field hospital. He was a seasoned Lt Colonel. His I.M.S. friends were amused that Lindsey had chosen to descend to the humble rank of cadet in this strange religious army, which apparently took little note of academic or military distinction. He was 33, and whilst it was true that many of the cadets had served in the forces, he was easily the oldest trainee.

'The powers-that-be have decided that since you are going straight to a medical appointment, half a session will suffice,' the Under-secretary at International Headquarters informed him with a smile.

'You'll be in India by June.'

'With my fluency in Urdu, I suppose that will mean the north, so June will not be an ideal time to arrive, in fact it is the hottest time of the year.'

It proved a hectic and at times, a bewildering experience. The academic work was not taxing, but the practical abilities required of a Salvation Army officer were another matter. He came to a new appreciation of his mother. It wasn't until he was finally on the liner bound for India, that he had time to contemplate the future. He found a quiet corner of the afterdeck and mulled it over. He had made the last major decision of his career. Becky's death had brought into sharp focus, the conviction that there was a purpose for his life. For the first time he saw this whole. He was destined to serve the needy in India, with the opportunities and restraints of a Salvation Army officer. It meant losing his independence. He smiled at the thought. In the war he had become accustomed to following directives on treatment, far more authoritarian than he would encounter in this other Army. When he left Burma, his commanding officer, Colonel Jones had said,

'I think you are capitulating; taking the path of least resistance in following the example of your parents. You're passing up the promise of a brilliant career.' As the throb of the engines lulled him to sleep in the Mediterranean sunshine, he wondered how to define a 'brilliant career'. But debate was over; he was at peace with himself, and enjoyed the voyage. He carried off two of the prizes for deck-quoits and table tennis; silver spoons with the ship's crest in enamel. He even dressed up as a Tibetan monk and joined the fancy dress parade. He preached at one of the ecumenical church services on deck. It was in the Mediterranean and there was a heavy swell. He would long remember clutching the portable pulpit, as he had alternate glimpses of sea and sky. The congregation slowly melted away.

He landed at Karachi. The port had expanded rapidly under war-time stimulus; it looked utilitarian. There was little in the town to interest him, although he was tempted to make a trip into the sandy hinterland to see the excavations of a 5000-year-old Sumerian city. The Lahore express had a long stop at Multan. The sight of a blue tiled dome gleaming in the sunlight, reminded him of that distinctive glazed pottery that his mother had not been able to resist in the Anarkali,

102

when he was a boy. The next stop was at Khanewal. He saw the Army uniforms on the platform. The khavi and red in dhoti and sari were worn by a Swedish couple, who brought him an appetising meal. Headquarters had done its homework well. They sat between great piles of grapefruit and chatted.

'We've had bumper crops this year,' they assured him. 'In fact the price of wheat has been so high,' the Major added, 'that the majority of the settlers have been able to pay up all their arrears of land-tax and now own their own land.'

'We hope you will be able to visit us sometime,' said Mrs Lindberg. 'All the settlers except the shopkeepers are Salvationists. The Sunday morning meeting is a sight to see. All the patriarchal white-beards are on the front row and full of fervour. They are generous too in their giving. They're grand folk. I sometimes wish that Commissioner Fakir Singh* could see the fruition of his scheme.'

Jonathan grew excited as the train drew into Lahore. It crawled the last hundred yards and he had time to pick out Jane, who was talking animatedly to a group of adolescent girls, their long black pigtails swishing with coloured bobbles plaited into the ends.

In the familiar bungalow on the Queen's road, he was soon exploring a new empathy with his mother. For Jane, Jonathan's return was the fulfilment of her hopes. Her son was assuming responsibility as a doctor, dedicated in a spirit that matched her own. Jonathan's ambition to run a first-class hospital hadn't faded, but he was now in tune with her. He felt a vast content that could live a day at a time.

The tiny branch-line station at Stewartpur, was crowded with white uniforms. They were led by the Scottish matron and the Indian manager with a flamboyant turban. As Jonathan glanced along the line, he picked out a tall blonde, 'Swedish I'm sure', he thought. So he was not surprised when Janet Fraser introduced her as Gunvor Sundberg.

'Your compatriots in Khanewal told me that there are about thirty Scandinavian officers in the territory.'

'Yes.' She had a Swedish lilt but spoke excellent English, he was soon to discover.

'Gunvor will be your theatre Sister,' said Janet Fraser.

Gulab Singh introduced himself; the Business Manager led the way across the tracks. Jonathan could see a level-crossing opposite the hospital gates, but apparently no-one bothered where one crossed. He was taking in the setting as they walked. The fertile plain stretched away to a horizon bounded by mountains. In June, the fields were mostly bare and the occasional clumps of trees covered with dust. But

* Booth-Tucker

103

here and there were rectangles of green – sugarcane. Looking back he saw the smoking chimney of the power station, that gave energy to the complex of buildings which comprised the woollen mills, which were the raison d'etre for Stewartpur.

'We've crossed here', Gulab Singh told him, as though reading his mind,' because the doctor's bungalow is at this end of the compound.' They passed through a line of eucalyptus trees and entered a pleasant garden, green from efficient watering, but devoid of flowers at this time of year.

'Your boxes arrived a couple of days ago sahib, and we've put them in your bungalow. We've engaged a cook-bearer. He's young but has worked as a deputy in one of the mill bungalows.'

Jonathan was making a rapid appraisal of his new home. The local bricks were a dull pink, not as attractive as the bright red of the houses at Glandford. He made the immediate comparison, though Glandford had never been his home. Here the brickwork was largely hidden by a climbing winter-rose. It improved it. Janet had seen his appraising glance.

'It's only twenty years old, and of a piece with the rest of Stewartpur. It's entirely a creation of British Wools Ltd. You'll soon learn,' she laughed.

The next morning he took stock of the hospital, before crossing the tracks to the mill manager's residence, in response to a personal note delivered by an office peon in peaked cap. The hospital reminded him of the Moradabad one. There was the long frontage; the pioneers had a knack of making impressive institutions despite limited funds. Outpatients' facilities, consulting rooms, office and operation theatre were all at the centre with wards stretching out in either direction. At the centre there was an incomplete cloister of smaller wards backing the main centre block. The wards had black cast-iron fireplaces.

'Imported straight from Britain, I bet,' said Jonathan.

'They're an anachronism,' Janet responded, 'for the average temperature is over a hundred in the summer, and in the winter we haven't the money for regular fires.'

'How do you manage then?'

'Fortunately the mills make coarse blankets, as well as fine worsteds and they're pretty generous with them, so we keep the patients warm.'

'It's funny really,' Gunvor chipped in,' the reaction of Punjabis to the winter, is to stay huddled in blankets, until the sun warms up the land.'

'And it does,' Janet responded. 'You'll come to love Punjab winters.'

'I think that you are both forgetting that I spent all my Christmas holidays in Lahore, when I was at school.'

The women joined in the laugh against themselves.

'We'll have to be careful in our comment,' they chorused.

'Tell me a bit about the mills,' Jonathan addressed this to Gulab Singh to draw him into the conversation.

'I remember hearing about the opening of the hospital whilst I was at school. I would have liked to visit then. I believe you had quite a tamasha.'

'I went to the Army's boarding school in Danepur. We had a pipe-band which was ordered on duty for the day. We boys thought it was a wonderful occasion. The Governor of the Punjab opened it, so there were loads of sahibs and gorgeous uniforms.'

'Where do the mills come in?'

'They own everything around here. With the mills they built the model dwellings for the workers, the bazaar, a dispensary and even the church: so they named their creation after their founder. We were sorry that the hospital wasn't built nearer to Amritsar, where the Army had land. Ranjitala is a walled town built by the Moguls. Commissioner Booth-Tucker had an aunt who used to visit purdah ladies there, in the last century. A hospital there would have been more like the Moradabad one. I have a brother there', he added, 'I used to spend school holidays with him.'

'Is Himmat Singh, the compounder there, your brother then?'

'Jihan.'

'So you see,' Janet took up the tale, 'the mills offered land and a contract to care for the senior staff. This was a contract promising a regular income, a prospect that could not be resisted.'

'I must tell you at once sahib, they don't pay enough.' Gulab was obviously dying to get this off his chest. 'Our finances aren't very healthy.' Everyone was anxious to give him the picture; he'd better get this vital relationship clear before he went further.

'Will you take me over to Mr Blickling. He's the manager isn't he?'

'Jihan. Let me slip back to the quarters to tell Pritibai, where I'm going.'

It was ten o'clock striking from the mill tower, as they picked their way across the railway and up a narrow path between bungalows, hidden behind dense foliage.

'This is the back way, I presume?'

'Yes. Much quicker than going round to the town and through the main gates.'

As they got among the two-storey mill buildings, the click-clack of the looms became deafening. Gulab was left outside as Jonathan was ushered into the manager's office to receive a warm welcome.

'We've been waiting your coming, hoping that none of us would get seriously ill in the absence of a Chief Medical Officer.'

'I'm equally glad to be here at last.'

'I know that the expatriate family of Stewartpur is comforted to have an experienced surgeon to care for it, the memsahibs particularly.'

'You have your own dispensary and doctor for your Indian employees, I'm told. That must be a tall order for one man.'

'He's only at sub-assistant-surgeon level and has no inpatients. We send all hospital patients to you; you bill us for them. That's a new arrangement I'm suggesting, since your people say that the old grant does not cover costs.'

'What is the size of your staff?'

'It is in excess of two thousand. Quite a lot have been sipathis. One or two, I'm told, claim to have been your patients in Mandalay. They are singing your praises so loudly that even the bungalows have heard,' he laughed, as a smart orderly brought in a coffee tray. Over their cups, Harold Blickling said,

'I know that you will want to get dug-in over at the hospital, but as soon as you find it convenient give me a ring and we'll show you round the works.' He had an afterthought. 'I must have a word with Christopher Jennings, who is secretary of the club. I think this is a good opportunity for a party.'

Jonathan chatted to Gulab as they picked their way over the metals. He had a premonition of the divide between Indian and sahib, which would characterise his working days – his leisure also, if he had any. It was all too predictably Kiplingesque.

The khansamah, whom Gulab had engaged, brought his breakfast on a tray the next morning. He had returned to his kitchen, when Jonathan heard an anguished shout from the side of the house that bordered a ploughed field. He dropped his toast and ran. The elderly mali, wildly excited, was flailing the hedge with his hoe, encouraged by the cook with his axe. A snake was writhing energetically in the tangled branches, which obstructed the hoe. It slithered to the ground. Jonathan could see its hood, as it came very near to the bare feet of the gardener, who was aiming wildly with more force than accuracy.

The cook was obviously reluctant to get too near; his weapon hadn't the reach of the hoe, whilst the cobra was four feet long and incredibly swift. The accompaniment of wild shouting continued, soon drawing a crowd of patients' relatives, emboldened to trespass on the doctor's garden. They shouted advice but gave no assistance. The snake had returned to the safety of the hedge, but the arrival of Sher Singh sealed his fate. Sher Singh was the hospital carpenter and odd-job man, an elderly Sikh, obsequious to foreigners, but given a profound respect by the villagers who came to the hospital. He was short, turbanned and bearded. He came at a shuffling run, brandishing a long iron rod with a forked end. 'He's done this before', thought the doctor, as the Sikh deftly hooked the snake from the hedge, jamming the fork over its neck, close to the spade-like head, jaws open and fangs flashing. Pinioned to the ground, it had no chance of evading the axe, as the cook came boldly forward, shouting gleefully.

'You know how to deal with snakes,' Jonathan said to the carpenter. One of the onlookers replied for him,

'Sher Singh makes good medicine from snakes. He cured my mother's rheumatism. She can chop wood now, as well as carry water-pots.'

Sher Singh took his trophy by the tail. The crowd, with an exciting story to while away the tedium of convalescence, melted away.

When Jonathan reached his consultation room, Janet was awaiting him with a series of administrative problems. Before getting involved, he asked her,

'Did you know that Sher Singh had another string to his bow?'

'I'm quite certain that he only does the comparatively mean task for which we employ him, because it affords him an opportunity to find patients for himself. Once or twice I'm sure that the malunited fractures that have come to us, were his failures. I don't know what hold he has over people, but we never get any complaints.'

As the weeks went by, Jonathan found himself spending more and more time with the theatre Sister, Gunvor Sundberg, the Nordic blonde who was only a couple of inches shorter than himself. Her English was not only good, it was often idiomatic. He had already learned that she was more at home with her patients in their own tongue, than any other of the expatriates.

His reputation soon attracted all the hopeless patients from other hospitals, even some from far afield. It was soon a matter for discussion at the meal-table in the Sisters' mess, that the mill wives and daughters were trying him out. These, for their part, discussed him in the club over their chhota pegs. Victoria Harrison, wife of the Weaving Master, of mature years and feminine judgement, volunteered,

'Mr Lindsey,' she'd learned that it was not correct to call a surgeon 'doctor', 'is falling for Gunvor; she came into the consulting room this morning, and I saw the look he gave her.'

'I'm not surprised,' her husband grinned,' I find her smashing myself. I wouldn't mind having my appendix out, to be looked after by Gunvor.'

His wife turned on him.

'You'd be disappointed, I'm afraid, for all her ministrations would be whilst you were unconscious.'

'But she might give me the anaesthetic; I wouldn't mind being put to sleep by her,' he teased her.

Jonathan had been relieved when he saw her competence and impressed by the unassuming manner in which she assisted. He had not known what to expect in a small hospital in the Punjab. He learned that she had completed her general training in Stockholm, but had then gone on to the Carolinska as a staff nurse, working with one of the new breed of plastic surgeons, who had trained at Sir Harold Gillies' unit at Rooksdown House, near Basingstoke. He was an Anglophile; some of his predilections had rubbed off on the theatre nurses.

After a few weeks' familiarity in the theatre, Gunvor felt sufficiently at home with the new Chief Medical Officer, to offer a suggestion on technique.

'I don't know whether you are interested, but I grew accustomed to the careful needlework of the plastic surgeons and determined to bring some very fine needles with me. Those packets of fully-curved cutting needles are still in my trunk. I could make them up with 004 and 006 black silk, and keep them ready sterilised in packs of six.'

'I'd be delighted to try it out.'

'Then I'll make up a few packs.'

It was a few weeks later that Mrs Jennings from the mills was driven over by her anxious husband. Four-year-old James had tumbled after climbing on his father's desk and opening his penknife. He had a nasty gash in his left thigh. The bleeding had seemed alarming to his doting mother. Janet took charge of the weeping mother, whilst Jonathan, discreetly assisted by his theatre sister, made a careful repair. He was pleased with the long line of fine stitches as were the grateful parents. The story quickly went round the club and was soon leaked to the bazaar. 'Surgery without scars,' was the message.

'What else have you got to teach me, Gunvor?'

'You'd be surprised.'

It was like living in a glasshouse, being the first unmarried doctor in Stewartpur hospital. Even the patients were pairing him up, he felt. Jonathan found two understanding allies across the railway line. One was Harold Blickling, but the other was Timothy Ramsay, principal of the mission school, a fifty-five year old American widower. He invited Jonathan to dinner.

'Do you run your school on American lines?' Jonathan asked.

'Well curriculum-wise, we have to follow the Punjab Government's pattern, but I suppose a bit of our style rubs off. We're rather less disciplined as youngsters in the States. I'd have hated wearing a school uniform as a teenager,' he smiled.

'You know what the psychologists say.'

'You're not talking about the Jesuits' claim to set the pattern of life before the age of eight, or is it seven?'

'No, I was referring to their aphorism that children need fences to teach them to fly.'

'I concede the sense in that.'

Timothy knew something of Salvation Army lifestyle from long association, so it was nimbu-pani with the meal, then unfortified coffee after it.

'This is something that you are better at in the States, Timothy.'

'Why, do you still use that coffee essence, with Queen Victoria on the label, being served by a resplendent bearer with a silver salver?'

'We all did when I was a medical student, though I thought it was a burra sahib rather than the Queen.'

'I don't suppose you've visited Southern India?'

'Only a brief holiday visit to Ooty.'

'I think you may remember the Brahmin coffee you get at any railway station. It's made with a ladle of boiling coffee elixir from one pan, diluted with two of hot milk from another. I always think that is the original of your "Camp" coffee – I confess I always enjoyed it.

'A propos nothing', he continued, 'the mill manager tells me that you are a Cambridge graduate.'

'That's true.'

'I'm Harvard myself, but you probably know that Harvard himself was a Cambridge graduate, and aimed to make his new college in memory of his alma mater.'

'I can go one better than that, for I am a graduate from the same college, Emmanuel.'

'Well that is something! Of course I know that many of the early settlers were from the puritan colleges.' He paused, and said, 'Some of them were my Presbyterian forebears, though you will find that most of the missionaries of my church have sound Scottish names.'

Ramsay had old-fashioned furniture, including the elegant recliners straight out of 'Tales from the Hills'. So they relaxed, swinging out the leg-extensions, on their brass pivots, sipping their coffee.

'I'm going to be a Dutch uncle and warn you that the club gossips are fixing up a marriage for you!'

'How fascinating. Who's the girl?'

'They're undecided, for they're betting on quite a large field,

109

including one or two relations in Lahore. However the odds are on one of your own. I gather that the firm favourite is your theatre Sister.'

As he walked home, Gunvor was in focus. He'd already enjoyed her company when the Sisters invited him over to their mess in the evenings. They were a happy lot. By contrast with the company at the club, they seemed satisfied with life. Seldom did a disgruntled remark surface. They took it in turn to cater for the group and there was much laughter over the variety of soups that appeared at the end of the month, when the kitty was empty.

Six months passed, by which time Jonathan was in a smooth routine, which was just as well, as more and more patients were coming, even from as far away as Amritsar and Kangra. Periodically he was aroused from deep sleep by a porter or the chowkidar.

'Hospital itifarquan', in staccato tone. 'Itifarquan' or 'ek dum' meant 'at once'. Particularly on cold nights, he'd find a group of frightened relations, crouched on the cold paving-stones of the out-patient hall. Usually one would throw off his blanket and spring up to implore his special attention, often claiming some particular link with the hospital or its staff, meriting a favour.

Tonight, blood was up and the whole group sprang up, chorusing curses against all Sikhs. Ghulam Mohamed had quarrelled with his neighbours over irrigation water. They had caught him unawares, whipping out their kirpans and whirling them around their heads. He put up his arm, instinctively covering his head from a slash. A blade had caught his hand and his brother had several of his fingers, wrapped up in a piece torn from an old sari.

He was already on the table and Hamid, the young Muslim doctor had started the anaesthetic, as soon as Jonathan had walked in. Dr Rani, the Christian doctor on the women's wards, was already scrubbed up with Gunvor and was draping the wrist in a sterile towel, before placing it on an armrest that had been slotted into the table.

'He must have grasped the sword, for several fingers have been severed. They've brought the very dead bits with them, sure that the English doctor can sew them back on,' Dr Hamid said.

Unbidden, a nurse brought a kidney dish with the grey bits in saline.

'I wish that I could. To judge by those sad fingers, the fight took place hours ago.'

'Apparently the fracas was at midday, since then they have been embroiled with their neighbours and the police. As usual it took hours to get that over.' Himself a Muslim, Dr Hamid spoke with animation.

It was all very military surgery. Jonathan soon made deft flaps to cover bare bone and preserve the stumps. Over the bandage, a wet

110

plaster-of-Paris slab was applied and moulded to the fingers. Finally, Jonathan carefully parted the covering of the finger-tips.

'Watch the colour, Hamid. We don't want to lose anymore tissue from gangrene. Keep the hand supported by suspension from a drip-stand and get the usual blood-tests done in the morning.'

Before he disappeared to his office to wash, Gunvor invited him.

'I've a flask of hot soup in the sitting room if you'd like to share it.'

The common-room of the Sisters' accommodation was a large square room, verandah to the front, serving-room, pantry and kitchen to the rear. The usual ring of cane chairs had a feminine touch with cretonne-covered cushions. The large and colourful Mirzapur rug, was beyond the spartan scale of furnishings approved by authority in Lahore. 'It must have been a kind aunt or a grateful patient,' Jonathan had concluded.

Gunvor opened the mosquito doors, and crossed the room, to sit at the table near the pantry door. Involuntarily they looked at each other, sharing an intimate sense of relief that another difficult task was done. There was a mutual respect and appreciation in all these relationships but tonight both were aware that they had passed beyond this. They were excited, yet at ease with each other.

'This is super. Did you make it?'

'Janet had a parcel of goodies from home and amongst other things were some packet soups. I knew you liked tomato.'

'And you suspected that I relish well-fried croutons as garnish eh?'

Again their eyes met. Jonathan put his hand over hers.

'You're very good to me Gunvor.'

'I think that I am falling for you; is that how you say it?'

She surprised herself with the admission. For Jonathan all tiredness vanished. He led her to the settee. His arm went round her and her head was on his shoulder.

'I had a fiancée during the war and was excited at the thought of marriage. But it wasn't to be,' he paused.

'I've heard about Captain Burdett's tragic death and mourned her, for we shared a weekend in Lahore shortly after I arrived here. It was your mother who introduced us.'

They were silent for a while.

'Something has been dead in me since then. I suppose I've been on my guard against an emotional involvement. It was such a sudden end to my expectations and crystallised the decision to become an officer. I knew it was the end of a comfortable life as a surgeon. In some ways I withdrew to the cloisters.'

He kissed her hair.

111

'You've drawn me to love again.'

She turned her head and their lips met, a mutual acceptance of decision. It was a long kiss. They parted for breath and looked at each other with new eyes and an exciting discovery.

'What a surprising emergency this has been. Are you sure that you didn't arrange it Gunvor?'

'I don't think that we are going to get much sleep.' Gunvor whispered as she closed the netting door after him.

Territorial Headquarters accepted their decision. The Commander, noting their age, granted a speedy engagement. It was in this state of definite commitment – what in mediaeval times had been called betrothal, that they went on holiday together in Naini Tal.

This would probably be Jane's last summer at The Gables. Sixty was the retirement age for women. She was delighted to have them under her roof; her happiness was evident in all that she did for them. She had prayed daily for her son; though she was aware that God knew what was in her heart, before she told Him.

Jonathan was impatient for the wedding. Back to his mind came the memory of a book he had read in schooldays; Charles Reade's 'The Cloister and the Hearth'. He felt a kinship with that hero. This was already the relationship of a lifetime. He had the typical male indifference to the trappings of marriage. It came as a surprise that Gunvor, no less committed than he to a lifetime of service, was nevertheless vitally concerned about the detail of the ceremony. And so was Jane.

The Sundbergs were distressed that they were so far away. Theirs was a long, long letter that Jonathan could not read, though he noted the fat kroner cheque. He asked Gunvor for a translation. She laughed and said,

'They say "do it properly", and that I intend to do!'

And so Jane and Gunvor had their heads together many mornings when Jonathan would have preferred to show his fiancée his school's setting. They managed one long trek to Sat Tal. That twenty miles in one day, marked the physical peak of the holiday. It was a spiritual highpoint too. A famous American missionary had established an ashram there and stressed that he welcomed all truly seeking a spiritual interpretation of life. Gandhi had stayed with him. The Mahatma had said that it was in this retreat, that he had come to sing and appreciate, 'Abide with me', and 'Lead kindly light'.

Jane had provided an excellent lunch, within the restraints of a knapsack. They sat on the shelving bank of the lake, which was so still that it mirrored the far side and the encircling forest. On the far shore was a simple wooden cross. Sometimes a whole house-party met here in worship. They sat for a long while after the meal. It was a benediction. All would be well.

But before they could complete their own plans, disaster hit India. Its future was clouded. As independence loomed, tension between Muslim and Sikh grew. Jonathan had warmed to the Sikhs he met in Stewartpur. The mills employed many. He learned more of their history as he took on a new responsibility, twelve miles away at Ranjitala. The Indian Quaker, who was principal of a Christian college there, asked Jonathan to be the official medical officer. The heart of the college was a Sikh palace, 150 years old. At the height of the Raj's exuberance, this college was envisaged as an Indian Eton, a school for the sons of the elite. Now it had accepted a humbler role as a university college. Jonathan had tried to imagine this crumbling stucco building as the seat of the ruler of the Punjab. Now its throne-room was a boys' dormitory. Boys gathered from diverse provinces and tongues, only bound together, as was the Raj itself, by the English language. From somewhere around here had come the prophet, who had attempted to blend the monotheism of Islam with a Hindu heritage. Moghul rulers had tolerated the new faith for some generations, but by the time of the tenth guru, Aurangzeb was on the throne in Delhi and persecution commenced. The pacific followers of Guru Nanak took to the sword so successfully, that the Punjab became a Sikh kingdom; Sir Henry Lawrance had been the British Resident before his ill-fated transfer to Lucknow.

Jonathan found that something of the Hindu legacy had remained. In Stewartpur he found that there was a group of Mazbee Sikhs, some of whom had become Christian. He rather fancied that in the dim past their ancestry was of the outcaste community. Amongst patients he found that the farmers might be either Muslim or Sikh. In temperament there was little to choose between them. They were all forthright and forceful, fodder for the conflagration which was to come. There were outward differences however. The Sikhs were the people of the 'five Ks', one of which was the kirpan, the sword which they all carried. He grew accustomed to seeing that a visiting husband, had hung his sword on the chart hook above his wife's bed. He was invited to meals in their homes and found that the womenfolk enjoyed considerable freedom and could be good in business deals. Many had been educated in Christian schools for girls.

113

As the tension increased ugly incidents began to occur around Stewartpur.

Seventy miles away in Lahore, a Sikh temple, a gurdwara, was burned down; nearer at hand, rioting broke out in Amritsar, which was the Sikh's holy city. The police force was mixed; the strain broke the loyalty to an impartial service. Jonathan returned from a long discussion with Mukerjee at Ranjitala College, mulling over the situation created by the Muslim insistence on a separate Pakistan. Negotiations under Lord Wavell, the Viceroy, broke down. Repercussions in Stewartpur were sad. Muslims and Sikhs who had worked together as colleagues, were now jittery. One morning the phone rang.

'Harold Blickling here doctor. Do you think you could come over for a few minutes. I don't want to talk on the phone.'

'If it can be at noon, OK.'

So he sat in the air-conditioned luxury of the manager's bungalow. The sitting room was furnished for the entertaining of important visitors. Here, Blickling held cocktail parties for visiting Governors or senior civil servants. Blickling launched into the problem without preamble.

'Trouble's coming, and we will be right in the thick of it. Have you made plans in the hospital?'

'My ear to the ground confirms your fears, but there is an equally strong feeling amongst ordinary villagers, that the British Army will preserve the peace. Despite their ancient animosities, and current friction, they've only known the Raj.'

'I think that scenario is unlikely. For if the country is divided, so will be the army. People are going to be caught in two minds. However I'm primarily asking about the plans you are making for the Sisters.'

'I've discussed this with them and none of them wants to go. I'm not quarrelling with their decision, for the hospital service is going to be needed more than ever.'

'We've always maintained the Gurkha guard here, and I'd like to offer you their cover, if you will accept it. I anticipated the reaction of your staff.'

'How would it work?'

'Herbert Hemmings is responsible for the guard, through their Subedar. They have a four-hour roster, and you can have twenty-four hour cover, if you can provide a guard-room.'

So the disused gatehouse was refurbished and within a week, Jonathan had grown accustomed to a cheerful Gurkha grin, when he came on duty. The Gurkhas became part of the hospital scene; their smart turnout and their distinctive slouch hats, gave the patients confidence.

With the appointment of Earl Mountbatten to succeed Wavell, plans for a partition of the sub-continent assumed a new urgency: the date for Independence was brought forward.

Alarm spread in Stewartpur, when the Muslim employees learned that the Pakistan border would be only 15 miles away on the river Ravi. They calculated the risks of being caught in a Hindu-Sikh state. They began to melt away, whilst the going was good.

Jonathan called a meeting of senior staff in his bungalow.

Dr Hamid was the first to speak.

'I'm sadly going to offer my resignation. My wife will not feel happy even in a Christian hospital. Most of her relatives have already gone.'

'We quite understand your position, though we'll be sorry to see you go. What about the other members of the staff, Hamid?'

'I can warn Ismail, the mason family that we employ. I find the malis and tradesmen already are trying to get out.'

Gulab Singh took over.

'We ought to go down to Amritsar as soon as possible and stock up medical supplies; strain our credit to the full. Headquarters will have to come to our help if money gets tight.'

Janet and Gunvor spoke together.

'What about food supplies?'

'I think that I will discuss that with Mr Blickling. I'm sure that the mills will have their plans, plus far greater storage facilities than we can provide.'

Alarming stories began to circulate, as the Union Jack was hauled down at sedate ceremonies, hundreds of miles from the trouble spots. Murders were already overwhelming normal police efforts.

On the first day, mutilated villagers were being admitted. The Gurkha guard was doubled. With rifle at the ready, there was now a man at either end of the flat roof. Before long panic spread amongst the simple shepherds, grazing their flocks on the high pastures of the Kulu and Kangra valleys to the north. They fled down the foothills, being knifed all the way. Flocks and women folk disappeared into the villages en route. Some staggered as far as Stewartpur and were provided with a dormitory in the empty mission-school.

Jonathan was called at 5 a.m., by the terrified chowkidar. The school had proved no shield. Mills' staff were carrying over the few survivors. Jonathan worked on until mid-day with Gunvor, then Kathleen Dobson called them to a snack meal in he consulting room. Janet joined them.

115

'The injuries we have been coping with all the morning, have been from sword thrusts. It's easy to tell who has been responsible.' She was horrified.

'I wouldn't be so sure. The universal hatred I've seen on faces in the last two days, beggars anything I've ever seen.'

'Where is it going to end?'

'When they can rout out no more Muslims.'

'There must be a fair number still in hiding. It was a relief to hear that most of the mills' staff got away.'

Even with them, I hear that word has filtered back, that some were attacked at the border post.'

'I have had the benches moved out of the chapel and filled it up with beds... Oh dear!' she became quite agitated as a nurse, looking quite terrified, beckoned her to the door. All watched the whispered conversation. Janet closed the door carefully as the nurse withdrew.

'Gracebai tells me that young Salim, our cook, whom we thought had made a good escape, is hiding in our bungalow. What do we do now?'

'We must get him out. Sooner or later,' said Gunvor, 'someone will see him, they'll strip him, see that he is circumcised and kill him.'

'Slip over and see that he's fed and well hidden', ordered Jonathan, then we'll find a way of getting him out this evening.'

So Jonathan and the theatre staff worked on throughout the afternoon, during which rifle shots could be heard, even in the theatre. He learned from the guard that he was sure there were marauders lurking in the sugar-cane, behind the hospital. They were intent on killing even those that had found sanctuary in the wards.

Jonathan was heartened by the fearless way in which the Christian staff had risen to the challenge, donning red-cross brassards and working tirelessly.

Jonathan had been particularly impressed by Lieut Christopher, a graduate of Lahore university who had been posted to the hospital to assist Gulab in administration. He was every inch a Punjabi, six foot and broadshouldered. He readily agreed to collaborate in the plan that his two seniors had concocted. They found an old red tunic that fitted Salim, who sat behind Jonathan and the Lieutenant in the ambulance, an authentic staff member.

There was the likelihood of a curfew, so speed was of the essence as they covered the 36 miles to Amritsar in an hour. The road was littered in places with the remnants of household goods and occasionally there was a corpse at the verge. Jonathan had warned Salim to lie on the stretcher and not to look out. The signs of carnage were more numerous on the last fifteen miles to the border post. There were indeed two

116

frontier posts to negotiate. The first manned by Sikhs, determined to see that no Muslim sneaked out. The guards took one last look at the legend on the ambulance, spotted the sahib at the wheel and called out cheerfully,

'Muktifauj, thik hai!' and waved them on.

Jonathan thanked God as they bumped over the broken tarmac in no-mans' land, towards the Pakistan check-post. Here the process was less speedy; Jonathan doubted whether the guard could read. He was pretty certain that the passport, which he had thought might do the trick, was held upside down. The frowning soldier started to look the vehicle over, but fortunately an officer strolled over and politely asked, 'What brings you out on this dangerous road after dark sahib?'

'You know our headquarters are in Lahore and I have important matters to discuss with my Colonel. You know how it is.' The Captain was a regular and smiled his understanding. The passport was reluctantly surrendered and they revved up.

As they entered what Jonathan remembered as a smart suburb they found many of the new two-storey villas were gutted. No attempt had been made yet to clear up. There were blood-stained saris, trousers and smashed trunks everywhere. Safely delivered in Queen's road, Salim's gratitude knew no bounds. He dropped to the ground and clasped Jonathan's sandals, kissing the bare flesh between the straps. He fell to sobbing as the doctor gently raised him. Captain Andrew, the H.Q. cashier arrived and took in the situation.

'You're alright Salim. We need another cook at the Girls' School, the doctor's mother will be delighted that you've come.'

So it was to Jane that Salim was assigned and Jonathan's last sight of him was in the kitchen, crowded with servants from all the bungalows around, sipping a cup of tea, whilst telling his dramatic story. Jonathan had heard him describe his fear as they halted at the check-point on the Amritsar side.

'I expected to be dragged out at any moment, stripped naked and mutilated before they killed me!'

'Jai, jai for the redcoats,' shouted Anwar and they all laughed with relief.

Jane found surprise swallowed up in relief too. She found it sheer joy having her son at such a distressing time. It was obvious that Jonathan was at the end of his endurance, but she insisted that he take a bowl of porridge and hot milk, before falling on the charpoy in the spare room. She peeped in before retiring herself. She was relieved to find him sleeping heavily.

It was a wrench to say goodbye to him the next morning but she

117

guessed the urgency of the situation to which he would return, so she busied herself packing a parcel of goodies for Gunvor.

The sun was well up by the time that they reached Amritsar. There was a deathly silence over the countryside. Life went on but voices were hushed. The road looked worse in daylight. Twice they stopped at strewn bodies and, finding life, gently lifted patients onto stretchers and into the ambulance. They passed several drunken groups waving swords and guns. They had to drive on, thrusting grasping hands aside. A solitary shot shattered the windscreen, showering John Cristopher. They drew to a halt at a safe distance, shook themselves free, finding comfort in the fact that the tyres were intact. Christopher staunched a facial cut with Jonathan's handkerchief, but they did not linger.

The Gurkha guard had been alerted, and shouted the good news as soon as they were spotted, coming along the bricked road to the railway crossing. Nurses rushed out to welcome them and unload their pathetic cargo. Janet spent no time on discussion. She took charge of the bloody patients, sending Gunvor off to the bungalow.

'Go over and get the doctor some coffee,' knowing that it would be a hug of relief that mattered more.

Jonathan inspected the guard. These cheerful little men seemed almost nonchalant in their confidence that intruders would be repulsed and calm maintained in the wards. There was a new cameraderie; cups of tea were handed round frequently. Milk was short and sugar rationed but there was ample atta for making chapatties. To ward rounds, Jonathan now had to make regular tours of the grounds with the guard. He noted that the dharmsala, a long shed at the rear of the hospital, was practically empty. Usually it was full of family groups, hunched around acrid fires of minimal wood eked out with briquettes of cow-dung. He enquired of Janet, 'What's happened to the patients' diet?'

'I presume you mean, who is supplying it?'

Gulab Singh gave the answer.

'We're having to feed everybody. Fortunately the mills have sent over atta and we have a first supply of milk powder delivered by a military patrol.'

The spirit of his Indian brethren delighted Jonathan. They seemed indifferent to fatigue, accepting menial tasks, even nauseating chores with helpless, often dying casualties. Many of these came from the charming little villages that were dotted along the wooded hillsides of the Kangra valley to the north. After a week it was possible to clear the beds from the chapel and restore the benches. It was crowded each morning for prayer. It was not only the nucleus of Christian staff.

118

Jonathan wondered how small a percentage of the Sikh and Hindu population had been involved in carnage and looting. Before long medical cases began to trickle in. The radio reported a rising toll of deaths from cholera. Cholera killed quickly, but the wards were filling up with typhoid and dysentery.

Jonathan called another emergency meeting in his bungalow.

'It is obvious that this emergency state will continue for a long while. I thank God for bringing us through thus far, and for the courage and grace you have all shown, in living these days unmindful of your own problems. You've shown a true example of impartiality, which isn't very popular at the moment. With new people moving in, our reputation in this respect is important.' The Chief Medical Officer paused for a while, glancing around the mixture of races with pride. 'For the time being we are cut off from headquarters and will have to fend for ourselves. Even a trip to the bank in Amritsar has its dangers; it is probably fruitless anyway. So we must be careful of supplies of all kinds. I welcome any suggestion that will help to eke out our supplies. I am judging our situation on three counts. First is our medical load, then our food supplies and finally security and particularly how we can safely dispose of convalescent patients, most of whom have no home to return to.'

Dr Rani was the first to speak.

'A Sikh doctor came to see me whilst you were in Lahore; I've been expecting him to come back, but he hasn't and in the rush of these days, I confess I'd forgotten him.'

'He must be new to the district,' Gulab Singh suggested.

'Yes, he told me that his family had fled from Sheikapura when rioting broke out there a month ago. He'd been with a relative in Govindpur, who suggested that he might find a place here. He's been qualified for about five years.'

'We certainly need someone to replace Dr Hamid,' Jonathan responded with animation. 'This is the way in which our prayers are being answered. Can I leave it to you to get in touch with him, quickly?' She nodded. Janet was next.

'I also had a visitor from the Frontier Defence Force, who left the milk powder. He too has not returned. He was a British Lieutenant, serving temporarily with the force. Mr Blickling sent him over. He asked about our food supplies. His platoon is grossly overstretched, but he promised flour, cooking fat, sugar and some milk powder.'

'Certainly without price. I hope it is also without payment.' The group had a welcome opportunity to laugh.

'I can report on the third count myself. I saw Herbert Hemmings yesterday. He is proud of the performance of the Gurkhas. He says that

119

the bloodshed is now effectively over. He thinks that Lieut Smythe, that's your boy I expect Janet, has power over rail movements and when we give the word, he'll commandeer a coach for our convalescents, and see that they are seen safely over the frontier. The Superintendent of Police came in this morning on a quick recce. He reassured me that law and order is now being enforced, and goondas – the lawless who have profited from the misery, are being rounded up. But he also confirmed that with a near fifty per cent turn round in population, land has been untended, so it is a bleak prospect for the rabi crop.'

But the new farmers who had escaped from the west, were busily planting. It was late, but there would be a crop of sorts, even though land disputes would take a long time to settle. Life was returning to normal in other respects. Babies were arriving in the Maternity Block as fast as normal. But, as the policeman had said, the population had changed, the old tranquility had gone.

Of course the new people were all Sikhs or Hindus; officials, farmers, tradesmen or artisans, all had a grievance if not stark tragedy to be forgotten. They had an in-built attitude that society owed them something. Though many of Jonathan's patients were of professional status, they all asserted, 'we are refugees' – pronounced with a very hard 'g'. This meant a prescriptive right to free treatment. Finances continued to be a headache.

Throughout the 'troubles', the lovers had little time alone. In snatched moments at the end of long days, they found renewal in quiet moments and long embraces.

'I wonder how many romances have been blighted by the bitterness around?' Gunvor had been troubled by the hatred evident in the wards. 'I've searched my own heart, to find whether there is anyone I can't forgive, or anything that is more important than being at peace with God and our neighbours.'

Jonathan remained silent for a long while.

'Being in love has helped me. I've been supremely aware that all love is of God. I've thanked God for you many times a day. Our love has helped me to see hope in some of our less attractive patients.'

'How could we have managed without a School of Nursing and the first class of probationers,' Janet said to him one morning over a shared coffee-break. 'They are so keen that they have worked like Trojans.'

Ruth Kendall, the first Nursing Tutor, was also enthusiastic. 'Of course there is so much competition to get in, that we've had the pick of High School graduates.' She gave him a broad smile. 'It was clever of you to get the school going and recognised, so soon after coming.'

It was true that Jonathan had wasted no time in writing to Colonel Palgrave on the subject. His department's approval was mandatory. Palgrave had sent his deputy, to inspect the hospital's facilities and records. Major Swift did not need any encouragement to visit Stewartpur. He knew quite a few of the senior mill staff; he met them on Defence Force manoeuvres, and in more leisurely state at the Masonic Lodge meetings in Lahore. He was the guest of Harold and Margaret Blickling, who'd promised him not only golf on the club's rather arid course, but also a half-day's shoot up in the hills, where the broad River Ravi issued from the Himalayas. Here an irrigation canal took off, on its long course through the Amritsar district. An old section of it flowed right through the mills. This backwater included the original ten-foot drop, which had provided the motive power for the first Victorian looms. Now it provided fishing on a Saturday afternoon.

'I didn't know that you would get into this outfit, when I met you in Kohima,' he greeted Jonathan.

'I didn't know myself, but the idea was germinating.'

'Don't you find it very quiet here? I suppose you have the mills' society to entertain you.'

'Wait until you have looked around the hospital and seen the work involved, then you won't wonder what I do with my time.' He laughed.

'I believe you get into the B.M.A. meetings in the medical college. I must have been on tour when you've visited.'

'Yes. I gave a paper on "Traumatic Surgery", particularly about gas gangrene. That was at Palgrave's instigation.'

'Now I'm with you; I read that in the journal.'

So the official sanction had come through and as Janet remarked, the very first class had proved invaluable.

There was no slacking off of the surgical load. Many of the new residents had mutilation, even though their wounds had healed. One had lost his nose to a sword slash and many more had bullet wounds leaving nasty scars on the face. Added to these was a new type of casualty from the railway. Trains were regular again, but the rolling stock remained unrepaired from the ravages of the fighting. Most significantly, every train was grossly overcrowded. Many hung precariously on the running boards, clothing streaming in the wind. Most alarming was the sight of groups, men, women and children, sitting nonchalantly on the roofs; many were swept away by low bridges. Most were ticketless. They were now independent; they remained poor.

The single track branch line, running right along the front of the hospital, provided entertainment to patients' relatives sitting idly on the front verandah. The coaches were almost completely hidden by banners of clothing. As the train slowed into the station, many dropped to the track, some leaving it too late, trapped legs between train and platform.

The great event before 1947 was out, was the arrival of another missionary doctor to share the load. Guntur Mann had met Brunhilde Stahl at a Salvation Army relief centre in Hanover. She was a secretary, grateful to find employment with this team of ex-enemies. She came to love them individually and to admire the spirit that motivated them. She had already donned uniform when she handed a cup of tea to the young doctor, still limping from a wound sustained whilst serving with the Afrika Corps.

'We used to be proud of serving under Rommel, but look at me now.'

She eyed him with pity, for his civilian suit was no fit and the pattern and material were atrocious. The beginning of their romance was the outfit she found for him in the donated bales of clothing, from a consignment delivered by the Swedish Red Cross.

In Stewartpur they were given a welcome which reflected the universal desire to open a new chapter. To Jonathan it was a delight to find that Guntur was a physician, with a Berlin M.D. To International Headquarters, a doctor was a doctor, another pair of hands, but as Jonathan confided to Gunvor,

'God was more exact in judging our need.'

They were now able to arrange a roster for full duty. So the lovers had evenings off and commenced to discuss the wedding. The border regulations were still not final. Foreigners with passports were able to pass back and forth across no-man's land, with no more difficulty than the long delay. The ambulance was given a permit for repeated passage.

In late February, Jane made the crossing and stayed with her son. She and Gunvor went into a huddle to make plans.

'I'm sorry you haven't your own mother with you; she'd enjoy it so much. A girl needs her mother around at such times,' she pontificated, unusually for Jane.

'Yes it would be lovely', she was dreaming a bit. 'But I couldn't have a better mother-in-law to help me – and perhaps chide me.'

They hugged each other as Gunvor continued, 'Mother has written to say how pleased they are to know that you are here. She sent their gift with the comment: "I wouldn't know what your guests will expect, or where to get the goods. There won't be a gown to be made because you will be married in uniform."'

Jane was also dreamy-eyed for a moment,

'I'm going to enjoy myself!'

'You're thinking of your own wedding in Simla nearly forty years ago, aren't you?' Gunvor kissed her cheek. 'Jonathan has described the scene to me second-hand. I certainly won't have Commissioner Fakir Singh to perform the ceremony. You know, I still think it was a benediction to have such a delightful saint marrying you.'

'Meaning that Colonel Chandrasekar is a bit prosaic?' She changed the subject. 'Jonathan tells me that he's fixed an arduous trek for your honeymoon. He's just like his father, Gunvor.'

'You'd be surprised how much your example influences his decisions. He wouldn't admit it, but he was quite starry-eyed when he told me of your honeymoon.'

'So you've heard all about our adventures on the Simla-Ani trail.'

'You'd almost think he had been on it!'

The Blicklings had offered to put up a shamiana in their garden for the reception. But Gunvor and Jonathan were determined that it should be a day that bound Indian and overseas Salvationists together. That meant holding it on the open land behind the hospital.

'Do you think that you could have the shamiana erected at the hospital?' Jane asked most innocently.

'That's O.K. by me.' He could never follow the reasoning of these unworldly folk. 'I'll send my men over tomorrow to map out the site. What you are passing up is my beautiful garden.' He smiled and turned to his wife.

'I'm sure that Margaret will be glad to make up for the loss, with pot-plants.'

'That will do famously, Mrs Blickling, though it is putting you to a great deal of trouble.'

'Oh Margaret is a born organiser, she'll love it.'

The hospital was agog. None of the Indian staff had seen a western-style wedding, even one scaled down to a Salvation Army hospital. Under the trees on the front lawn, a canvas top had gone up on a bamboo frame. The reading desk had been carried out from the chapel. Everyone, with or without an invitation, came to the ceremony, conducted by the Territorial Commander, Colonel Chandrasekar, in his elegant Punjabi puggarree and red tunic. The mills' elite had chairs, but in front of them, a hundred children sat and chattered on the ground. On the fringes were farmers and their families, men with scars

123

from successful Stewartpur surgery, wives with small children across their broad hips – Stewartpur babies. Hindus, Sikhs and Christians mixed happily. Only the Muslims were missing. Jane moved among them, asking questions in Urdu or Punjabi; patting babies on the head. She'd never got round to the more familiar Punjabi greeting of pinching the babies' cheeks.

In the shamiana, Jonathan and his bride moved amongst the guests, glad to see that Yorkshire weavers were chatting happily with their Indian subordinates or district officials, despite the absence of whisky or gin. Even one of the tall bearded Sikhs, with an elegant blue turban, twitted the surgeon,

'What Sahib – no Scotch?'

'Shame on you Sirdarji. Doesn't the Guru prohibit strong drink?' There was a general laugh.

'Come on – try some of my mother's secret lemon concoction.'

Bride and groom slipped away to get changed as it grew near to their time for the train to Pathankot. They crossed the line to the station, followed by a motley crowd, carrying garlands. The train puffed in, driver and stoker curious at the crowd, putting so many garlands around the necks of the bridal couple that they bid fair to suffocate them. Before boarding, the garlands were removed and fixed to windows all along the train; passengers pouring out to get a better view and to join in the fun.

Timothy Ramsey had arranged that the newly-weds should spend their first night with his friends, the American miss-sahibs at a girls' boarding school. They had a large rambling Victorian bungalow, on the lantana covered hillside, facing the high range of the Dhaulat Dhar.

'Our pioneers looked at the foundations dug by the local builders, thought them too modest in size, so ordered, "Make them a yard wider all round". You see the result.' Miss Macdonald explained. She had been Jonathan's patient and was very happy to play hostess.

Jonathan and Gunvor fell asleep in each other's arms, with a glorious content which outweighed the excitement. They awoke to the aroma of brewing coffee. There were waffles and crisp rolls as well. Susan Macdonald was serenely middle-aged, but she watched her companion, Pat Maclean, little older than the bride, wondering what was going through her mind. She knew her coming to India had followed a broken engagement. Jonathan had told Gunvor that Miss Macdonald's speciality was a cashewnut cookie. In the unhurried moments of waking and rediscovering each other, she reminded him. So it was a knowing glance that they exchanged, when their host handed them a little parcel, as they boarded the crowded, ramshackle bus for Mandi.

They were now in the Kangra valley, with the long high ridge of the Dhaulat Dhar filling the sky on their left. Forest climbed the first five thousand feet, but above the tree line it was bare crags and snow. A hundred feet below them on the right lay the little town of Kangra, crowned by its temple. They could scarcely make out the course of the Beas river beyond the town. But on the low hills in the distance they caught the puff of smoke, as the little mountain train struggled up to Nagrota.

'We must try that toy railway some time,' enthused Gunvor.

'Up on the hills to the left' said Jonathan, pointing, 'is the little hamlet created by the first British tea planters. They built the tiny church. There, you can just see it. Next to it is the Canadian mission hospital. I expect we'll get a call from there before long.'

'I wonder what sort of time they had in the rioting,' Gunvor asked. 'Some of the Muslim shepherd-casualties must have been known to them.'

'Dr Edith Slingsby at Palampur is quite a character. She is an Anglo-Indian schoolteacher, who came from a comfortable home in Agra. She was appalled by the lack of medical help for the villagers who were her pupils' families. So she went off to the then new, medical school for women, in Ludhiana. She was the only non-Indian. But she won her sub-assistant surgeon's diploma and returned here, the only doctor for twenty-five years.'

'I've heard of her, for we've had patients sent down by her. The locals, especially the women, love her.'

The bus pulled up outside a wayside teashop. They sat on the flagstones of the verandah and opened up Miss Macdonald's packet. There, sure enough, below the egg-sandwiches was a cardboard box of the renowned cashewnut cookies. On the cobbles sat a villager, selling the small fat cucumbers from his smallholding. They bought some, together with the brown rock-salt, which he crushed on the pavement and supplied in a screw of newspaper. The tea was piping hot and they ordered refills from the smiling pahari. It was fun to watch his technique. It was a dramatic performance which he never tired of creating. Holding the soot-covered aluminium kettle high, he poured the boiling water with unerring aim, into a cheap gauze strainer. It was already nearly filled with tealeaves from earlier customers, topped up with a pinch of fresh ones, tossed in with his left hand. It was a strong brew.

The shopkeeper was anxious to know where the sahib and memsahib came from.

125

'Kahan se aya?' In his experience, sahibs usually went sailing by in private cars.

'Jusqua Stewartpur hospital,' Gunvor told him. His face lit up.

'Aah Muktifauj shifakhana!'

He salaamed afresh and launched into a tale. Two years previously, he had had to close his shop, to escort his sick wife to the hospital. It was the only time that he had been out of the valley. If he had been too anxious to enjoy the adventures on the downward journey, with anxiety relieved, his bibi vigorous again, he'd found the return – his first railway experience – exciting. As the toy-engine snorted through tunnels and cuttings on the climb to Nagrota, he saw for the first time, from a distance, majestic mountains, under which he had lived the whole of his life.

He poured them an extra cup of tea, on the house, as he summed up a crisis that had been well resolved by the skill of the doctors and nurses.

'Bahut acha tha', it was very good, he summarised. The bus-driver was honking his klaxon urgently, as they bid farewell, promising to have a full rice and curry when next they passed that way.

By the time that they reached the end of the valley they were in the native-state of Mandi. Here the river Beas, escaped from the Kulu gorge and bending ninety degrees, flowed into the lush vegetation of the valley that would take it down to the plains and its confluence with its neighbour, the Ravi, until they joined the mighty Indus.

'You remember that I had to come up to Palampur six months ago, to see a Rajah's daughter. She had been taken ill at a party, given by a Maharajah who has a summer palace in the valley. The court physician thought that she might die, so her father was overjoyed when she made a full recovery.'

'I know the rest.' She squeezed his arm. 'The grateful prince wanted to make a handsome presentation, which the doctor felt he must refuse. But he did accept the offer of a night in the state guest-house, when he found the right girl to share it with.'

'Spot on!'

The bus driver, always ready for a diversion that promised a tip, drove right up to the steps of the large old house, set amongst trees and overlooking the spot where a major tributary joined the Beas. The staff were obsequious in making them welcome. It was a tray of tea, with English bone china, this time. They were in the mood to enjoy it. Watching the devout, bathing from the broad stone steps of the temple, with its pagoda-like roof which lay below them, Gunvor thought aloud.

'These hill people are quite different from the plains Hindus, I think.

126

Hasn't Hinduism had an amazing ability to absorb other religions through its three thousand years' history?'

'I agree, for this area was animist, then Buddhist, before becoming Hindu. Each has contributed to present ideas and practices in the region.'

'That temple certainly looks more Buddhist than any I've seen on the plains. It explains the attitude of some of our long-term patients.' Gunvor reflected. 'They are fascinated by their first contact with Christianity. The warmth and kindness of their treatment, makes them want to absorb all that is new and attractive, without any break from their own traditions.'

'It reminds me of the ashram at Sat Tal, built by a Methodist, but quite acceptable to Gandhi.'

Jonathan was relieved to find that the Rajah of Mandi was away at a conference in New Delhi.

'That saves the need of making a formal visit to the palace.' Gunvor was grateful.

'Though this is one of the smaller states, the ruler is dedicated to sound government. He was so impressed by the standard of administration in neighbouring British districts, that he sought experience, in another area.'

'I think that Indian rulers have an immeasurable advantage if they wish to rule well, for they start with the devotion of their people.'

'It even helps in the tourist trade,' laughed Jonathan, 'for the ruler has a traditional role in the programme of the temple, which attracts a vast number of pilgrims.'

'Have you been in it?'

'No, but I understand that, despite the Buddhist architecture, it is a shrine to Shiva, and his stone lingam is central.'

'Like the one you've described at Bageshwar. I bet most of the pilgrims are women looking for babies.'

That night was the real honeymoon. They found each other in the cool that required blankets. They could have lingered the next morning, but the bus came honking up the drive quite early. The driver was apologetic, explaining that the route lay through a gorge, only wide enough for one vehicle. They must reach the southern gate before 9 o'clock. But before they reached the ravine, so steep and narrow that the sun could not penetrate until noon, they were in trouble, due to the narrowness of the mountain road. It was a graphic reminder of the hazards of travel. The bus had to inch past a lorry laden with potatoes for Amritsar market. The passengers got down and watched the drama, giving advice freely to both drivers. The truck had the safe, inside position, Gunvor watched with anxiety as the bus with their luggage on the roof, inched nearer and nearer to the edge of the steep drop to the river below.

'Don't these people love excitement? They're almost willing the bus to go down the khad,' whispered Gunvor.

At Barejadi, they passed the further check post. They were awed by the broader valley opening before them. Tree-clad hills climbed one upon another; snow peaks dominating the head of the valley. But for the annual migration of the sheep, the villagers knew nothing of the outside world. They eked out a living from the terraces that climbed a thousand feet up every slope. For countless generations, they had depended on the melting snows to water their plots of vegetables and millet or barley.

'No wonder they are animists primarily,' Jonathan mused aloud. 'Their god lives in those snows on which their lives depend.'

'You mean that they are only Hindus by adoption, or absorption.' Gunvor took up his thought.

'I once heard Mr Ramsay telling the story that one of the Aryan gods came over the Rohtang pass and liberated a sort of Pandora's box of lesser deities, so that every village has its shrine, related to a local spring or a massive boulder.'

'I wish we were here for the Dussehra festival. Again it is Ramsay who is the informant. He says that from every village, a palanquin bearing the silver masks of the local god, is taken from the temple. The temple devotees, jogging the palanquin to simulate a living occupant, wend their way down dozens of mountain tracks, preceded by musicians with flutes, cymbals and drums. There is a great fair on the maidan in Kulu, with traders from over the Himalayas.'

'It's all very Old Testament, isn't it? I can see Isaiah watching the animists from Ammon and Edom, luring his people from the more austere worship of the true God, of whom no graven image could be made.'

'The Canaanite hilltop shrines to Baal, must have resembled Shiva's, in their erotic practices.'

Before they went to bed that night, they sat on a rug, before the wood fire that roared on the rough stone hearth, and read Isaiah satirising the folly of worshipping man-made gods.

'To whom will ye liken God, or what likeness will ye compare unto Him? The workman melteth a graven image and the goldsmith spreadeth it over with gold, and casteth silver chains. He that is so impoverished, that he hath no

128

oblation, chooseth a tree that will not rot; he seeketh unto him a cunning workman, to prepare a graven image that shall not be moved... Hast thou not heard that the everlasting Lord, the Creator of the ends of the earth, fainteth not neither is weary? There is no searching of his understanding...'

They read on to the end of the chapter.

'They that wait upon the Lord, shall renew their strength, they shall mount up with wings as eagles; they shall run and not be weary; they shall walk and not faint.'

'It's powerful writing and apt, though it is three thousand years old.' They looked long at each other, till Gunvor suggested, 'Let's go out for a few minutes and watch the stars.'

They stood with arms entwined, listening to the voice of the wind rustling the trees. In the stillness, they felt the reassuring presence of the God who is like Christ.

They had rented a small cottage, woodframe filled with roughly squared stone, smashed and chipped from the boulders lying all around and pointed with mud plaster. The roof was of deodar shingles. The whole blended with the forest.

'It's very Swedish,' Gunvor commented the next morning, lips parted, as she watched birds circling in the thermals near the ring of snows that enclosed the head of the valley. 'And so is the food,' she added as she spread the breakfast table. They were to cater for themselves, so the previous afternoon, she had been up to the big house and bought apples, butter, homemade bread and a jug of milk. The property belonged to a family descended from an Irishman, a Captain in the East India Company's army. He had been cashiered, so the story went. True or not, he had ridden up the valley, bought land for a song, married a local girl and settled down. Before long his masterful personality had been accepted by the villagers, who regarded him as a local chief.

'They're certainly the valley aristocracy now,' was Jonathan's comment as he sipped his coffee. 'They are the postmasters, own an orchard and a lot of property, arrange tours for bigwigs and run the panchayat – the traditional Indian group of five elders controlling all local affairs.'

There was one street of little shops that looked like garden-sheds. These were open all day, with their goods spilling out onto the rough paving of the bridle path. Even these irregular booths were parted by

129

occasional massive boulders, as though a giant had planned the place and left it unfinished. Women washed garments in enamel bowls, spreading the garments out over the great stones to dry in the sun.

March was turning into April, wild flowers were appearing in profusion whilst the first flocks were beginning to stream up the street to the bridge. Giant deodar logs made a cantilever across the noisy torrent which was the young Beas. They stood watching the kilted shepherds, for all the world like Greeks in national costume. Meat was mutton or goat, cut from the whole carcase, hanging in the grazier's shed. Eggs were heaped in baskets woven from the willows fringing the river.

'The eggs are small but only a few annas a dozen.' Gunvor reported.

Never had food tasted better and for the first two days they had no desire to explore further. Eventually the snows lured. The Rohtang pass was in their sights. The O'Reillys had advised them, since they spurned hiring ponies, that coolies to carry bedding and food would be essential. They also loaned them six-foot cherry staffs, with three inch spikes.

'It is a very steep track and more difficult coming down than going up, you need a long reach on the return.'

They set out at dawn. That night they spent at Kothi, which was the last traveller's hut before the crossing. It was very near the treeline. To Gunvor, it was the most lonely place that she had ever seen. 'Just what the doctor ordered for us I'm sure.'

They sat outside the hut, in the steely light of dusk. The infant river had carved out a deep ravine. It was just below them and though they could not see the torrent, they heard its thunder. Across it they could make out a few two-storey wooden houses. Women in bright kerchiefs and coarse woollen skirts, were bringing in the cows and goats and feeding the chickens. Soon smoke began to curl up from isolated chimneys and the soft light of oil-lamps, appeared from upper storey windows, before shutters were bolted for the night.

They huddled companionably over their own fire, before falling to sleep before its embers.

With another early start they made it to the snow-saddle, the lowest point in the range, by middle day. One or two great rocks were clear of snow, providing them with a table on which to set out their lunch. They gratefully uncapped a flask of tea. A strong wind was already blowing from the ice-bound north, fluttering dozens of tiny cotton flags, strung from a couple of bare boughs anchored in a cairn.

'Prayer flags from Buddhist monasteries, blowing prayers for travellers in danger,' commented Jonathan.

They had been warned that it was unwise to linger long in the pass. After midday, the wind usually reached gale force. But the view held them for a long while, despite the cold. As far as they could see, it was range after range of snow slopes and bare peaks, the greatest desolation that either of them had ever seen. They were on top of the world and it brought that elevation of mood, experienced by mountaineers reaching the summit. Eventually the cold drove them down.

As they retraced their steps towards Kothi, they had to climb off the path to allow women bent double with large, funnel-shaped baskets on their backs, carrying Kulu produce for the barren valley beyond. Some of the younger ones had a baby atop the vegetables.

They bought another load of wood from the chowkidar, cooking their evening meal on a roaring fire, blazing on the open hearth. When last in Lahore, Jonathan had picked up a tiny volume from his mother's bookcase, 'Harvests of the East'. It had been small enough to fit into his jacket pocket. So they read to each other by turn, recreating an India before even Jane and Stephen arrived. They were silent as they thought their separate thoughts of the zeal, enthusiasm and tenacity of the Salvation Army pioneers. Again as the fire died down, they unrolled their bedding and cuddled up in the warmth.

Jonathan came-to slowly. It took him a few seconds to grasp his situation. There was still a dull glow on the hearth, but light was filtering in from every crack in the shutters and door. He'd been dreaming. The imagery was from Mogul paintings, vaguely Persian, full of tailored gardens and delicate marble buildings, the creations of masons who were masters of curves and arabesques. The men were princes and all the women beautiful. They were raven-haired – scantily clothed in silks that the faintest breeze breathed life into. Even the trees were shaped to man's design, every fruit and every leaf carefully delineated. His own princess was tranquil in sleep, so he moved cautiously to avoid waking her. Was she dreaming too? She looked more desirable than the ranis of his dream. Did loving refine the features and leave an imprint on the expression? He pondered the immense mystery of sexuality. Gunvor was one to debate every subject that surfaced in their conversation. She had skills of the hand and eye. He recaptured her childlike ability to enjoy food and to revel in rambling, tennis and swimming, whenever opportunity afforded. Yet in all this appreciation which they shared, she was different, and the difference was subtle – exciting.

He'd known moments of inspiration throughout his years; moments when difficult concepts became simple and all life whole... this was one of them. His life was still being built on the certainty of a God who was righteous but rich in giving. This morning the richness was in this new companionship, which would endure and grow.

She stirred, her eyes opening and very slowly focussing on him. Life flooded that dear face and held him for an eternity before she stretched out her arms to draw her to him.

They lived in the present; it demanded all the skill and stamina that they could bring to it. The hospital grew more and more busy. Gunvor continued her duties in the operation theatre until she was six months pregnant with Alistair, who arrived on a bracing December morning of Punjab sunshine.

A new sister had arrived soon after their honeymoon. Irene Osborne, a Devonian, came fresh from a period as staff-nurse at the Canadian unit of the Plastic Surgical centre, that had grown like a parasite on the cottage hospital of a Sussex town. She was well suited to take over from Gunvor.

'She's more up-to-date than me – or is it "I"?' Gunvor said, a trifle wistfully.

Teaching nurses took more and more time, but Jonathan was able to leave medical tuition on the wards, as well as in the classroom to Guntur Mann. Brunhilde volunteered to look after their physical education and to provide a cultural programme for relaxation. The waiting list for the course grew longer, as both Hindu and Christian parents saw that their daughters would be safe in the care of the sahib-log. But they had outgrown the adapted property that Major Swift had inspected. Something bigger and custom-built was called for. There was an animated evening in the Sisters' bungalow when each made his – or mostly 'her' – point on the requirements of modern training.

'Don't forget that we have to find the money too,' laughed Jonathan.

But between them the main issues were settled and a blueprint produced, which received the official stamp of the Municipal Council. With help from the mills' engineer, foundations were dug. Major new buildings were a rarity in the rural society; curious sightseers were a menace to the labourers, flailing their mattocks or hoisting their hods. Cheap supplies of well-burnt bricks were purchased from the mills' vast stockpile. Cement and iron for reinforcement were still in short supply, so Jonathan had to go and plead his cause for priority. Having operated on the Deputy Commissioner, certainly strengthened his case!

A dear old lady who lived in one of the earliest thatched houses, built on the cliff at Kulanur after the Mutiny, when the Punjab of the Raj was in its infancy, gave Jonathan 200,000 rupees, swearing him to secrecy. She had hailed his arrival at Stewartpur with delight; this charming blue-eyed boy, was the best thing that had happened in her world for many a moon. The little colony in which she lived, was in a beautiful setting above the Ravi, at the point where it issued from the mountains. One looked across the rapidly flowing waters – very wide after the monsoon – to the jungles of Jammu-Kashmir. It was here that the canal took off from the river to irrigate widely all around Stewartpur. Mrs Jameson was a little thing, an I.C.S. widow, who 'Wouldn't go home'. She gave the money in one hundred rupee notes. As she handed them to him, she said,

'Both my boys were shot down by those tiresome little Japs. I haven't anyone to leave my money to, so if you are stuck, I could find a little more.'

Major Swift, five years earlier, had been true to his name; he had made a rapid appraisal of the hospital and its potential. He commented in his report. *'The hospital has a great asset in its staff of well-trained expatriate nurses.'* To his superior he added, 'I wish we were as well off in Lahore.'

Not one to miss the opportunity for a tamasha, Jonathan launched the opening of the new buildings with a party. The Collector* performed the opening ceremony. Himself a 'refugee' from Sialkot, he said, 'This is the kind of function that puts new life into this scarred country.'

Guntur had brought Mrs Jameson down for the occasion. Krishna Gupta, the Collector, was overjoyed at the sight of her. He had been a trainee assistant under her husband. She greeted him as 'my dear boy'. She was enthusiastic over the young women in their white uniform dresses. She approved the starched caps perched precariously on coiled masses of well-oiled hair, gleaming jet-black.

Jonathan had been appointed, 'Certifying factory inspector'. It made him the official assessor for damages in factory accidents. He was issued with a printed copy of the scale of damages that tallied with the penal code, established by Macaulay a century earlier. It had the merit of simplicity and acceptance. However, it did not prevent litigation.

'Why hasn't Sundar Singh gone home?' Jonathan asked on the morning round.

'He's prevaricating, which I suppose means that he is hoping to spin out his stay beyond the three weeks required to uphold a legal claim of a 'serious injury'.

* i.e. Deputy Commissioner or collector of taxes

133

'I get it!'

He found that his X-rays had to be guarded, and the staff constantly warned against receiving bribes to part with a patient's records. They could be produced in court by the vakil with a flourish.

The locals adapted to the cold but sunny Winter season. Even the dignity of the court had learnt to bend to the weather. At the District Sessions in Govindpur, Jonathan would often drive up at the last minute to find the judge moving out into the sunshine; warmer than his unheated court. Jonathan came to enjoy his relationship with the court. He had to overcome his initial distaste of the legalistic attitude to human suffering, plus the waste of his time.

The court officials, particularly members of the Bar, took their cue from the judge, who treated him as an honourable and busy surgeon, but never as a foreigner. Red-tape was commonly dispensed with as the medical implications of criminal cases came under discussion. Evidence was recorded by clerks in both English and Urdu, and he was looked to for translation of anatomical and medical terms.

'Kindly repeat that in Urdu, I can see the clerk has not got it down,' When they sat out in the sunshine, Jonathan could watch barristers, 'pleaders', they called them, as they prepared cases for illiterate villagers. Some sat under trees at the fringe of the proceedings dictating their needs to a professional letter-writer. A far-away relative must learn that Ram Das had gone to prison, for something they were certain he had not done. These 'writers' had boxes with sloping lids, portable desks like the one he remembered seeing in Apsley House at Hyde Park Corner. The Duke of Wellington had used it for despatches on campaign. It gave Jonathan a picture of the young general camped outside Seringapatam, watching Tippoo Sultan. Jonathan was often importuned by the same villagers, baring chest or thigh for an alfresco consultation. In the court he was an 'expert witness', entitled to a regular fee and expenses, which would be handed over in cash on the spot.

For a year or two the expatriates crossed the border on their passports although a new H.Q. had been opened in Delhi. But Jane was now an honorary Pakistani. She was beyond retirement age, but in the hope that she would see something of her son, she had agreed to stay on at the girls' school for a while. In the event, it became a full five years, for the two headquarters agreed that they would never find a better matron for The Gables in Naini Tal. She also crossed the new frontier without challenge.

She could have no more rewarding holiday for herself. 1951 was significant. It would be the last.

One morning she stood at the northern end of the verandah and watched the first sunlight gild Cheena peak. It was quiet but for an altercation between coolies on the road 150 ft below. Not a ripple disturbed the waters of the lake, a perfect mirror for the mountains. Forty years rolled away; she was looking at the scene with the eyes of a bride of twenty-five. Stephen, with memories of the neat alps and homesteads of Switzerland, had found these mountains unkempt and disappointing. Her own home in Norfolk, was little above the level of the sea, a mile away. She was seeing the high-point of her childhood world, Wiveton Down, with its bluebells and golden gorse. By this time next year, she would be with Mary and her other grandchildren in Sheringham. What a benediction it would be to revisit all her old haunts. She was surprised at the intensity of her feelings. For the moment it was to be her Indian grandchildren, Alistair and Gertrud, who would come for their holiday. She saw the three-year-old boy, questions pouring endlessly and feet pattering on the bricks of her kitchen, spying out the cookies that Grandma must have made for him.

Her reverie was interrupted by Yakub, the new Majordomo.

'Do I get No. 1 ready for the doctor-sahib?'

'Of course.' The room, over the dining room, had a corner window above where she was now enjoying the view. Jonathan had loved it since he was a boy. She must get on. She totted up the number of guests as she hurried to the pantry. The cook was sitting on his haunches whilst his underling, the masalchi, was busy washing the dishes. They already had breakfast ready; she only needed a few minutes to check the meat and vegetables for lunch and dinner. Back in her room, she sat, 'just for a minute' to continue her reverie. She remembered struggling with a Hindustani primer – it was 1907. More than forty years on she still believed in her mission, but as she pondered a divided India, she was less certain that the Raj had done all that it should for the poor. Perhaps she was more Indian herself now; not in economic terms but in her empathy with villagers and their constant struggle for survival, the women particularly. Her thoughts moved on to her girls in Lahore. For thirty years Jon said she had 'queened it'. A smile flitted across her face – the girls called her 'hamari rani' – our queen, for her mixture of almost regal command of the institution and her patent love for them.

'I bet the idea came from their frequent sight of the marble Victoria seated at the end of the road.' Now it was a separate country and

135

tempers flared quickly, so near the frontier. For a year now Jonathan had not been able to visit her easily in the ambulance. Customs had apprehended the driver of a Miss-sahib's car, for smuggling gold in the chassis. All vehicle permits had been cancelled. So she would make the most of these three weeks.

The overloaded bus panted round the last bend in the road, steam hissing from its radiator. It creaked to a halt, but it was impossible to get near it for the fighting, gesticulating mob of bedraggled hillmen; but a little fair head, peeping out expectantly, shrieked, 'There's Grandma – there's Jane!'

It made her young again.

The term was drawing to its end for Jonathan and Gunvor. Patients who had long postponed needed operations, had their minds made up very quickly. You could never be certain that the doctor would come back. Invitations to farewell meals poured in and there were garlands galore, which delighted the children. Gertrud was eighteen months and toddling into everything. Christmas had been a new wonder to her, especially the crib-scene in the chapel. Twice she had gone missing and been found kneeling before the manger, with the baby Jesus in her arms. The highlight for Alistair had been the arrival of Father Christmas on a camel. The gangling beast, all awkward legs, had actually kneeled to let him mount with his father. Then they careered across the bare fields behind the hospital, the mount grunting bad temperedly, thought Alistair.

New year was ushered in for the staff, with a watch-night service in the chapel. For most of them, painful memories of the partition riots were still vivid, so they thanked God with genuine fervour, for a good and peaceful year. Then with the heartiness of Salvationists, they shared a meal of vegetable soup in the out-patient hall. It was not long then until the children were helping their mother, on her knees before the open trunks. Going home was becoming real. The whole staff of the hospital and most of the convalescent patients, streamed across the lines to the station as the Pathankot train pulled in. The station master dived into his office, to put on his best jacket and come out with his garland. He wouldn't have been there if the doctor had not got his duodenal ulcer in time, when it had perforated.

Jonathan stood at the open window of the compartment, his arms round Gunvor and the children, as they steamed past the hospital. He kissed her hair and whispered, 'What a confirmation of the decisions that led us into this kind of life.'

136

She turned to him and kissed him on the lips, 'I'm so happy that I can't talk.' The tears were running down her cheeks. Alistair turned away from the view of the fields rushing by and distant mountains fading, to find his sister staring in bewilderment at her mother.

'Why is Mummy crying?' Grown-ups were so illogical.

Chapter Five
A BROAD CANVAS

The sons of want.

Jane had left India at the beginning of November, so was well ensconced in her retirement home, by the time that the Lindseys reached England. It was a tiny cottage, built a century earlier for a fisherman; therefore near the sea. Jane rented it because it was near Mary's big, clifftop house.

'It's big enough for her brood of four, with spare for you when you come home,' Jane had written to her son.

So Gunvor and Jonathan had their first long view of a blustery North Sea, from the bow-window of their bedroom. Alistair and his sister meanwhile explored the adjoining dressing-room which was to be theirs for the holiday. 'Gert' was the best that Alistair had been able to manage of his baby sister's forbidding name.

The sisters-in-law explored each other's history and interests, whilst the children, after a brief shyness, joined forces and ran down to the beach. Mary's house was to the west of the town centre. A miniature clocktower had been erected to celebrate Victoria's Jubilee. It conferred a permanent landmark on the fishing village, that was rapidly becoming an East Anglian resort which catered particularly for families. Children were usually instructed to wait at the clocktower if they lost contact.

Beyond the slipway, where the lifeboat was launched, the cliff fell thirty feet to the esplanade and beach. There was a staged wooden stairway up the cliff to Mary's back garden. As the days warmed, Jane had a winged basket chair in the sun.

'In which she can doze or daydream,' Mary confided to Gunvor.

Despite Jonathan's enthusiastic letters of a few years earlier, in which he broke the news of his engagement to a Swede, Mary had to be convinced that her brother had been right in not marrying an English girl. Even Jane's periodic sharing, whilst she was ironing, had not converted her. She had come to enjoy those moments of peace before the children burst in from school. It was the prime time for catching up on India, which had obviously changed a lot since she had left it. For Jane it was a chance to relive busy years at leisure. Although Mary could remember her wartime upbringing, with a father away in France and Serbia, whilst her mother looked after cheerful, amorous sailors in Harwich, she had settled into life in Norfolk in the manner born. Even the years in India, with friends of several nationalities were rapidly being forgotten.

'She has developed a parochial outlook,' Jonathan explained to his wife, mystified by Mary's views. Robert, Mary's husband, was a man of long silences. He eschewed casual clothes. Gunvor became accustomed to his hurried departure after breakfast, with his rolled umbrella and Homberg hat. She lingered with Mary over a second cup of coffee and asked, 'What does Robert do?' She had learned that the abbreviation, 'Bob' was frowned upon.

'He's a bank-manager; you pass his branch as you turn into the High Street.'

'I sometimes wish that Jonathan had office hours,' she smiled, 'What a hope!'

Mary eyed her cautiously. Was she criticising their comfortable life-style? Her second thought was not new; she was frequently surprised by Gunvor's near perfect English, even her correct use of colloquialisms; 'what a hope' had surprised her.

'I've had a job too for quite a long while,' she volunteered. 'With all the children at school, I needed to be occupied. The headmaster of their school, told Robert that he needed a secretary so I volunteered. I enjoy it.'

'But you've not been working since we descended on you?'

'I'm treated on a par with the teaching staff, so am entitled to a sabbatical. I'm taking it now, to enjoy your furlough.'

'Not my understanding of Sabbath rest,' Gunvor laughed, 'but I'm sure that Jon and I appreciate it.'

'He tells me that you are an artist.'

'Jon's exaggerating as usual, when he talks about me. I sketch, usually in pencil or watercolour. It fixes memories for me, but I'm never satisfied with my results.'

'Well, we'll explore Norfolk together; you will be able to sketch to your heart's content.' She slipped her arm through Gunvor's and they joined Jane. As usual Jane was busy. She was in the kitchen with flour up to her elbows, as she prepared scones and cookies for half-a-dozen appreciative grandchildren.

On Sunday, they all went to the Salvation Army hall. Robert, as befitted a banker, was the corps treasurer, with a woven 'C.T.' on the shoulder of his uniform. Mary had no insignia, but loved her job as leader of the Primary, the kindergarten end of the Sunday School. Children under five weren't angels, but they easily looked the part. Their guileless enjoyment of dressing-up for bible scenes and action songs, endeared them. They always stole the show at a demonstration. It was all new to Alistair and Gertrud. Sunday was as exciting as any other day. There was not an idle moment. They liked to be early enough to get seats behind the band. Alistair was quickly hooked on the trombone, intrigued by its brassy tone and the easy transition from note to note, by the deft operation of the slide. Jonathan watched the boy's fascination.

'Jack Fisher is a bit of a showman,' commented Mary when her brother told her.

The children returned from their run along the Front, climbed the cliff stairs and opened the garden gate, panting.

Their chatter awakened Jane, who had been dozing in her special chair. Jonathan had come down from their bedroom, having watched for some time from the window. It struck him that in a life of coming and going, with his mother as the anchor to his living, he had never seen his mother asleep. He had seldom seen her resting. It was a dear face, and the hair, though greying, still had golden tints. He sat on the grass beside her. He was seeing her in this Norfolk setting, which held her beginnings. He marvelled at her achievements. Hers had been creative living, but she travelled light; even in retirement she had few possessions. But her simple faith had endured, and become the anchor not only to her family, but to an unnumbered array of little people, to whom she had been a mother, a confidante or a provider. She implicitly believed that God would provide the inspiration, direction and the ability to make dreams come true. Her faith had refined her. With the years had come not only content, but a very human divinity. Somewhere he had read a Wesley aphorism, 'There is no holiness but social holiness; Christianity is a social religion.' Jane seemed to have grasped this instinctively.

It was typical of her, that as the children woke her, she immediately comprehended his presence, leaping up with the agility of a youngster and a cry of,

'What am I doing? I was to have coffee ready for you.'

All too quickly a month flew by and Jonathan was off to London by the Poppyline train to Norwich. The single track meandered through the low hills to the edge of the Broads; then through lush grazing land to the provincial capital, with its elegant wrought iron and glass station. The express was waiting with steam up and a dining coach to provide city gents with breakfast before they reached Ipswich.

He had landed the appointment of Senior Registrar to Sir James Grafton, at the West End hospital in which he had held the junior post fifteen years earlier. It was still his first choice. Sir James was a dignified consultant of the old school. He treated Jonathan as a colleague, was keen to wine and dine him, but he expected absolute loyalty, with enthusiasm for the chosen craft.

He had been intrigued by Jonathan's curriculum vitae; attracted by his varied experience in war, as well as that in an India he did not know. It would enrich the practice. Tuberculosis was still the scourge of London's poor. Tuberculosis of the bones and joints was Sir James' speciality, as it had been of Sir Christopher Raymond in 1938. The country annexe still had open-air treatment for patients with varying degrees of paraplegia. Its long verandahs were full. The Chief still operated to relieve the pressure of pus on the spinal cord. It was early days in the antibiotic era. But penicillin had already worked wonders against the common staphylococcus, the microbe that caused the

141

common bone infection – osteomyelitis. The children's wards were no longer filled with very ill bairns, whose drilled bones oozed pus. This was a memory of his student days. Now there was a specific for the tubercle bacillus. Streptomycin had been purified and was rapidly changing the scene. The possibilities for surgery were greatly widened.

Jonathan intrigued Sir James; his attitudes and interests were so different from his previous registrars. He was of course older, with a wealth of both foreign and military experience. There was none of the Puritan arrogance, that he might have expected from one who had followed the distinction of a Colonel in an Imperial service, with all its perks, by a missionary career 'on a shoe-string', as he explained to his wife. He invited him to a leisurely lunch at his club. He opened the conversation, on his own pet subject.

'Do you see many tubercular spines?'

'Yes. We're seldom without two or three.'

'What do you do for them?'

Jonathan smiled. He knew that Grafton was famous for his laminectomies; by removing bone he released the tubercular debris, which was creating pressure on the spinal cord.

'We've found that streptomycin is making it possible to deal with many cases without surgery. If paraplegia has not developed, we extend the spine and apply a plaster jacket.'

'It's expensive treatment with antibiotics, isn't it? We're cushioned by the National Health Service. Is there any state medicine in India?'

'There is, within the restraints of a tiny budget, set against a population of three hundred million. Before independence, the Raj set up a commission to advise the way forward for the health of the nation. The present government is basing its programme on the Bhore report from that commission.'

'Then how do you manage in a mission hospital? I suppose you get a good subsidy from England?' He paused, studying Jonathan intently for a moment. 'I have always comforted myself that the donation I send to your headquarters may help the sick poor overseas.'

There was a pause, whilst Jonathan silently debated how best to answer that one. He knew that only a small proportion of the budget came from international funds.

'You've probably read of William Booth's ardour for giving the poor a chance. He never had enough money, and there were always too many enthusiastic officers, tackling urgent causes all round the world. So two cardinal principles have operated since the 1880s. I have no quarrel with them. The first is that every institution aims at self-support. In Stewartpur we've been able to develop rapidly in the last six years, because we've earned money and also attracted enthusiasts with money.'

'But you can't have many who can afford to pay, surely?'

'You'd laugh at the fees I get for major surgery. R100, is about seven pounds; that is a healthy payment for us. Given our careful expenditure, it permits us to treat a large number free.'

'Are you saying that you get nothing personally for your surgery?'

'I'll tell you the second principle, shall I?' Jonathan replied.

'Go ahead.' A waiter cleared the dishes and took their orders for a sweet.

'For many years now the organisation has harnessed the idealism of youth. There is no guaranteed salary, whilst the scale of allowances is based on a simple cost of living, which therefore varies from country to country. I get less in India than in the U.K. I can see that you are raising your eyebrows. It is certainly the reverse of the situation in the I.M.S., where I had an overseas allowance paid into my bank in England, to cushion the increased cost of living abroad.' Sir James frowned.

'That certainly keeps the cost down, but it's tough on your personnel.'

'I think you have to take into account, the satisfaction of running a hospital that is better equipped than the norm of the country, with a happy staff and a true team spirit.'

'Someone has told me that your wife is Swedish. Is that correct?'

'Yes, Gunvor is in her native Stockholm, introducing our children to her parents, as we talk. You see, being an international outfit, we draw like-minded recruits from all over the world. And we're all accustomed to the same discipline.'

'I take my hat off to you. I still don't see how you can survive on a tiny allowance, when you have a family to support.'

'It means that we live off the land. It's quite healthy I assure you.' The Chief gave him a quizzical smile, as Jonathan continued 'It means that I've enjoyed your lunch the more. Thankyou sir.'

Jonathan had been offered a staff-room at a hostel for homeless men, situated near to the Houses of Parliament. He not only found it convenient but fascinating.

'My Chief thinks we're heroes in Indian hospitals,' he said to the Captain one day, 'but I hand the palm to you – up at all hours with a skeleton staff. Give me a wounded man any day rather than a drunk!'

He stood in the gardens by the Victoria tower of the Lords, looking across at St Thomas's Hospital. He was seeing Florence Nightingale walking those wards with her first probationers. Her burning conviction must have cost these young women dearly, but it had changed the world. He remembered those very long, wooden-floored wards from a visit in student days. His Stewartpur wards were not so long, but fortunately they were of a similar shape; a single nurse could see every patient. His sisters were equally dedicated. He sat down on one of the wooden benches, paid for he noted, in memory of a local worthy. The quiet in the midst of the continuous hum of London, was conducive to reflection. Miss Florence had supplied the world with her eager recruits. Becky had told him that nursing had started in Australasia, with the arrival of one of St Thomas's apostles, at the Sydney General Hospital. He remembered another, with a memorial in his alma mater, as the foundress of the nursing service that had replaced the Sarah Gamps of Mile End. His thoughts came full circle to India again. The oldest Salvation Army hospital was in Travancore with a like tradition; one of the pioneers there had been a probationer from Florence's satellite school at the Marylebone Infirmary. So the teaching had reached Tamil girls. He took a fresh grip on the truth that a well-trained, disciplined staff, was of more worth than an endowment.

He heard Gunvor saying, 'though I wouldn't sneeze at that!' She knew he would be proud of another colloquialism.

After the ward round the next morning, drinking excellent coffee, from Sister's Worcester porcelain, he raised the subject with Sir James and a fascinated Sister Allsop.

'I think there is such a delicate balance between discipline and independence. So much has been given to medicine by loners. But even the most ardent individualist needs inner discipline, if he is to contribute to the community.'

Sister Allsop, a Catholic by upbringing and a nun in her dedication to nursing, intervened.

'I wish the postwar generation of student-nurses were as single-minded as we were. Money is becoming far too important.'

Sir James frowned.

'It's a reaction from wartime austerity; that goes for discipline as well as money.' He got up to terminate the discussion. He was unhappy with the subject. At heart, he agreed with the Sister's dictum. He himself belonged to the era of nurses in starched uniforms, with a disregard for the clock. But he found the discussion on present trends depressing and unprofitable. Jonathan had been watching him; it was sad to see the Grand Old Man's normal courtesy and charm disappearing under strain.

Jonathan went off to the outpatient department over the road, where he had a long line-up of elderly ladies, whose hips he had pinned

144

following fractures. He was proud of them, as they walked between parallel bars, or graduated from Zimmer frames to single sticks. Vast strides were being made in orthopaedic surgery, since antibiotics had lessened the fear of infection in bones. In my student days, he reflected, a fractured hip meant months in plaster. How many of them died of pneumonia? Now he handled most of Sir James' cases; they were usually walking in a few weeks from the insertion of a stainless steel pin.

He related every new treatment to the Indian scene to which he would return. In London, he had a trained team and a mass of new instruments and equipment. He would need a special operating table; one which could be largely dismantled when the operation was over. He'd need to work out an X-ray routine, for here, it was a dozen plates to each operation. Stewartpur would not be able to afford such largesse. When it came to the pins and plates – any one would cost more than the average operation fee he could expect. Sir James had a private patient in which the pin had worked loose. He said to Jonathan,

'I'm going to try something new, so put her on my list for Thursday.'

He removed the loose pin and gently hammered in a length of living fibula that he had previously removed from the patient's left leg. He was very pleased with his idea. As they shared a pot of coffee in the interval before the next operation, he asked,

'Will you be able to do that in India?'

'I've spent a good many hours and used a whole notepad in working out the equipment I'll need.'

'Now I've found a way that I can help you.' Jonathan had never seen him so gleeful, prolonging a pause whilst he put more sugar into his coffee.

'When you get back to the Punjab, as I know you will, I will send you all the vitallium bits and pieces that you need. I can collect them from my friends, who retire from Harley Street, or move to newer types of gear.'

'That will be a great load off my mind. I'll still have to find some essential equipment. I've made a detailed sketch of your orthopaedic table; I'm sure that our local blacksmiths are clever enough to copy it. That leaves me with some of these stainless steel specialist tools.'

'I've an idea for raising the funds.' Sir James was as happy as a conjurer, whisking innumerable silk scarves out of his hat.

'My wife writes a weekly column in one of the women's journals. Now I believe that you could write-up some of those racy stories that you have told me, particularly those Himalayan ones. I am certain that Dorothea could sell them for you.'

145

Jonathan not only started writing that evening, but also found illustrations in his albums. Captain Jenkins set him up with a desk and a typewriter in the private office in Peter Street. He even opened his store, for a 100 watt bulb and a table lamp.

He rejected the typewriter for his letter to Gunvor.

'We're home and dry,' he wrote, 'there's another expression for your little note-book.'

The news from Stockholm made him envious.

'My parents are thoroughly spoiling the children. They've turned Gertrud into a true daughter by fitting her out in a Dalkalia costume, with a flowered cap and blouse and a golden yellow skirt. Of course mother had done her hair up in plaits, with big bows in the yellow of her skirt. You'll eat her! I miss you very much. This holiday is giving the children a real idea of their double inheritance. Perhaps next time, we will be able to spend most of our furlough here as a family.'

The voyage to Bombay became a novel experience to Jonathan and Gunvor, because of the awakening understanding of the children. 'They seem to have become persons on this visit to their grandparents.'

Gunvor was in a flowered dress with a long full skirt.

'This is a new one to me,' said Jonathan, fingering it.

'I picked it up in one of the "realisations" in Kungstragordan, that mother insisted that we go to.'

She laughed at his puzzled look.

'That's Swedish for a bargain offer.'

'I like it.' He slipped an arm around her pliant waist and gave a quick kiss of understanding. They were returning to India with renewed zest and optimism. Partition was behind them and they had a host of new ideas for Stewartpur. They had discussed the issue of sending Alistair to a boarding school, a month or two before his fifth birthday, or the alternative of another year at home.

'Could we not glaze in the front verandahs? It would give us two more rooms; one could be a classroom.' Gunvor was loath to part with him; he was already reading and would be a delight to teach.

They had the usual four-berth cabin down in the bowels of the ship. The holiday had renewed Gunvor's love of reading and writing in her own tongue. It was a pleasure to scribble long letters to Stockholm. 'Though our porthole is near the water-line and consequently closed most of the time, it was open whilst we were in Port Said. An energetic salesman steered his boat under it, to sell us Turkish Delight. The

146

youngsters were in a laughing fit, for it was no easy operation, with the little boat bobbing up and down in the wake of a launch.'

The children had been awake early, clamouring for their breakfast, which the purser scheduled an hour before that of the adults. A parent had to be in attendance. So they had it, turn and turn about, to enjoy a run around the promenade deck, whilst the other saw fair play with the children in holiday mood. The catering was first-class even in the tourist dining saloon. To go down the whole menu at every meal was added pleasure for Alistair. This was marred on the third day out, when the Bay of Biscay lived up to its reputation, tossing the 20,000 ton liner about. There were many queasy parents, reluctantly supervising toddlers, still enjoying their prunes.

'What can we be,' asked an excited Alistair, as he listened to his mother, as she read the notice on the Purser's board, which announced a fancy-dress parade, 'with a special section for the under-tens.'

'Well, son. It's easy for Gertrud, she can go in her Dalkalia costume.'

'But what about me?'

'How about going as S.S.Travancore. We could make you a robe, covered with menus, notices and picture postcards... and what about an admiral's hat, made as a model of the ship?'

'I'll steam in at knots.' The boy was already into the part. Gunvor bought a roll of tinted paper from the ship's shop, cut and painted, then pasted together for his disguise.

'I'm lucky to have a clever mum; Tom Shipley's can't think up anything for him.'

So the ship's band played a suitable medley of 4/4 tunes, as the children marched past the Captain and his panel of First-class notabilities, on their dais.

'It's easy to spot the entries from the First-class,' Gunvor whispered as one or two flamboyant rajahs and ranis simpered by.

Neither child won a prize, but they could be philosophic with the lavish ice-creams served to all the losers. In their turn they enjoyed their parent's success the next day at deck tennis, in which they carried off the set of silver and enamel spoons.

The Punjab had settled to an uneasy peace. The century under the Raj now seemed idyllic. There was a new blend of peoples; most had grievances. There were deep family wounds and a general loss of possessions. There was a questioning of authority at all levels. The fields had recovered, more quickly than society. For his part, Jonathan constantly examined the shortcomings of the service the hospital offered, and with the experience obtained in the past year, set himself to improve and extend it. With Guntur in the practice, he confined himself to surgery; he found that with patients coming from all over the province, another doctor was needed. They found a calm and smiling Christian, a Syrian from Kerala, a state formed recently by the merging of the old princely states of Cochin and Travancore. The state was new, but the church from which Dr Jacob came was a very ancient one. He had graduated from the Christian Medical College, which had developed from an earlier foundation, only for women. He was competent and had great charm. He was an immediate success with Gertrud, who tripped across the lane to him, to be picked up. She would study his face, running her fingers through his eyebrows reflectively. He took to buying wrapped sweets from the mills' shop in the bazaar; he always had a few in his trousers' pocket against seeing her. There was a gentleness in this relationship which brought tears to Brunhilde Mann, as she watched them from her house. She had no child and the years were passing. Guntur told her,

'He's just as gentle with the patients; I find him refreshing. He tells me that his Christian ancestry goes back to the fourth century, when his forebears fled from Persia in a Zoroastrian persecution. Sailing down the west coast of India, they found a maharajah who permitted them to settle. They've remained almost a separate caste within an Hindu society.'

Jonathan warmed to this latest recruit. More and more he realised the truth, that the hospital's strength lay in a compassionate staff. It's roots were spiritual and he set himself to nourish them.

Periodically, Major Prabhu Das, the Divisional Commander of The Salvation Army in Ranjitala, came to see him. It was usually with a request to visit one of the villages in his district. The requests were usually to a feast followed by a meeting. It was commonly occasioned by someone's son passing his school finals. This was father's way of thanking God, 'in the presence of his neighbours', as Prabhu Das put it.

'It's all very old testament,' was Gunvor's comment.

So Jonathan would sit on the ad hoc dais, with Gunvor and sometimes Krishnancoil Jacob. The little hall doubled as a school all the week. They sat watching the excited crowd. Before them, in a small clearance, a men's singing group gyrated, to the rhythms of a small barja, their hands clapping or striking pocket-size cymbals as they sang. The box-like reed organ, was on the floor before the cross-legged player, who pumped the bellows on the back with one hand, whilst running the fingers of the other over the three-octave keyboard, with a

148

swaying motion in tune with his fingers. They played and sang by ear, producing the most oriental harmonies despite the western instrument. The leader sang a line with operatic passion and the others took it up with equal drama. Jonathan had a momentary vision of the Stewartpur sahibs downing each other's whisky in club or bungalow. He felt the great gulf between the two areas in which he moved. He had a moment of doubt, that such a gulf could be bridged, despite the shrinking world. Yet he remembered that many of his mills' friends had grown up in Britain in Methodist families. Some had been Sunday school teachers. They had no church now: mammon had won. He discussed this with Timothy Ramsay, whose fluent Urdu was in demand at the few Presbyterian chapels in the neighbourhood.

Timothy was not to be drawn on starting a weekly English service.

'You do your own thing,' he encouraged Jonathan, who promptly put a notice on the club notice-board, announcing an ecumenical worship. So every Sunday evening, the patients were intrigued to see sahibs and memsahibs in their calling clothes, wending their way along the front verandah to its southern end, where a small hospital chapel had been created. Very quickly, a crowd of women and children formed around the open door, listening to the unfamiliar singing accompanied by a portable organ.

Alistair had settled well at the American school in Mussoorie, which made it easier for Gunvor to part with Gertrud, when she too reached the age of five. Childless, the parents rediscovered each other. Gunvor returned to regular duty in the hospital.

The telephone was ringing, as he awoke with the realisation that it was Saturday morning, with a prospect of some leisure, since it was Guntur's weekend on call. He scrambled up and ran to the strident machine.

'Is that Dr Lindsey?'

'Yes. Good morning.'

'This is Dr Slater of Kangra. I am very sorry to alert you so early, but my colleague here in Palampur needs your help. Could you come up immediately?'

'Sure. What's the trouble?'

'It's an acute abdomen, and in my opinion needs rapid intervention.'

'Right, I'm on my way. Do I need to bring anything?'

'No. I think we have adequate instruments: I have crossmatched a couple of donors with Edith.'

'O.K. You can work out how long it will take with the car. Till then, goodbye.'

'I heard that,' Gunvor was beside him. 'I'm coming with you. I'll be your theatre sister again.'

'As well as companion and co-driver?' He hugged her.

It was spring, a delightful time anywhere in the world, but short-lived in the Punjab. There were daffodils in their garden, but unlike Norfolk they would only last a week at the most. Then the rapidly rising noonday heat would finish them. Bushes were green and grass at its lushest, as they drove up the mountain road. The towering Dhaulat Dhar was still crowned with snow. As they turned from the Kulu road and commenced the 3000 ft climb to Palampur, they passed solitary houses lost in fruit blossom. They reached the tailored slopes of tea bushes. Tea was not much of an industry now, but this had been one of the first areas planted by the British long before Assam took over.

They drove into the hospital compound to find Dr Claire Slater waiting on the steps. She had heard them labouring up the hill; she had even glimpsed the moving vehicle in the valley.

'I'm sorry to take your only break this week, Jonathan.' They were of an age, and enjoyed an uncluttered relationship common among missionaries, whatever their label. At home differences in dogma, liturgy and nationality might loom large, but 'on the field', the common task, especially amongst medics, was all important. He took her arm as she continued to talk to them both.

'Tea first and then I'll tell you the story.'

The Palampur tea had a China flavour which Gunvor liked; she sat back sipping appreciatively, as Claire described Dr Slingsby's symptoms.

'You know her don't you?'

'No, we've never met, but we've heard the legend of the teacher turned doctor.'

'She's a gem. The pahari-log around here swear by her. She's not one to fuss about herself; she dismissed this tummy pain as premenstrual initially. I was called over yesterday afternoon. She has a raised white-cell count, but no other lab abnormality.'

It took Jonathan but a few minutes to confirm the suspicion of acute appendicitis. He noticed the doctor's wince of pain, as he lifted his fingers from her abdomen. He turned to Claire and ushered her out of the room.

'I fear that it may have ruptured already. Have you put her on penicillin?'

'Yes. At the moment she's on it four-hourly. Can I change it to the long-acting variety?'

150

It was a very drowsy Edith that was wheeled into the theatre after premedication. Claire induced anaesthesia, with a steady drip, drip from the chloroform bottle on the open mask. She changed to ether for the twenty minutes that it took Jonathan to complete the operation. She watched pus well out of the incision; their eyes met momentarily. He felt his way to her left flank, made a stab wound, introducing a corrugated rubber drain, ensuring that it was adequate before closing the abdomen. He left the nurses to apply a many-tailed bandage, which isolated the drain. She was coming round, as the trolley reached the small side ward at the end of the verandah. A saline-glucose drip was already running.

Gunvor, Claire and Jonathan, sat on the verandah of the doctor's bungalow, with its awe-inspiring view of the snows, towering over the trees. Between the craggy snow-covered rock and the last of the stunted rhododendrons and junipers, were grassy alps. Jonathan could make out a gaddi, with his mixed flock of sheep and goats.

The coffee tasted especially good.

'You'll stay until Sunday morning, won't you?'

They relaxed by a roaring log fire that evening and in the morning shared matins in the wooden church, built by the tea planters nearly a century earlier. They had one other memorable experience. A few miles from the hospital, the Canadians had built a leprosarium. Leprosy had been common in the unhygenic intimacy of mediaeval European poverty. It had lingered in cold climates, where families huddled together for warmth. This was obviously the reason, thought Jonathan, why the disease was found in these mountains, when he saw none on the plains. On the other hand it flourished in the Tropics. It was apparently most common in South India. Sir James had heard Paul Brand give the Hunterian Oration at the Royal College of Surgeons, on his experimental work in the hospital at which Dr Jacob had been a student. He had restored function that was permitting leprosy patients to earn a living again. Sir James was full of admiration for this historic breakthrough, in what he automatically concluded must be primitive working conditions.

The buildings of the leprosarium were simple, and furnished with the basic, metal-frame beds produced by the local blacksmith. These were woven with a cotton tape which could be easily washed and sterilised. There were thirty patients, both men and women, all eager to be seen by a new doctor. Hope never seemed to fade; surely something could be done. They stretched deformed hands, lifted roughly bandaged feet, gave the grotesque smiles that ravaged eyes and noses produce. They were taken to the stone chapel. It was very simple, its altar a plain stone slab. But over it was a stained glass window that was beautiful. They studied its portrayal of Christ healing a leper.

'That's excellent,' said Gunvor, 'how have you been able to get that in so isolated a place? It has all the marks of a Renaissance painting.' she added.

'Thereby hangs a tale,' Claire responded. 'In the war we had 10,000 Italian prisoners of war from North Africa in camps up this valley. It's not surprising that among so many, there were a few artists. One of them designed this; several more co-operated in cutting and staining the glass. It was their way of thanking us for the hospitality and comforts we were able to supply. They asked permission to come here sometimes with their chaplain for a Latin mass.'

Jonathan made a final visit to Dr Slingsby, already smiling and free from pain. Her fever was abating and she was sipping sweet lemon squash.

'I have a little present for you, Dr Lindsey. I gather that you have been to see my leprosy patients and have admired the chapel window. Here I have the original black and white cartoon that the artist drew. The Italian Corporal gave me the cut canvas as they were leaving. I'd like you to have it.'

It was Gunvor, with excited fingers, who took the twenty or thirty pieces of canvas with the drawing in Conte crayon.

'I can glue these onto a large panel of hardboard, and work it up in oils.'

'You'll probably find it hanging on the wall in our hospital chapel, the next time you come,' Jonathan smiled at her.

They drove home in the late afternoon, lost in thought.

Guntur, Jonathan, Janet and Gunvor sat around the table in their dining room, to discuss a scheme arising out of the Palampur visit.

'Could we set aside a four-bed ward and commence the rehabilitation of lepers, do you think?'

'Nothing would give me greater happiness than to commence such work.' Guntur was visibly surprised and moved.

'Do you believe the time is right?' Janet was more judicial. 'I know there is a widespread fear of infection among villagers.' she elaborated.

'On that score, I wonder how the mill staff will react?' Guntur was now reflective.

'I agree with you both that tact will be necessary, as well as education. But to answer Janet, since the sulphones were found to be effective against the lepra bacillus, the infection can be controlled. The surgery will be safe; there will be no danger to others.'

'I would certainly be happy to take responsibility for them medically; of course there must be complete laboratory clearance before we accept a patient. We can make this fact clear to everyone.'

Guntur was going to be a stout ally, Jonathan could see.

'Then I'm all for it,' Janet was coming along too. 'It will be valuable teaching and training for the nurses.'

So there was another trip to Palampur.

'It's a good opportunity to give Janet and Kathleen a weekend off,' suggested Gunvor.

Kathleen Dobson was the Obstetric Sister and Tutor, Jonathan's accomplice in many a midnight drama.

At the leprosarium, the patients lined up, each hoping for a miracle. Dr Slingsby stood by him, beaming at them all. He chose a woman with a hole where her nose had been.

'She's only thirty though she looks like sixty', said Edith. 'She has considerable skill in weaving and in embroidery, learnt at the mission school.'

Jonathan's mind leaped ahead.

'If we could give her a nose, it would help her self-esteem. Then perhaps she could teach her skills to other patients.'

Then came two women with extensive ulcers of the feet, and finally one with a palsy of the right hand, which had not yet progressed to the loss of fingers or even marked stiffness. He had his tally; all women this time. The men looked glum, if not frankly angry, that all the patients selected were women.

'Cheer up!' He admonished them. 'It will be your turn next time.'

The Canadian padre drove the quartet down in the next week.

'They've been singing all the way down, doctor. Into their grey world has come a ray of hope; they are like children at a feast.'

It touched Jonathan. Here were women, rejected by family and society, who could be lifted from their slough of despond. In the ensuing months, he was to discover that no patients were more enduring and enterprising than lepers. They had a determination to be creative in the community, which made them indefatigable. Suffering had simplified their priorities; to be healed and to be of use was heaven.

Sumitra's story soon got round the hospital and she became famous in the district.

'They've made another living Ganesh in the Muktifauj shifa-khana.'

Then with a laugh for turning the myth on its head, 'But this time it's a woman!'

Word quickly crossed the lines. Margaret Blickling called one morning full of curiosity. Gunvor slipped into her husband's consulting room ahead of her.

'I know you do have reservations about these poor women becoming object lessons, but I think it would be a good thing, if so important a person as the manager's wife, were allowed to show that she has no fear of infection; it would convince the district. In addition if she is impressed by what she sees, she might become a useful supporter.'

So Sumitra met Stewartpur's leading lady. Jonathan described the scene to Gunvor over lunch.

'It reminded me of the London Hospital tradition. After Sir Frederick Treves had operated on her husband, Queen Alexandra took to visiting the hospital. The newspapers picked up the story that she had seen the "elephant man". He was a young man that Sir Frederick had rescued from a circus, where he had been a sideshow because of his grotesquely deformed face. It led to the Queen becoming the patron of the hospital.'

The Manns were over to dinner that evening and the story was repeated.

'We'll have to start thinking of what we can do to train these patients, not for a return to a leprosarium but to their own villages.' Jonathan launched the subject.

'That will mean more building and more money, won't it?'

'Yes. I wondered whether Guntur had any ideas.'

Germany was making rapid progress in recovering from the devastation of total war. Brunhilde was an enthusiastic correspondent. Her letters brought a response; she could usually find the marks to fund small projects.

'Tell us more of what you have in mind?'

'I'd like to start a weavery, particularly to get crippled hands going again.'

Guntur took a sheet of paper and quickly pencilled a sketch map of the land at the rear of the hospital.

'There's the site I'd choose.'

'Are you offering to finance it too,' Jonathan gave him a quizzical look.

'Certainly. I've been discussing it with Brunhilde for a week now.'

It was Jonathan and Gunvor's turn to be surprised.

'I've costed it and the price of three looms. I saw George Harrison yesterday. The Weaving Master says he'd be happy to coach Virginia in the art of the hand-loom. "She's itching to find a role in the hospital", he told me.'

154

'This is beyond my dreams, Guntur.'

'I've not finished. George became quite excited when I showed him the improved loom that Major Maxwell invented – only a drawing of course,' he laughed.

'Where do you propose to get the looms; the Army's factory closed down long before Independence.'

'That's easy, for George said, "I could get our carpenters to knock up a couple of those in a week."'

Jonathan turned to Brunhilde.

'Do you share your husband's enthusiasm?'

'Obviously we've discussed the subject. I've a notion to become proficient in occupational therapy and perhaps even vocational training too.'

'She's a pretty good tailor, and has been looking for a place to install her sewing machine, to start a class for staff wives.'

'It's symbiosis,' said Gunvor. 'We give an ever expanding service to the mills, then we have all their resources to draw on.' She continued to turn the matter over.

'We'll need the help of Charles Ferguson – though that engineer is a tough customer; and a womaniser!'

'That's true, I agree. However I get on with him and plans go through the Municipal Council, bricks become available and the club gets to know.'

'We certainly don't have to bother about publicity!'

Joginder was a hillman from Gurmukteswar, near Manali. At twenty his right hand had suddenly become numb. He soon found that he couldn't bend his fingers properly. His young wife watched him comparing the working of his right hand with his left – ruefully. When the doctor saw him at the leprosarium, she made a definite diagnosis. The shocked relatives were happy to transfer all responsibility to the missionaries.

One Saturday morning he was in the long line, watching Jonathan as he moved from one to the next. These eagerly awaited visits only occurred every three or four months, depending on the availability of beds in the growing department, which was broadly titled The Reconstructive Surgery Department; leprosy was never mentioned. There was a new charity in England with a Salvationist on its board. It had quickly become popular, for it was perceived as more humanist than Christian. Stewartpur's imaginative experiment was brought to its notice; grants commenced to flow. A much older charity, that had pioneered compassionate care of lepers, had taken a new lease of life from the discovery of curative drugs. It too offered assistance.

Dr Mann's first project had resulted in another of those gala days for the district. The Sikh Governor of what had become Himachal Pradesh had cut the tape, and been the first to enter the new block.

'The greatest success of this brave new scheme, is that public opinion has changed. Leprosy patients are getting a fair deal.' He told the crowd. Then looking up from his notes continued, 'And I think that Gandhi would have loved to hear these looms clacking.'

And so Jonathan moved along the line of Kangra patients, each willing the surgeon to choose him. He took Joginder's hand and with a pin, outlined the area of anaesthesia. He then assessed the mobility of the clawed fingers. He had developed the habit of carrying a tennis ball in his pocket. It had started with the unconscious training of Alistair to catch a ball, thrown suddenly at any height or angle. It continued as the simplest method of demonstrating the nub of the disability, and eventually of its cure. He put the ball on the table in front of the young man.

'Pukaro,' he ordered in staccato tone, so that the man who knew he couldn't 'pick it up', was startled into attempting it. But the tips of the fingers bent on themselves and could not grasp. He had failed he thought. 'He won't take me.'

But to his surprise the doctor smiled and said,

'Thik ho jaega.' It will be alright.

On this occasion he had brought Irene Osborne to assist him. She sat in the back of the ambulance, as it sped down the valley, talking with the pathetically grateful hillman. Guntur continued the medical cover started in the leprosarium, but confirmed the fact, commonly true with paralysed hands and feet, the patient was not infective.

In the theatre Jonathan's newest equipment was available. He could now work on such hands with an automatic tourniquet, that gave him a bloodless field. A little cut in the third crease of the third finger enabled him to detach the long tendon. Through another cut at the wrist he drew out the tendon and with a gentle scalpel, slit it into four tails. Each of these was then routed through to the back of a finger and attached with the finest of stitches. Delicately he tested his work, drawing slowly on the tendon at the wrist. It flexed the fingers reassuringly. With the hand balled into a fist, he applied a plaster cast and released the tourniquet.

A month later and Joginder was proudly demonstrating the result. Not only could he pick up a tennis ball, but on a tiny loom he was commencing to weave the nawar tape that was needed for the hospital beds in Palampur. He quickly became Brunhilde and Victoria's star pupil.

The new block on the eastern boundary of the hospital soon became the happiest place in the compound; a place where laughter was infectious and the looms gave tiny echoes of the mighty machines on the other side of the railway line. No joy, Jonathan reflected, exceeded that of being creative.

❖ ❖ ❖ ❖ ❖

'It's Saturday, Jonathan. I hope you can take a half-day this week and enjoy a game of tennis at the club.'

'Yes, my love. I'll do a quick round of the post-operative ward after lunch; always barring emergencies, it's on.'

'You and your provisos,' she poked him affectionately.

'I'll tell the Sisters; they always look forward to a break.'

'They certainly deserve it this week. Every afternoon has had a long operation list, and they've had half-a-dozen midnight babes, including one that required Caesarian section to escape the womb.'

It was April, with midday temperatures already in the nineties. At four o'clock half-a-dozen, single-filed across the permanent way and up the lane between the bungalows to the club. The one-storey brick building surrounded by trees, had a spacious compound, divided up by hedges six foot high. One hedge surrounded the swimming pool, popular at any time throughout the summer. Gunvor and Jonathan often slipped over for a refresher at dusk. But on Saturday afternoons, the senior staff of the mills gathered at the four hard tennis courts. A long line of folding chairs had been set out for them in the shade of a hedge. The looms were silent until Monday morning. For the thousand or so employees, this was family time. There were pilgrimages back to home villages, or shopping expeditions to Amritsar. There was a staff recreational centre, which attracted younger men particularly; amongst them were some badminton players of championship standard; whilst the volley-ball team often won the district shield.

From any angle it was a model-town, created by the company. It had literally grown out of the local clay, for every brick had been kilned from the clay on the spot. The power station was coal-fired; the coal dust was passed to a contractor in return for a quota of bricks. There were lakhs of them stacked in the mills' compound.

At the club Victoria Harrison greeted Brunhilde affectionately. They spent much time together over weaving patterns, or on the finish of

157

gaily-coloured place-mats. These were being made at steady pace by their protèges in the workroom behind the hospital.

'I want to get Guntur to have a word with George about printing some advertisement sheets for our products. He says that he is sure that Harold would be willing for them to go out with the Company's catalogues.'

George was playing a singles match with his arch-rival, Sen Roy, the Sales Manager, a Calcutta Brahmin. Sita, his wife in an elegant silk sari, was in deep conversation with Janet. She wanted to secure a place in the next nurses' intake, for the daughter of her bearer. The Brahmin couple were the only Indians, to date, to be admitted to the elite, 'Covenanted staff'. Only they enjoyed club membership. Gunvor, with her command of English as a foreign language, had a keen ear for the medley of accents in the buzz of conversation. The majority of the British staff were from Yorkshire or Ayrshire. Even Harold Blickling was recognisably Bradford. Owen Spring belonged to neither area. Jonathan said that his parents had worked for the company elsewhere, sending Owen to school in Darjeeling. There was one other who didn't fit the pattern and he would be sleeping at the moment. Louis Strange, was officially Night Supervisor, knowing nothing about the art of woollen manufacture. He was an artist, stranded on a visit to India when war erupted. He took no part in the social life of the community. Though Jonathan could have a philosophical, or even biblical discussion with him, he belonged to an esoteric religious group which prevented him from worship in the hospital chapel. He was a solitary. Only Gunvor made real contact with him and this was on the artistic level. She had bought one of his Himalayan landscapes and he had helped her with the reconstruction of the Italian masterpiece, even supplying tubes of oils that she lacked.

The only other unmarried man was John Stevens. He was twenty; a recent arrival. Gunvor kept a motherly eye on him, for the older men seemed bent on making him an alcoholic. Jonathan had been called out one midnight in the previous week, to find a drunk and dishevelled John, who had been brought home, cut and bruised from horseplay that had landed him in the undergrowth on the canal bank.

'It's fortunate that it didn't plunge him in the water', Gunvor remarked, when Jonathan crawled back to bed. He had seen John safely tucked up in the European ward. The night-sister, Jamilla, a matronly Punjabi was not unaccustomed to the follies of the 'mill-log'.

Only one of the Sisters, Irene Osborne, had a racquet, so she partnered Jonathan in a game of doubles against the Security Officer, Herbert Hemmings and his daughter Susan, who had just finished at

158

the American school. Her mother, Florence, had taken Gertrud and Alistair to tea at the boarding house in Landour, where she spent part of every summer, whilst her daughter was at school. Florence watched her well-groomed daughter with pride, as she volleyed the doctor and won the point.

'They don't just leave school, those American girls, they "graduate". They all graduate, whatever their exam results. What a fuss they make! I had to give a party for Susan and buy her a gown. I tell you, marriage will be quite tame for Susan after that.'

Gunvor studied Florence. She knew that Florence was excitable by temperament, and she made no secret of the fact that she was on treatment for a difficult menopause.

There was a buzz of conversation all along the row. Home news was always worth sharing. Not the least attraction however of the Saturday afternoon programme, was the tea. It seldom varied. Salmon and cucumber sandwiches and unlimited cream cake. After a week of austere living, the nurses enjoyed being spoiled.

'It's a curious example,' Gunvor paused, as she wrote her weekly letter in Swedish. But with the passing years, speaking nothing but English, she sometimes found herself pausing for the correct Swedish word. She found it and proceeded, 'of male chauvinism; only men can be members of the club, but all their womenfolk can enjoy the amenities on his subscription! So Jonathan, as Chief Medical Officer considers the sub worthwhile, because all the Sisters benefit. He says, "What a harem I've got!"'

The conversation was brought to a startled halt, when Genevieve Grindall, wife of the Office Superintendent, who was partnering Guntur in another doubles match, mis-hit badly, sending the ball into the bearer, delicately balancing a tray laden with steaming cups of tea. There was a horrified silence as the cups smashed on the concrete path. Hot tea splashed down the servant's thin cotton trousers, scalding his legs. He was led away to the club-house kitchen and the first-aid box rifled by two of the nurses.

Genevieve was a tall athletic Devonian.

'Her face is pleasing rather than beautiful,' Jonathan had commented to Gunvor, when he returned to bed after delivering her of her first-born. That was six months earlier. Jonathan knew that with many women, this sharing of joyful intimacy, created empathy. Although this birth was more special than usual, for Genevieve was over thirty, she had been withdrawn and unsociable. She was seeing Guntur professionally, he knew. Now she was over-reacting with plenty of friends to fuss her. The games were renewed. Irene Osborne had a useful volley, low over the net, which often disconcerted her opponents. She wrapped up the match now with one of her specials.

'That was pretty convincing Rene', Jonathan congratulated her. 'You must be ready for cream cake!'

By convention, barring tournaments, matches were limited to one set, to allow maximum participation. Genevieve had been escorted to her bungalow and conversation resumed by the time that they sat down. The topic was the summer exodus of wives to the nearest hillstation at Wellesley. It was interrupted by a bearer who approached Jonathan.

'Muaf kijiye Sahib,' he apologised for interrupting conversation, as he pointed to the uniformed male-nurse, who stood at the corner of the court.

'Trouble I imagine,' Gunvor said to Irene. 'I expect it will involve you.'

Irene had already seen the familiar figure of Christudas.

'It always happens.' She was already on her feet. It took but a minute to confirm with Jonathan, that the summons was for a surgical emergency. This one sprang from a village quarrel over cattle grazing. Whilst the farmers had been shouting abuse at each other, the errant bull had gored one of the wives. An anxious but still volatile crowd met them in the waiting hall. Every relative of the patients in the wards, swelled the number. They entered into a familiar drama with alacrity. It had all happened before.

Arjan Das, the Sikh doctor, already had the patient, a grandmother of forty, on the operation room trolley. She was holding her guts in her blood-soaked sari. The blood-soaked clothing was removed and she was lifted onto the table. Whilst Irene, Arjan Das and Jonathan scrubbed up, Guntur soothed her and commenced the anaesthetic.

Sister Osborne checked the instrument trolley laid up by a staff-nurse.

'Doctor may need to resect intestine,' she whispered to the nurse. 'Put rubber-covered clamps into the steriliser, with half-a-dozen more of the long curved artery forceps.'

The bull had produced a jagged six-inch wound, obliquely across the lower abdomen. After liberal swabbing with cetavlon and then normal saline, sterile towels were draped to obscure all but the wound. Jonathan examined the coils of small intestine, lying outside the rent in the belly. The blood vessels were fortunately undamaged, but he noted the enlarged uterus.

'She's five months pregnant, but the bull's horn appears to have missed it.'

He patiently excised ragged tissue and after gentle bathing, gathered the torn peritoneum with Allis's forceps before easing the

160

final coil of errant gut inside. He called for No 1 catgut and commenced the repair of the abdominal wall, layer by layer.

'Will you see to the drip and lab-work, Guntur?'

The anaesthetist was watching the breathing and checking the blood pressure.

'I think we'll have to give her some blood. I've cross-matched some of that great crowd of relatives!'

As he walked home, Jonathan thanked God, that out of the horrors of war, he had been given a colleague from the Afrika Corps.

At 2 a.m. the doorbell rang. Staff-nurse Rani stood with the chowkidar. She waited while Jonathan threw a dressing gown over his pyjamas.

'Routledge Memsahib taiyar hai, doctor sahib.'

'She's ready eh, but she's been in labour a long while?'

'Ji han."

They crossed the lawn behind the bungalow. It was bathed in moonlight. The chowkidar, hugging his pole with its sinister axe-head, accompanied them as far as the gap in the perimeter hedge. Only the breeze, rustling the shisham leaves, and the far away hoot of a train-whistle, broke the silence; until they neared the blaze of light from the maternity block, when a frightened scream rent the night. As they passed under the brilliantly lit frosted glass of the delivery room, there was another scream, this time partially muffled.

Jonathan entered the anteroom, and quickly gowned up before seeing the panic-stricken woman.

'How's it going Felicity?'

Another scream was his answer. Sister's quiet voice as she swabbed the woman's sweating forehead, encouraged her to keep up the push until the pain faded.

"It won't be long now dear. Doctor is just on time, as usual.'

'Not a touch of envy there, Kathleen?' Jonathan whispered. But she side-stepped the sally.

'She's having quite a long second stage for a multip.'

Jonathan laid his gloved hand on the perineum, as he swabbed the scalp of the baby almost launched.

'It won't be long.' He echoed the midwife's assessment.

With the next cry, he delivered the head from the straining perineum.

'Take it easy now. No more pushing. You can leave it all to me.'

161

The head was hardly free, before the tiny lips parted with a mewing cry. He held the baby boy aloft by his ankles and nurse Rani swathed it in a warm towel, carrying him to a prepared trolley to bathe and fondle. Jonathan kept his hand on the mother's belly, gently massaging the uterus through the flaccid abdominal wall. Presently he felt it rise up under his hand. With steady pressure the placenta was free with a final gush of blood. He turned to Felicity, whom he knew as the mother of two, still proudly conscious of her beauty. She knew that she still had the power to arrest a man's gaze. She looked almost wan now, her hair matted with sweat and her eyes closed.

His eyes met Kathleen's. They were puzzled by Felicity's dejection. A smiling Rani brought the baby to his mother. The infant's eyes opened and closed, as though puzzled by the bright light; its tiny fingers were seeking something to clutch. Felicity could hardly be roused to put the child to her breast, for that first happy cuddle. This usually had the nurses cooing, but now the room was silent. Mother and babe were lifted onto a trolley, and swung through the double doors to a private ward along the corridor. John Routledge was waiting there. The staff, once sure that Felicity was comfortable, left them discreetly to express their affection without an audience.

But something was wrong. As the days passed, Felicity was not only depressed, but developed a paraplegia. Jonathan conferred with Kathleen Dobson and Guntur, after all his lab-tests had been completed.

'She's afebrile, the lochia is normal and she hasn't lost more blood than normal. I'm baffled.'

'Well it's good nursing and kindness for the time being. I presume that she is eating.' It was really a question from Jonathan.

'Not normally.' Kathleen responded. 'She pecks at her food without relish and it is quite difficult to get her to nurse the baby.'

A fortnight passed, Felicity being pushed around in a wheelchair. She was a wan shadow of her previous glowing, feminity. Despite his hectic schedule, Jonathan found his thoughts constantly turning to the sad Routledge family.

The Lindseys discussed the situation under their mosquito-net one night.

'I keep thinking of Felicity,' Gunvor whispered, her arm around Jonathan's shoulder. 'Could it be a rare form of puerperal depression?'

'Guntur is toying with the idea of hysteria. How well do you know Felicity personally?'

'She's always been so gay. Always ready for a laugh.'

'Do you think she could be afraid of something?'

162

'She's only twenty-eight, whilst John Routledge must be nearer forty,' she paused. 'He seems fond of her, but I have heard of her complaining, that Stewartpur is such a boring old place. I know that she looks forward to going to Wellesley every May.'

'Unless she gets some life back into her legs pretty soon, I can't see her getting to Wellesley this year.'

The next morning, Guntur came into Jonathan's consulting room, in a preoccupied manner.

'Could you spare a quarter of an hour to give Felicity a Pentothal anaesthetic. I'm going to see whether she will abreact. John has agreed to the procedure.'

'Certainly. We've never done it here before. I remember some bizarre scenes during the war, when servicemen became voluable as they recovered consciousness.'

Guntur seemed lost in reverie. He too had wartime memories. He was thinking of the horrors of a Casualty Clearing station in Italy, of snow and unheated dug-outs, not the hot, lush scenes of Burma which Jonathan was recalling. It was a long and bitter retreat that Guntur would rather forget. Jonathan had moved on to happier thought. He thanked God for the happy band of brothers to which he now belonged. He still loved his homeland but loved this international family more. He suddenly noticed the sadness of his colleague's face.

'A pfennig for your thoughts,' he jollied him.

'I was away at Anzio, with an enamel bucket full of empty Pentothal ampoules,' he waited a moment, collecting his thoughts, 'but I have one of a happier hospital in Hamburg. It was there that I first met the Heilsarmée.'

'We still have a few minutes before Sister is ready. Tell me about it.'

'I was coming into the theatre, after a minor operation, when I was stopped in the passage by Captain Florence Becker. She always charmed with her schoolgirl German. She was the first Red Shield relief-worker that I met. She not only introduced me to this Army, but also to Fraulein Brunhilde Stahl.' He was smiling now. 'She was already secretary-interpreter to the team. I'm miles from Pentothal now.'

'I must say my funniest experience with Pentothal was the time when it was given to a casualty by a woman anaesthetist. She was scarlet, when half round, the man spilled the beans on his amours.'

They entered the room where Felicity lay, listlessly fingering the pages of a woman's magazine. All her normal coquetry had gone, Jonathan noticed as he moved to the washbowl to scrub his hands. A trolley was all ready at the bedside. She made no demur as he took her left arm and swabbed in front of the elbow joint.

'Just a prick' he warned her, as he selected a vein and pushed home the needle.

'Why don't you count to ten for me. See if you can beat me to it.'

But she was not cooperative and fell asleep silently.

'That will be enough, Jonathan.' The needle was withdrawn, a Dettol swab applied and the arm folded over it. Guntur started to talk to his patient.

'Something is worrying you Felicity,' he paused and Felicity stirred. She slowly opened her eyes, then wearily closed them again.

'Can you tell me what is troubling you? It's a great help to share it. The woman turned her head away from him and tears started. There was a long silence. Inconsequentially Jonathan remembered a line from a poem he had to learn at school, 'the minutes pricked their ears and ran about.'

She was frankly weeping now.

'I shouldn't have done it,' she wailed.

'Done what?'

'Gone to Ralph's bungalow after the Club-dance.'

'Was that in Wellesley last summer?' asked Guntur, the truth dawning on him.

To the whole community it was a miracle. Felicity returned to her three children, walking! The mill-folk congratulated John on his happy family, and praised the skill of the German physician. Jonathan would always remember the scene, when the husband and wife were reconciled, then assured of medical confidentiality.

March had turned to April before Felicity returned to tennis teas on Saturday. She was reluctant to bring a racquet, although she was walking quite normally in her own bungalow.

'She's got her hands full with three bairns under five,' John explained, 'young Archie is proving a sturdy lad; the other two love him.'

Medical confidentiality was trusted implicitly by the mills' staff; the women didn't need agony aunts. It meant for Jonathan and Guntur, that the consulting room or bungalow bedroom became a confessional. Probably, the unspoken sense that these Salvation Army doctors were not only competent medicos, but wise and understanding in the ways of men, helped the revelations to flow.

'If I were only a reporter, I could write my own "Tales from the hills"', Jonathan told himself as he left the Hemmings bungalow. It was May and one of the end doors of the line of rooms, that was the standard pattern of the mills' engineers, had been replaced by a three-foot induction fan, drawing a cold blast of air through the khuss-khuss screen. It was a delightful coolness, compared with the hospital, but very noisy. It was against this racket that Jonathan, having examined Jennifer, who was bleeding heavily, told her,

'I'll have to get you over to the hospital for a little operation. It will only require a short anaesthetic. I hope you haven't had any breakfast.'

He offered to take her immediately, sending word to her husband to follow.

'Let Bert bring me over. I'd like a word with him. It's a D.&C. isn't it?' She didn't wait for his answer, but ploughed on with her confession.

'He's sure that I've had an affair with Charles. I've certainly stayed too long at his place, on the one or two occasions when I've been to ask a favour. You know how it is; Charles can have so many things done about the house.'

Jonathan had learned to wait. Charles Ferguson was the Chief Engineer, a divorcee, who was too fond of women. Stories abounded. Gossip had been busy behind hands at the tennis tea on the previous Saturday. Charles was a heavy whisky drinker, who sometimes was shut up in his bungalow for days. 'He's on a binge', his colleagues said. His house was secluded behind a high hedge of oleanders. He was known to have 'strange women', on some of these occasions. On Saturday it had been whispered that Gabrielle, the Weston's daughter had been seen by the chowkidar, coming from the house, long after midnight. Gabrielle had recently graduated from the Mussoorie school and was at a loose end, until her mother could take her home to Huddersfield. She was a peaches and cream beauty, with a skin-deep sophistication.

Imagination made up for a paucity of hard evidence.

They would never get anything out of Charles. He was not gregarious, played no games, and his sardonic humour was not relished by his colleagues. Jonathan had only once been asked to visit him by the manager. The 'binge' had lasted too long this time. He'd given no explanation or apology. Despite his unsatisfactory behaviour, he was still treated with some deference. He knew his job; kept the looms moving and the power-station had not been known to fail.

Jonathan found an enlarged liver.

'You don't have to tell me Doc. I know my liver is packing up; but I've got through a bottle of whisky a day for a long while. I've no intention of breaking the habit.'

'I'd advise you to keep to nimbu-pani for a week, Mac. Give your liver a breather. You like your food still, don't you?'

'Och aye. I'll see what I can do.' He changed the subject. He maintained a curious relationship with the doctor, solitary though he was by inclination. One might have thought that the Salvationist's rejection of alcohol as a norm of life, would have antagonised him. But not so. With a strange twist, he rather admired these cheerful cranks, without any desire to emulate them.

He proved consistently helpful with all the doctor's schemes, was ready with technical assistance; would procure building materials or undertake emergency repair of the ambulance, or a physiotherapy machine. Further he could be relied on to keep his promises. He was not chatty, but seemed to enjoy the doctor's visits. He always plied him with excellent coffee, and his cook's speciality – potato chips, double baked to a crispness that made them crumble under the tongue.

'I can't imagine what he finds to talk about to the ladies,' Jonathan confided to Gunvor, in one of their nightly sessions, when they reviewed the day's events before turning over to sleep.

'I wouldn't know. Many of them have little to do and are frankly bored and –' she turned to Jonathan with a conspiratorial smile, 'they have husbands who are no longer attentive. They probably find Charles with his known reputation, titillating.'

'That's a big word. I hope you know what it means!' He slipped his arm around her, drawing her in for a kiss.

'I can't complain that my husband is inattentive, can I?'

A new block was on the drawing-board. It was a complex proposal. The School of Nursing had grown, and so had the standards required in a free and self-conscious India. A new nurses' home was mandatory. But this would give the opportunity of converting the old building, to provide a training centre for orthopaedic cripples. This would include leprosy patients, with newly useful fingers. Like those with birth deformities, or paralyses from poliomyelitis in childhood, there was nothing for them if farming was ruled out. They must be taught modern skills of the workshop, if they were to be able to earn a living. Charles Ferguson had already helped by finding a lathe at a bargain price; he complemented this by taking one of Jonathan's young men into his own workshop, to train to be an instructor for others. It stirred a perverse enthusiasm in the old cynic.

'Get it going Doc. There are dozens of minor metal-working jobs here. It would be more profitable to put small jobs over to you, at agreed rates.'

So as Gunvor wrote to her parents,

'Strings of donkeys have started to arrive again; bricks, sand, gravel; and by lorries, soft iron rods. I don't know which I dislike most, the braying of donkeys or the clatter of unloading lorries.' The braying and klaxons even punctuated morning prayers.

Few of the sahibs and memsahibs shared the Salvationists' faith, but all of them admired their enthusiasm and achievements. In clubs and offices around the province, and even across the border in Pakistan, Stewartpur was being discussed, not for its worsteds, as much as its human saga.

The periodic opening ceremonies were attracting wide publicity. In a different way, Government departments were sending foreign guests who needed to be entertained, and shown what new ideas were abroad. Within the hospital itself, educational opportunities were attracting students from as far away as Kerala. Private patients were also coming from further afield. Many of the locals had relatives in Delhi or Jullunder. The surgeon who had saved Sita's life would be the right one to operate on grandma!

In the club, they quizzed Victoria Harrison.

'What's this newest scheme? You spend a lot of time over there.'

'Sister Kendall the Nursing Tutor is becoming an enthusiast for teaching convalescent patients. Everything from embroidery and weaving, on frames small enough to go on the bed, to learning a trade.'

'I thought that they already had a little weavery and tailoring shop behind the hospital.'

'That's right. That is my baby, you should come over and see it. But this new scheme is to upgrade nursing; passing over their old building for an extension of vocational training in engineering. You'll find that Charles has a finger in the pie.'

'Isn't he perverse? He'll push a thing like that. He knows some of us aren't enthusiastic that lepers are being admitted to our hospital.'

'Well I must be fair. I've taken home sets of those colourful tablemats they weave; my family was delighted with them.'

'Glad to hear it. George and I designed some of those!'

If there were sahibs who were less than enthusiastic for the doctors' projects to rehabilitate lepers, there were villagers who still feared contagion. Only slowly was the prejudice overcome. The company had given another wheatfield east of the hospital. A low brick wall had already gone up to isolate it, and a line of sapling trees looked well established. The trees had to be protected by chicken-wire from the depredations of the omnivorous goat. 'The greatest enemy of our young saplings.' said Guntur, as he paced out the site for the new building, 'is the old granny with a family in the ward. She scavenges for twigs to

167

feed her cooking fire, and has no compunction about breaking down one of our precious trees if she thinks no one is looking.'

The scheme took off in a big way. The occasional visitor sent by a government department soon became a steady stream. Sociologists and medicos from the South came to evaluate the project which could have even greater potential in their part of the country. The whirr of powered lathes, mingled with the cries of paddy-birds and hoopoes in the self-contained colony of handicapped young men, some patiently plodding in callipers and a few in wheelchairs. They employed the long evenings when the workshops were silent, in the nurture of their kitchen-garden. A widespread musical talent was apparent, for soon their male-voice singing party was being invited to the villages for concerts. The string band helped. Gunvor donated her guitar, whilst Guntur was encouraged to bring out his flute, to be copied several times over in the workshop. They were immensely proud of their achievements.

'Will our family ever stop growing?' The Sisters asked Jonathan.

The clock in the mills' tower, which was its landmark, had struck ten. The Lindseys were abed, when a loud banging on the front door disturbed them. The chowkidar was there with his staff of office, his pole-axe, but instead of a nurse, it was sixteen-year-old Susan Hemmings who was banging in agitation.

'Mr Weston has been taken very ill. Joan says he's unconscious; can you come at once please.'

Joan was a second wife, twenty years younger than her husband. She had a young brood, three children under ten. Horace had met her, a buxom mill girl, in his hometown of Bradford. She was a down-to-earth, jolly girl who took his fancy. In Stewartpur she was a little too noisy, for those who had become self-consciously of the Raj. But the men liked her; her talk over the bar counter in the club could be provocative.

'Horace is a bit too old to satisfy her,' was the comment.

As usual, it was Gunvor who had to remind the doctor, who was drowsy.

'Your bag is still in your den, where you left it after your last call. You may need some more morphine and atropine ampoules; you'd run low, you may remember.'

As the trio crossed the railway track, only the signal-lights were showing in the dark night. He chatted to Susan, but she could tell him no more about Horace Weston.

Joan, in her nightgown and a light wrap, was flustered. Her children were whimpering beside her. It was a household where nothing was private. Joan's scream had wakened them all. She piloted them to the bedroom, and was scarcely out of earshot of Susan, who was ushering the children into the lounge, when she burst out,

'He would insist on making love to please me.'

There was a shaded bedside lamp, casting long shadows across the bed. Even before the doctor could see the patient, he could hear his stertorous breathing. His mouth was open and slack; his right cheek flapped limply with every snort. His left arm lay inert on the coverlet. It took Jonathan but a minute to confirm a stroke, with a left-sided hemiplegia.

'What's going to happen?' wailed Joan, tears pouring down her cheek. He put his arm around her shoulders, in an attempt to soothe her. But she clung to him crying bitterly.

'For the youngsters' sake quieten down Joan. Perhaps Susan could take them home with her. I'm sure her mother will gladly look after them for a few days.'

Susan, girlishly curious yet not quite mature, as she took in the situation, was already at the door and immediately responded.

'Mum will be happy to have them; she's got me to play with them.'

Horace regained consciousness, but his mouth remained distorted and his left limbs flaccid. As a purely medical condition, Jonathan handed Horace over to Guntur. Joan wasn't too sure. She had a lingering discomfort at the thought of her Horace being looked after by a doctor who had served with Rommel. Horace had been in the 8th Army. But she was soon won over by Guntur's understanding and counsel. She, normally so ebullient, was now depressed.

'I feel so guilty, Doctor,' she took him aside and offered him coffee, after his morning visit.

'I think I understand your reaction. But guilt is a crippling emotion, Joan. It certainly won't help you to get Horace on his feet again.'

'There's no medicine for it, is there?' She looked so dejected.

Guntur wished that he had Brunhilde with him, she was better at this than he was. But his sincerity and patent concern for her, broke through.

'You have the kinder, who look to you for comfort and certainty about their future.' It was the measure of his hesitation, that he had lapsed into German. '"The children", I mean.' He smiled at her. 'The only remedy that I know for guilt, is the realisation of the forgiveness of God.' He hesitated. 'Would you like me to pray with you?'

Back in her childhood, she had been sent to the nearest Sunday school. The memory of those Methodist folk, who spoke so naturally of

God, flooded back. They sat quietly for a long while, before she gave him an affectionate kiss.

'I won't forget this morning Dr Mann.'

Christmas '58 brought Alistair and Gertrud down from Landour, in the Amritsar party, excited with the knowledge that there would be no school for the next year. Homeland furlough was scheduled for Mum and Dad. Gunvor was at Amritsar station to meet them, as they said goodbye to their friends.

'Lucky you!' echoed on all sides.

This was the Christmas that would figure in their memories of an Indian childhood. For the first time, Alistair entered into his father's concept of the significance of the festival. From his own boyhood, Jonathan had been conscious of the disparity, between the opportunities for fun and games given to Christians and their Hindu neighbours. The Hindu calendar had a galaxy of red entries; its mythology was studded with events that called for celebration. So melas, or fairs, abounded. Their temples offered glamorous processions and easy hospitality, with the chance to forget the hard and humdrum existence of the village.

So he made the maximum of Easter and Christmas, not only to make their significance clear, but to give vent to the craving of the human spirit for fun. So he made the maximum of Easter's exuberant triumph, of good over evil. They had a march on the Sunday, which started as they caught the first glimpse of the sun. On the Monday they let their hair down.

But Christmas was the greatest opportunity of all. The senior staff literally became the servants of all. Alistair found plenty to do. There was the usual life-size nativity scene in the outpatient hall to be created. Mum came into her own with the backdrop. She'd had hardboard nailed to half-a-dozen frames, which together hid the whole frontage of the work-a-day world of consulting rooms and offices. It was Alistair's first job to slosh white paint all over it, before the artist could rough out a compelling glimpse of the Judean landscape; a scene framed in the open doorway of the stable. It wasn't the limestone-cave-stable of the antiquarian; it was the timber frame farm building of her Swedish childhood. Gertrud was already showing her mother's aptitude for painting. To her, this was a magical opportunity to re-create a huge picture, that you could see when you closed your eyes. It was Louis Strange's opportunity to make a contribution. He took Alistair in hand,

170

mixing generous quantities of distemper in old soup-plates and battered aluminium cooking pots. They painted with outsize brushes made by the carpenter, from straw well-beaten and bound. On crude bamboo frames, old rags and hessian were bound to create life-size figures of the principal characters in the Nativity drama. Louis even managed sheep and cows, cut from hardboard and vividly coloured. The Sikh carpenter had never imbibed so much of the gospel, as he did in getting an authentic thatched roof over the whole tableau.

For the first time, many of the village women glimpsed the hope of a new dawn for humanity, which fired their Christian neighbours. They came from far and wide for the morning meeting. There was no mass reaction, but there were individual ones, when saried figures knelt before the manger to place a personal gift; eggs, vegetables or precious pots of pure ghee.

'And my best doll was the baby Jesus,' Gertrud wrote to both of her grandmas. Of course there were carol parties to tour the township, with mountains of mince pies prepared at the sahib's bungalows. When they got back to the hospital at midnight, Kathleen Dobson showed them the Christmas baby, born only a few minutes earlier. The 26th was a day of merriment. It started when the Punjab sun had little warmth. Father Christmas came on a camel, with sacks of goodies for the patients and the staff children. Even the camel seemed to enter into the spirit of the day, kneeling most co-operatively for the children to mount, for swaying tours of the neighbouring countryside. Dinner was served, first to patients who were not inhibited by caste rules; though there were curries at the patient's choice. There was a vegetable one for the Hindus, whilst the Sikhs, Christians, and some of the sahib-log that Victoria Harrison had brought over, dipped appreciative fingers into a mutton pilau. They sat on a long line of coir matting, plates of banana leaves in front of them on the ground.

They needed a little rest after that, before sports and sideshows commenced. Alistair won his first coconut and insisted that Gunvor help him to make coconut-ice.

Harold Blickling had heard of the mammoth preparations for Christmas so sent over carpenters to erect bamboo structures, on which hired experts rigged an impressive fireworks display to end the day.

It was all great fun; classless and raceless.

As Gunvor and Jonathan climbed wearily into bed, it was Gunvor who had the last word.

'The high spot was seeing that Christmas baby. Jesus was just like that, yet the shepherds could believe he would save his people from their sins.'

171

Jane met them at Sheringham Station. Her hair was grey, but her skin still had life in it; the only creases were laughter ones, Jonathan noted. With the children, the years slipped away in minutes. As they piled into Uncle Robert's car, they were chattering away about the voyage, darting affectionate glances at their Grandma.

Jonathan found it a disturbing furlough. There was to be no study this time and there could only be short stays at Sheringham and Gattonside, for it was the turn of the Swedish grandparents to indulge their Indian grandchildren.

'I'm getting old,' Jonathan confided to his excited wife, as they made their selection from the smorgasbord display on the ferry-boat from Newcastle to Bergen.

'I don't like all these partings.'

For Gunvor it was different. She had enjoyed the time with her husband's family but now it was a reunion with her own. She kept silent.

Alistair and Gertrud were old enough this time, to enjoy the old town in Stockholm, but the fairyland of the city's fashionable shopping streets was an even greater delight.

'You can't understand, Mum,' Gunvor told her, 'they never see anything like this in Stewartpur or Landour. It's not that they want you to buy them things all the while.'

Their first outing was to Skansen, with its re-creation of the life of an older rural Sweden. Ancient properties had been brought stone by stone or timber by timber, to complete this old-world village in the heart of the capital. There was a forge and the bakery, but the workshop that Alistair could not be prised away from was the glass-blowers'. Open-mouthed, he watched the incandescent blob on the end of the craftsman's hollow rod as it lengthened, was rotated and blown until a flask took shape. Every time he glanced at the bowl in the dining room in Stewartpur in later years, he could recapture the glow of that experience. For his sister, the 17th century farmhouse, with its single living room, was the highspot of the visit. The walls of that room were a series of sleeping cubicles, elaborately painted with flower designs or carved like trailing vines. She ran her fingers over this fine handicraft, seeing men of long ago, whittling away time as well as wood, through the bitter cold of winter. Now the sun was shining and Gunvor had her sketchbook open on her knees, as she captured the church, with its timber spire. It was Lutheran of course, not Anglican.

In the easy acceptance of children, Alistair and his sister brought tears of pleasure to the eyes of their grandparents, by the speed with which they picked up Swedish expressions. Before long Birghita was taking them out on visits to friends, or on shopping sprees on their own. It left Gunvor free to introduce her husband to all of her old haunts, and to meet old associates. She took special pleasure in the morning spent at the Carolinska Hospital. Her contemporaries were now senior and authoritative. Jonathan found two of the surgeons had worked with Gillies and McIndoe in England. They were employing the most modern techniques in plastic surgery. They had their own experimental programme in tissue transfer, which they discussed enthusiastically over coffee – repeated cups of the thickest, blackest coffee Jonathan had ever tasted.

One day they were invited to the headquarters of Frelsingsarmeen, to find that the Commander was a grandson of William and Catherine Booth. The Commissioner complimented Gunvor on her perfect English, a point she understood when introduced to his wife. Her voluble English had an unmistakable French overlay. To Jonathan he recommended a trip to the fortified city of Visby on the Baltic island of Gotland.

'It had strong ties with England in the days of the Hanseatic League. The boat trip starts from the heart of the city here.' Stockholm was certainly a capital on the water.

What a summer it proved. The sun shone every day. Swedes seemed to have a hedonist ability to bask in the sun, as though winter would never come; perhaps it was because they knew it would. All too soon the Lindseys had to leave the Sundbergs. It was back to hard work in a country where the sunshine was less attractive.

Alistair and Gertrud had to pack again as soon as they reached Stewartpur. It was off to Landour for the winter term. They had so much to tell their friends. They also had a secret language between themselves, which excluded the uninitiated – they kept up their Swedish.

The hospital engulfed Gunvor and Jonathan once more. There were many patients who had waited anxiously for their return. Surgery had been limited in their absence, but this had not affected the leprosy wards. The records showed an alarming fall in the surgical fees, but little difference in the number of operations.

Krishnancoil Jacob had served his apprenticeship with Jonathan, proving quite capable of maintaining the rehabilitative surgery. More and more Guntur had used the physiotherapy students in aftercare routines in the Vocational Training Centre.

The new year brought an exciting invitation from the British High Commissioner in New Delhi. Queen Elizabeth II, and the truly princely Philip, were to visit India. All the English nurses on the staff were invited too. It was an afternoon event, for Delhi was cold in January, once the sun had set.

The High Commission had broad lawns and it was a colourful occasion – 'a Delhi Ascot', Gunvor heard a grande-dame say, lifting her gloved hand and arm to her large flowered hat.

'It's more likely modelled on the famous Buckingham Palace garden parties.' Jonathan explained to Gunvor.

Gunvor had to write it all down, to share with the family in Sheringham.

'There was a shamiana with flags fluttering over the canvas top.' She could hear Jane describing that to the other grandchildren. 'The long trestle-tables covered with mouth-watering food, reminded me of the chef's extravaganza on S.S.Kerala; the dresses...!'

'Where did you get "extravaganza" from, Gunvor?' Jonathan was looking over her shoulder, laughing.

The most memorable part was the slow progression of the royal party, along the red carpet lined with guests. Any man entitled to a uniform, wore it; with as many medals as he could muster. You could tell the few that went back to World War I, by the clink as they turned. It was all carefully stage-managed. Those to whom the Queen was expected to speak, had been instructed where to stand; little islands in a sea of gentle noddings and curtseys.

The Queen must have been informed of their achievements in leprosy.

'I wish that I had time to visit you,' she said. 'You really do care for the most needy. How did your Founder put it, "Go for the worst"'. She gave them a smile that was warm, before moving on.

'She is a most gracious lady,' Gunvor wrote in Swedish. 'But Prince Philip is different. He doesn't smile, he laughs. He had a bit of fun with Jonathan.

"Ah." he said, "The Salvation Army. You bob up everywhere we go. But I thought that India had prohibition!"'.

It was an opportunity for them to explore Delhi at a leisurely pace. Jonathan described his first visit as a schoolboy, preoccupied with the need to do well in the exam on which his admission to Cambridge would depend. Then he made her laugh, as he rehearsed his interviews with the top-brass of the I.M.S. at the outbreak of the war.

They took a tonga to old Delhi. Exploring the Mogul city, they came on echoes of the Mutiny. The brickwork of the Kashmir gate was still

174

pockmarked from the cannonade which preceded its storming by the dare-devil Brigadier, Nicholson. Just inside they came on the church that Colonel Skinner had erected. They stood in the nave, reading the memorials. Jonathan was back again in the India of General Claude Martin and his Muslim wives. Skinner had raised the famous regiment of irregular horse; he too had local wives, hadn't he?

They idled in the churchyard with the distant hum of traffic and bargaining in the Chandni Chowk, still lost in the past. The golden cross and ball, which Skinner had placed on top of the spire, was now on a stone plinth by the West Door; its copper had been ripped open by the gunfire of that ancient tragedy.

'Of course, Jonathan couldn't come to Delhi, without a visit to the surgical instrument maker's shop,' Gunvor's pen was in full flight, 'though to be fair, I was just as interested. Jonathan is never still, physically or mentally, even though he's seated in an armchair. He was looking at newer types of hospital furniture – not to buy – but as examples of what his workshop for the handicapped might produce.'

Prosperity was returning. In Himachal Pradesh, the Sikh refugees from the debacle, had now become farmers, earning a handsome return from their hard work. Many had launched into industrial undertakings. Returning from a visit to Ranjitala, Jonathan was met by an unusually preoccupied wife.

'What's bothering you?'

'There's been a breakdown in the V.T. workshop. It will need more than one of Charles' repair jobs.'

'I suppose it's time we had some new machines.'

'Couldn't those new plants in Ranjitala produce what we need?'

'Now that's a bright idea. I'll go down with the engineering instructor and see what it possible.'

Harnam Singh was one of the Ranjitala entrepreneurs. He'd started as an apprentice on a lathe in Sheikapura, then lost both parents as the family fled through Lahore. He proved an enthusiast for the Stewartpur enterprise. It was something he might have attempted himself.

'We were close friends with the Muktifauj-log in Sheikapura, when I was a boy. I still remember Fraser Sahib. He used to give us mangoes from his garden.'

Guntur showed him round the whole hospital, then took him home to Brunhilde for tea. He became more than a business associate. He returned and returned, until he was accepted as part of the whole venture.

As more and more training schemes were started, the number of resident students increased. There were now more than a hundred of them. They couldn't study all the while, so to fill their evenings meant developing a recreational and social timetable outside the curriculum.

'Why did you come a thousand miles to study physiotherapy here?' Gunvor heard Victoria Harrison in the salesroom in the V.T.C., talking with Joseph Kurian, who was helping her price the handwoven goods on sale from the looms.

'Well, the course has a good reputation even as far away as Kerala. Students write home,' he smiled. 'I heard that it was an international team, so I thought I might learn something about the world, into the bargain.'

'They're an interesting lot, these Salvationists. Aren't they?'

'That's another attraction. You see I come from Trivandrum. Though I'm a Jacobite, I finished my education at the Salvation Army High School.'

'I didn't know that they had any!'

'Oh yes. We youngsters were proud to belong – a thousand of us. You see the school was only a hundred yards from the gate of the Maharaja's palace. He actually came to open a new science block when I was a senior. I helped to line the route in a scout uniform.'

Victoria laughed. 'Do you remember what the Roman Procurator said to the apostle Paul?'

'No!'

'Almost thou persuadest me to become a...' She paused, then continued, 'I'll let you into a secret. The last recreational meeting for this season, will be on Saturday afternoon. Mrs Lindsey has invited us to a party at her bungalow. We have a surprise up our sleeves. See if you can come.'

Victoria had worked her own inclusion, by offering to help with the eats as well as in serving them. It showed her a side of her friend that she hadn't seen before. Jonathan had a whole string of parlour games she remembered from her Yorkshire childhood. It was all very new and fascinating to Indian youth. They must have been given the run of the Lindsey home on these occasions. They didn't take liberties, as far as she could see, but they were intrigued to see something of a foreign way of life. They ran into the bungalow now, thirty or forty of them, to take books from the shelves and a pencil and paper. There was to be a quiz game. She noted a freer atmosphere between the young men and

176

women than she had observed in the past. Even this must be exciting to many of them.

The last game was the most hilarious of all. They had obviously played it before, for they divided into two teams in a trice. Brunhilde sat on the front steps of the bungalow, with two trays on a table before her.

Jonathan called out. 'I need a hair grip.'

With squeals of delight, they set hairstyles tumbling, in their haste to be the first to deposit one on the trays.

'I need a piece of chalk', was the second request. It set them on a chase to the main lecture room. It was for Sumitra a chance to put 'A' team into the lead. She stood panting, as Joginder for 'B' team, came struggling through the bushes.

Eventually Gunvor came to invite them all for a glass of cool lassi, made from the pulp of unripe mangoes mixed with sugar, milk and ice. They sat in groups on the grass conspiratorially. They munched their cakes, knowing what was coming next.

Aleyamma, a post-graduate nurse from Cochin, also studying with Joseph in physiotherapy, was the spokesman. After they had all chanted,

'We want Dr Lindsey. We want Dr Lindsey. We want...' and the cheers were thunderous as he appeared. With the stage thus set the tall nurse stood on the bottom step. Addressing particularly the staff members, she said.

'We are a very happy band here and admire the way that you treat us all as your family. A little bird has told us that you sometimes find the time to play chess,' she stopped, and there was a roar of laughter, 'though we don't know how you manage it.' She turned to Gunvor, 'We also know Memsahib, that you admire Indian handicrafts, we've seen so much in your bungalow, which you have opened up to us frequently.' This caused much scattered comment, and so many private giggles and jokes, that she had to pause again.

'We'd like you, Memsahib, to accept this set, made to an ancient pattern by the Amritsar carvers. It comes with our love.'

As Gunvor took the gift, Aleyamma put her hands together in a 'na maste', but she quickly gave way to a more intimate gesture, impulsively embracing her.

'We want a picture', and a camera appeared from nowhere, whilst Dr Jacob posed them for a group. They insisted on one with Jonathan and Gunvor, then another with all the staff, and finally the amateur photographer backed far enough down the drive, to get the whole group and the bungalow into his frame.

177

That evening the quartet sat in the Mann's sitting room sipping coffee. Guntur handed round his wife's cookies, before asking, 'How many years is it since you commenced here Jon?'

'Nearly twenty for me and even longer for Gunvor.'

'What a wonderful family we have become.' Brunhilde was pouring more coffee from her large German percolator. 'We've a different pattern of a league of nations, small but with true affection and common ambition...' She had no further words to describe her feeling, so she waved her free hand eloquently.

'Where do we go from here?' asked Gunvor.

There was a very long silence before Jonathan answered.

'Truly the Lord only knows.'

Chapter Six

THE HUNDRED YEARS' WAR

The Riots of Partition were almost forgotten.

1965 started with an unusually cold January in Stewartpur, there were several hail-storms. Village women scavenged the sidings beyond the station, where shunting engines turned out their fire-boxes. There was still life in the cinders; a kerosene tinful sold for four annas. Gunvor bought them and eked out with an occasional bag of coal from the mills, she managed a fire in the sitting room each evening. Grandpa Lindsey had paid a bookclub subscription for several years. Now he added another, for the weekly air-mail edition of The Times. Jane had told him how much Jonathan longed for good English prose to read by lamplight on these winter evenings.

The Manns would often join them after dinner, when a carom board was brought out. They sat on the floor and played a foursome of this Indian game. It was a sort of poor-man's snooker; the counters, which were draughtsmen, replacing ivory balls. They each had a distinctive heavy striker, which they propelled across the board with a flick of the crooked finger, driving the counters into the corner pockets. A tin of talcum powder stood in the hearth to keep the surface polish. Jonathan had played the game at school; it was always in demand at The Gables, when the officers were relaxing.

Jane's last letter had been full of the Centenary Congress being organised in London.

'It is hard to believe that it is sixty-one years since I attended my first Congress. The world of 1904 is like another age from today but I'm recapturing it. I was such a single-minded enthusiast when I boarded that branch-line train from Sheringham, for my first visit to London. I know so much more than I did then, but I don't think that my love for God could be any greater than it was then.'

'She is too harsh in her judgement of herself,' was Jonathan's comment as he read the letter to Gunvor.

'She is the least selfish woman I've ever met.'

'To me she is the proof of God's love, living in us.'

Gunvor was about to say jokingly, 'What about your wife,' but the words faded instantly, when she realised how deeply moved he was. He recovered his composure and said,

'There is another letter here. it's from headquarters, probably asking for more statistics.' He slit open the envelope and glanced down the letter. He paused, then gave her an unexpected kiss.

'Do you want to know what it says?'

'It's good news, I can tell by your face.'

'It certainly is; Jane won't be alone at the Congress!'

He handed her the letter, which explained that though homeland furlough was not due until the end of the year, the Lindseys were to be official delegates at the Congress. They must fly at the beginning of July.

'How excited Alistair and Gertrud will be; they've always wanted to fly.'

Sure enough Alistair's response was couched in terms of seeing the pyramids and alpine peaks beneath the wings. It meant a lot more. Alistair would have to prepare for university. Gertrud had other ideas;

180

she was pursuing her mother's interest in art, but thinking in terms of a career.

Back in Britain after six years, Jonathan found the gulf between the society he had known in the Thirties, and present tastes and mores, had grown wider. Life in India, particularly with the absorbing life of the hospital, masked the passage of time. In London, decorum had flown. Respect for age and experience had gone. Junior doctors were no longer prepared to slave away for long hours, as the price of future competence in skill and income. It was no longer fashionable for music to be tuneful, or art intelligible. God knows, thought Jonathan, there has always been discord and tragedy, but now it seems to dominate the arts and the press. Television was ousting the cinema; folk talked of being 'glued to the box'. Young mums appeared to be vocal in everything, particularly for a reordering of society, that would permit them to have careers and babies.

There were some gains in this reckoning. Opportunity was more genuinely available to a wider spectrum of society. Despite this, there were loud voices stressing class division, and a divided north and south. There were now arbiters between native born and immigrant, mostly with stridently alien culture. There were even tribunals to ensure fairplay between the sexes. There was talk of a multinational community, a multiracial society. Some older people felt disinherited.

But to Jonathan, the comparison with his childhood was healthy. Most youngsters had secondary education. New universities were burgeoning, not only completely new red-brick ones, but new colleges at Cambridge after centuries with little expansion. He asked the registrar in the Dean's office at the London Hospital, what changes he saw.

'In your day, Mr Lindsey, eighty percent of the students paid their own fees. Many of them were the sons of doctors – all were men. Now the proportion is only twenty percent; many of them are women.'

He found himself comfortable with the new fashions in clothing. 'Separates' were acceptable for men. Consultants no longer wore cravat with pinstripe trousers and long black jackets, for formal rounds. Few students wore collar and tie and there were diverse accents in the refectory.

The Salvation Army Congress was already acclaimed by the press as a celebration of 'The hundred years' war'. The Lindsey family had been allocated the top flat in a five-storey Highbury terrace. It included two attics which needed renovation. They were draughty and would be freezing come winter, but in July the children loved them.

'I can see Clissold Park from my attic window', Alistair wrote to his buddy in Landour.

But for Jonathan, Highbury was crumbling rapidly from the Victorian elegance, which had still lingered in his student days. Forty years on it had become an immigrant area. Many of the broad boulevards were cluttered with broken-down cars. On many days, and always at weekends, running repairs were made at the kerbside, children watching and picking up tips on how to keep tin-Lizzies on the road. Railings had been offered up in the national fervour to defeat Hitler. Now the walls were going too. A few bricks salvaged could always be used to build a hut in the garden. So flower beds or shrubs in front gardens were giving place to concrete parking spots or unsightly rows of dustbins, always overflowing. Some enclaves, mostly cul-de-sacs, preserved their antique dignity. A few had cachet; there were some famous names in the telephone directory.

Jonathan was summoned to International Headquarters and had his lunch in the canteen.

'Hi! Don't you remember me?' He held out his hand to Jonathan.

'Captain Bramwell Bloggs. We last met at Denmark Hill in '45.'

'What are you doing now?'

'I'm the C.O. at Downside in South London.'

'You wouldn't know of a secondhand car going cheap? We're home for five months and will need one.'

'You're talking to the right man, Jonathan. I'm getting a new car and the dealer has offered me two hundred pounds for my old Austin. If you want it, you can have it for the same money. It's in good shape, though it has done a pretty good mileage.'

So Jonathan had a test run, then drove up to Highbury and parked proudly outside the flat. With Alistair's assistance, it was washed down and lovingly polished. But it would be a fortnight before they could take off for Scotland. For the nonce, the Congress dominated the programme.

Salvationists in Britain were accustomed to mass meetings, though the crowds in London in the summer of 1965 broke all records. Reporters said there were fifty thousand in the extravaganza at the Crystal Palace in Sydenham. The Albert Hall was packed to the pillared gallery. There was hardly any room for the fanfare of trumpets.

The Lindseys were together as a family, and that heightened the pleasure in every occasion. Highbury was merely a dormitory for ten days. It was just as well, for Gunvor had to convert the living room to provide sleeping for the extended family, using camp beds and sleeping bags. It was great fun. The cousins got to know each other as never before; the laughter in the attics delighted grandmother's heart. At 79,

182

her eyes still twinkled. Memory suffused the present. She recalled the vision of a glorious future which was hers, as she threw herself into the congress of 1904. Now she was seeing its fulfilment and it was equally exciting. To don her sari once again and march with her son, behind the Indian flag, was a bonus. She saw none of this as born of her own faith and hard graft. It was all the goodness of God. There is no more rewarding emotion than that of gratitude.

For Jonathan, his whole experience of the organisation which had shaped his life was of small numbers and lonely places. By contrast this was an overwhelming occasion. His Swedish wife, often holding his hand in this welter of powerful feeling, was part of an international company, rejoicing in the oneness of mankind.

There were so many happy families like his. Black hugged white, and there was a babel of languages, but a universal hallelujah. Every event witnessed reunions, which were not strictly family ones. Most were old comrades who had shared a happy but hard life, anywhere from Tranas to Timbuctoo. They laughed over remembered hardships and embraced over personal tragedies.

Jonathan was unprepared for the reception that London gave them. From the little woman who sat next to them on the 29 bus, to the Queen, in her lime green dress on the Albert Hall platform, all spoke well of them. The Archbishop of Canterbury, a diminutive Friar Tuck, with his high pitched voice, said after a telling pause,

'I've never met a gloomy Salvationist!'

In one of the meetings, a Swedish officer – a headmistress – spoke of the impression an Indian officer had made on her. Her English was heavily accented, but translators around the building managed to pass on her story in French, German and Spanish. Jonathan turned to his wife and noted the silent tears. They gripped hands. On his left, a quiet Jane was reliving the Congress of 1914; she poured it out to them over their cocoa that night.

'That Congress opened in that same hall, with the news that half the Canadian delegation had been drowned, when their liner sank in the St Lawrence estuary, at the outset of their voyage.

We didn't know that a world war was to erupt very soon or that it would take us away from India.'

There was an initial meeting at the spot where William Booth had spoken in the open-air meeting, that was to alter the course of his life. It had a personal poignancy for Jonathan, for it was on broad pavement opposite the frontage of the London Hospital.

'There is a divinity that shapes our ends', someone was quoting tritely of the Army's Founder. In a flash of intuition, Jonathan recalled his experience as a schoolboy in the Himalayas, seeing its truth for him. His was a healing mission, but it had a spiritual dimension. As he stood in the crowd, with the noise of traffic and the cries of vendors competing on the soapbox platform, he heard Christ saying, 'It is better to enter heaven with one eye, than to be in Hell with two'. He had his handicapped patients in focus.

Packing their suitcases into the boot, they said goodbye to Highbury, and drove off to Sheringham, calling at Cambridge en route. Jonathan wanted Alistair to have a peek at Emmanuel.

With their own transport they were able to explore freely on this holiday. Gunvor was introduced to the whole north Norfolk coast, from Cromer to Hunstanton and even on to Castle Rising and King's Lynn. They made several trips to the Glandford area. The narrow coast road wound uphill and down again, with innumerable bends; an ancient track that had skirted fields and forded streams long before tarmac.

'This is the oldest farmland in Britain; settled by Saxons who felled the forest and ploughed the uplands.' He told her.

'Aren't some of my forebears supposed to have devastated it?' she chided him.

'True, the Vikings raided this coast. But eventually they settled and inter-married. Who knows, we may be distantly related.'

'I prefer this close relationship.' At the risk of driving into the ditch, she gave him a hug.

'Is it twenty years that we've been wed?' Then reverting to history. 'Even in the eventual settlement that King Alfred made, Norfolk was in the Danelaw.'

They drew into the verge and turned off the engine. There were little bays with low sandy cliffs and shingle beaches, quite deserted. The North Sea was calm and on the horizon a cargo boat. On their left a lane, little more than a farm track ran inland.

'That goes up through the woodland to the mansion where mother was a servant sixty or more years ago.'

'It was pretty country to grow up in.'

They started up again, passing a sentinel windmill on the seaward side, as they dropped into Weybourne with the ruins of a mediaeval priory behind the parish church. The road wound over heathland to Kelling.

'That sounds Viking.'

Then the road wound downhill to the level of the marshes. They pulled up at a green and found the carved village sign declared this hamlet to be Salthouse.

'Pretty obvious, this time.' They looked in at the post-office and general store and bought a couple of postcards for Stewartpur. A low hill topped the clustered cottages, crowned by a large church with massive plain tower. They were tempted across the green to the pub, which had a board, 'crab sandwiches always available here.'

'I've never tasted one,' said Gunvor.

'Now's the time then,' and Jonathan took her elbow and propelled her up the steps. They sat outside with their sandwiches, salad and lemonade.

Around a final bend and they were in the High Street of Cley-next-the-sea. This time there was a mixture; large Georgian houses and small cottages, with flower baskets. There were hollyhocks seven feet tall and valerian in great bushes. Wallflowers were literally growing from the flint walls. Jonathan stopped at the garage for petrol, and then turned up a lane towards the sea and a local landmark, the very high, eighteenth century windmill.

'Your mother has told me about this place. She used to walk here for the family shopping when she was a schoolgirl.'

They stopped on the quay, looking across the river with its bank of reeds to the grazing land beyond which stretched to the great shingle bank that kept the sea at bay. It was high-tide and a holiday party was noisily boarding a small cabin cruiser, for a run out to the sea at Blakeney Point.

They sat on a low wall, behind a terrace of old cottages at right-angles to the river. As they looked up-river it was to another line of hills forming the far boundary of the Glaven valley. At the seaward end it was dominated by the grandiose tower of Blakeney's church.

'It's funny' said Gunvor, 'it's got a miniature tower beside it. What can that be for?'

'Mum's told me the answer to that one. She went to church school just behind it. Before the days of lighthouses with optical beam, that little tower had a flaming brazier to guide the mariners who brought Newcastle coals and Flemish cloth into the prosperous Glaven ports. That beacon gave them a line for the navigable channel.'

It was a grey day.

'Not the best of days to visit,' Gunvor commented. But to Jonathan, it was as he had often seen it. His mother's brother had shown him round, when he was a small boy. It was this grey, silent mood of the marshes that had lingered in his mind. He remembered homemade toffee from the general store in the High Street. The store was still there as they discovered, but there was no toffee.

185

They looked in the old forge at the junction with the Holt road, but there was no blacksmith. But the half doors from a century ago were still there, as were the ship's cannon buried in the path like bollards. They went along this time to Wells, where they found that coastal craft still unloaded at the quay. A crane and a gantry across the road, were carrying sacks into high brick and timber warehouses.

'Seamen have always been credited with a fabulous thirst for beer. All these little ports seem to have a malthouse.'

'I don't suppose the appetite has changed but the brewers are not locals. Most of these maltings are derelict or used for other purposes.'

They meandered down tiny back roads to Glandford then via Wiveton back to Cley. The 'town house' on their right as they approached the High Street, was now a bungalow. Gunvor had looked out for it, for the little local guide, that she had bought in the sub-post-office said, 'It was built as a poorlaw institution to provide for eight female and eight male vagabonds.'

Their holiday in Sweden would be their last as a united family. The parents had to accept that the children were now embracing their own careers. Alistair was full of 'Emma'; bombarding his father with questions. It made Jonathan feel old. It was such a long while since he was an undergraduate.

For Gertrud it was other. She had been to see Newnham and Girton but was not attracted. She had inherited her mother's artistic ability and was increasingly drawn to study design in fabrics or advertising. Her mother raised the subject one evening in Stockholm. Grandma Sundberg's eyes lit up.

'There is a new Art College here. I'm sure it would suit the girl. I'm going to get a prospectus.' Her mind went racing on.

'She could live with us here; there's an excellent bus service.'

'Give the girl time to look around Mamalein,' Gunvor laughed.

The next morning Grandma persuaded both the youngsters to join her. With vivid memories of their previous stay, they persuaded her in their turn.

'You promised that you would take us up to that revolving restaurant at the top of the big store. We'd love to have those views over the city that you described.'

It suited Jonathan and Gunvor to be alone. They still had a physical attraction for each other. It was good to be out on their own. They skipped off to Skansen, where an orchestral concert was billed. Gunvor

186

met some old friends and found her Swedish deserting her. They went again to the Carolinska with the plastic surgeons. In bed that night, Gunvor was coy.

'I expect you've seen too many breast reductions today!'

His only answer was to put his arm around her whilst he explored with his fingers. She had all the reassurance she needed that she still drew him.

At breakfast, Olaf introduced his plan for the day.

'I've been given an invitation for us to visit Kurön today.'

'That will be a lovely drive,' Gunvor responded in Swedish.

'Do you think that we will have time to stop at the old palace en route?' He responded in his careful English.

'We'll take a flask of coffee and make a break there.'

The Sundbergs were an unusually sensitive couple, alive to their guests' differing background. As they drove, Birghitta stole frequent glances, intrigued that these English children were truly her grandchildren. Gunvor was her only child, so there was no prospect of any more. She had already made it clear that Alistair could spend part of his long vacs with them. Her thoughts wandered on as she smiled at him. Perhaps he would fall in love with a Swedish girl. It would be better still if Gertrud married a Swede. There would be an even greater possibility of having her nearby. Birghitta was well away now in her daydreams. There were many Swedish Salvationists who had gone to India over the years – many mixed marriages.

'Sweden always seems to lose one in these romances,' she confided wistfully to Olaf, as they reviewed the day later.

It was mid-morning by the time that they reached the shore of Lake Malaran. Sunshine sparkled on the rippling water curling up to a jetty, but the surrounding hills were misty. A tall man of about forty, flaxen-haired and blue-eyed, hailed them from the stern of a launch.

'There's a textbook example of the Swede,' Gertrud whispered to her brother. 'I like it.'

They climbed aboard and the pilot got the engine spluttering, turning the prow towards the island that looked quite near, but took them twenty minutes to reach.

'Are you on the staff?' Olaf asked the pilot.

'No, I'm only one of the patients.' He was very serious, so that Olaf's 'Obviously they don't think that you will run away,' died on his lips.

'You look pretty fit', Gunvor smiled at him.

'You should have seen me when I arrived here from the clinic in the city, three months ago. After five years as an alcoholic, I was a wreck!'

'It's a healthy life on the island then?'

187

'Ja.'

They were met at the landing stage by Major Kjellgren. Birghitta recognised him and whispered to her daughter, 'They're a wonderful couple, the Kjellgrens.'

'Careful now, I understand a little English,' the Major warned an embarrassed Birghitta. He put her at ease by taking her arm with, 'Solveig has the coffee-pot on.'

They sauntered up the gentle slope towards the highest of the timbered buildings, set amongst mature, deciduous trees. The Mansard roof was topped by a flagstaff, from which an Army flag was stiff in the strong breeze.

The youngsters' eyes widened as they studied the coffee table, laden with plates of fresh fruit tarts and a jug of thick cream.

'There are about fifty in our family at present,' the Major explained to them. 'Family is about the best way to describe us. A very mixed company in the background, but a strong bond of common experience. The men love the farm, with its wide variety of tasks. When they get over their physical disabilities, they are a hard-working lot. We produce all our own food.' He turned to Gunvor. 'They're all men, of course.'

'Is it a purely male disability then?'

'Oh no, though the women who suffer, tend to hide it within the home.'

'I think you should have some women in the company then. Men need women to civilise them,' challenged Gunvor.

'I don't think the "powers-that-be" have ever thought of that. I'll bring it up at the next board meeting. My wife would love that development.'

They commenced a tour of the village and market garden. Gunvor was soon chatting with the men bent over the rows of carrots, beets and onions. As they reached the flower beds around the meeting hall and lounge, Major Kjellgren introduced Hans.

'He's an artist by profession. Take Mrs Lindsey along to your room and show her some of your paintings. She's an artist too.'

'I'm joining you,' Gertrud ran after them.

When they met again over lunch, Gertrud showed them a watercolour sketch signed by the artist. On the back he had written, 'To my dear friend Gertrud'.

'You've helped his recovery, my dear.' Mrs Kjellgren turned to her husband, 'Now you see, Johan, what it would do for this place if you had a few women around.'

'They'll all have to be like Gertrud and her mother!'

Drowsy with a day in the Autumn sunshine, and replete with the lavish hospitality of the Kjellgrens, Alistair and his sister were in that state of youthful euphoria which can see present bliss as permanent.

'I think I'd be happy on the staff here.' Gertrud was thinking aloud. 'What a grand idea.' Her grandmother immediately latched on to the possibility. 'Wouldn't it be wonderful to have her so near,' she enthused to Olaf. The whole prospect was turning out better than she had anticipated.

Back in Stockholm, the art school prospectus was carefully dissected by the quartet. Although all students completed the basic course in drawing, painting, composition and life classes, there was ample opportunity for choice in aspects of applied art. So Gertrud could specialise in design if she wished. There was one snag: she could not start until she became eighteen.

One warm evening they drove out to Dalaro, through forest brilliant in Autumn tints, for a woodwind concert at a residential college. They enjoyed the concert, but Alistair and Gertrud enjoyed equally the fun they had with the students. Without hesitation, they accepted an invitation to spend the whole of the next weekend there. They found that many of the students were Salvationists, some even from England. The high quality of musical education appeared to be the major attraction.

'It's a folkschule.' explained Olaf. 'It is part of our national pattern of education, permitting secondary education to include a wide variety of interests. Folkschules are run by many groups with state subsidy.'

'It's just what I am looking for Grandma.' Gertrud hugged her. 'I could stay with you.'

They quickly confirmed that there was an art department in which Gertrud could prepare for entrance to art school.

'I'll certainly come over to see you in my long vac. So bully for you,' Alistair capped the discussion.

'They've got it all worked out,' said Gunvor wistfully to Jonathan. For the first time, they sensed that the children could get on without them; they were embracing careers with enthusiasm.

So Gunvor was triste as the return voyage was planned. Jonathan sought to deflect her by obtaining a brochure from Lloyd Triestino, with a new route they might try. He felt that it would ease the parting in a way that a few hours' flight could not do. Headquarters gave permission as long as he accepted responsibility for any increase in cost. It was a quiet departure from Liverpool Street station.

Only the under-secretary from the India section was there to assist them in boarding the boat train for Harwich, and the ferry to Hook-of-Holland. Lloyd-Triestino already had their trunks, so they travelled light, enjoying the Germany and Austria they could watch from the train. Gunvor had never been up the Rhine before. Neither had Jonathan but he had read a journal of his father's which described the forest, the castles and the vineyards.

In Munich they had several hours between trains, which gave them the opportunity for a little exploration, before returning to the station restaurant for a meal. It was noisy; too much strong beer around. It was now November and as the train sped on towards Innsbruck, its lights hit banks of snow. The taxi which took them to the small hotel, where Jonathan had booked for two nights, drove through falling snow.

'How romantic,' Gunvor reacted to the legend on the door, as the porter deposited their suitcases and fumbled with the key. 'The Goethe Room' it stated.

The snow continued all night; they parted their curtains in the morning to see the sun giving shape to a landscape uniformly white.

'Would you like to go up in the ski-lift this morning, Gunvor?' He looked up at the gleaming summits and mused, 'I haven't many regrets, but I would have enjoyed skiing had there been the opportunity.'

They left immediately after their croissants and cherry conserve, and achieved the first lift. It was already crowded with energetic, bobble-hatted, siren-suited young people, whose skis clattered and cluttered the gondola. At the hut they felt on top of Everest, there was such exhilaration in the cold wind, whipping plumes of snow from the crest. It seemed a perilously narrow slide on one side of the ridge, from which the skiers launched themselves. They sped down at break-neck speed, so that they became specks far below, in the matter of seconds. Even so, they were still above the Tyrolean houses on the river bank opposite Innsbruck.

'I agree with you, I'd love to have a go,' Gunvor confided over a bowl of soup in the diminutive restaurant at the summit.

An hour ticked away; they were loth to descend. They found consolation in window shopping in the old town, and a lunch of Wiener schnitzel. There were attractive windows of fine wood carving. They admired the character of the work but the prices could not compare with those in the Amritsar bazaar.

The train climbed to the pass and they were into Italy, with great limestone crags on either side of them. There was evidence that the Dolomites attracted skiers too, for there were racks for skis all along the corridor of the coaches. As they alighted at Trieste platform a bitter wind was blowing down from the mountainous border with Yugoslavia. They hurried to a taxi and made for the harbour. It was pleasurable to go aboard and find a warm cabin. Then they hit trouble. A seaman's

190

strike kept the liner at her berth; departure would be delayed indefinitely. They sought for the silver lining. At least there would be time to explore the town.

It was so cold that they spent as much time as possible in a well-heated departmental store, and in the numerous bars where they nursed cups of cappuchino in the fug.

They were permitted to sleep aboard, but on the morrow were sent ashore with meal tickets at a restaurant in town. The sun was shining and it seemed less cold. They found a bus that went up to a village on the plateau at the border. This was where the prevailing winds came from, so they did not linger long.

The buses were overcrowded, chiefly with middle-aged women, who all appeared to be widows in voluminous black. They were grim and experienced. They knew how to use elbows unobtrusively but with telling effect. They got on the bus! Gunvor laughed as they sat in the cabin that evening, writing postcards. She recorded Jonathan's efforts to be gallant, which left her perilously near to travelling alone.

They sailed the next morning, though the atmosphere with the stewards was tense. They stood about in groups, more intent on discussion with histrionic gestures, than in serving the meal. By the time that they reached Venice, trouble surfaced again. Once more they were on the streets, or more often this time on vaporetta or gondola. Cold had given way to wet; now it was into churches to avoid the rain. Several times it was an art-gallery that permitted them to dry off. The lagoon was high, slopping over the paving outside the Doge's palace with every wave. Outside St Mark's, the water was so deep that planks had been laid on tubs. Jonathan attempted the crossing in too cavalier a fashion and went into water above his knees. It was all a joke to Gunvor, as she drew him into a dark corner of the basilica, to wring out the ends of his trousers as best she could.

The ding-dong battle between master and man continued, although a truce allowed them to sail the next morning, but the scenario was repeated at Brindisi. Jonathan judged that some of the crew had family there. Once again they felt like schoolchildren with meal tickets and orders to stay out until the evening. This time the restaurant proved too small; the only attraction for most of the company was the free wine, which the proprietor judged might turn away wrath. Jonathan and Gunvor were highly popular for passing on their full carafe.

They found a Norman chapel and sat down.

'This is part of your history, Gunvor.'

'How so?'

'The Vikings who sailed down the English Channel, settling in

191

France and England, were so warlike and land hungry, that within a century, they had sailed on down the coast of Portugal and through the Pillars of Hercules into the Mediterranean. They ousted the Muslim conquerors of Sicily and southern Italy; they built many churches like this.'

'I was taught that the Norwegians went to Scotland, the Danes to England and France. My ancestors, I learned, also reached Byzantium but by way of the great rivers to the Black Sea.'

The remainder of the voyage was uneventful, there were no more ugly incidents.

They sat on the after-deck as the sun went down over Africa and made the ship's wake lurid.

'I'm glad that you suggested this voyage, Jon. It has been a lovely introduction to a new chapter in our lives. I'm even enjoying being on our own once more.'

'It has given me time to look backwards as well as forwards,' Jonathan responded.

'Do you know what was going through my mind on that very cold afternoon that we stood on the heights above Trieste, and looked into Yugoslavia?'

'I knew you were thinking of your father.'

'We were looking towards Zagreb. He was there forty-five years ago.'

There was a long silence, punctuated only by the throb of the engines and the cry of the following gulls.

'I'd like to see his grave sometime.'

When Jonathan passed through the outpatient hall, on his way to morning prayers in the chapel, there was already a waiting crowd of patients in subdued, and what looked like anxious, conversation.

'Would you mind carrying on for me?' Guntur had caught him up.

'I'd better see what this is all about.'

The crowd opened up to let him approach the charpoy, the string-bed that was being used as a stretcher. The patient was elderly, his long white hair spread over the pillow. Across the blanket that covered him, lay his right hand swathed in bloodstained, improvised bandages.

A tall young Sikh explained.

'My master is the Mahant of Vihala shrine. Do you remember me? You operated on me last year. I'm the Mahant's chela. I've been his disciple since I was a small boy.'

'Ah then, it's Sher Singh, isn't it?'

192

'Ji han. The Mahant decided to feed the buffalo himself, for he sent me on an errand. He put some fodder into the chopping machine. He's not used to it; his hand was drawn in with the bajri.'

Premala, the night Sister had not yet handed over to the day staff, so took control. The lights went on in the operating theatre, the wounded man was undressed, and covered with a sheet on a trolley in the anaesthetic room. Jonathan sent one of the male nurses to call Dr Jacob. Guntur had sent a laboratory technician from the chapel and Jonathan instructed him.

'Go ahead with the blood tests. He'll probably need a transfusion.' As he cleaned up the mangled hand, now bloodless in the control of the automatic tourniquet, his thoughts drifted back to Stockholm. The plastic surgeon was teaching his students. The maestro held up his left hand, flexing fingers and thumb.

'All that differs between the human hand and that of the apes, is that peculiarly human ability to oppose the thumb and the forefinger. Even if there is only one stiff and crooked finger, a pinch grip is still possible. This is man's master tool.'

The memory simplified his challenge. Only the stumps of the fingers remained but the thumb was unharmed.

His plan clear, he bared the unconscious man's abdomen and laid the crippled hand across it; with a sliver of bamboo as pen, and the antiseptic dye, gentian violet, as ink, he marked out a two inch strip. He would design a pedicle, and at the next operation in three weeks' time, one end could be divided and attached to the stump of the index finger.

'You can usually cheat the abdomen of some tissue,' he explained to Dr Jacob, to whom the procedure was new. Each stump was neatly repaired and the two-inch strip of skin and underlying tissue raised and the edges sewn together leaving what looked like a baggage handle.

The Mahant was a cheerful patient. He had spiritual perception, claiming Jonathan as a brother.

'He's my guru,' he explained to his many visitors. Each morning when the surgeon was on his round, the Mahant treasured the opportunity for conversation, welcoming a final prayer. He came to the periodic operations with a quiet dignity, and a growing sense of wonder, as the surgeon's planned result was clear.

When the new index finger was complete it lacked rigidity, until at the final operation, a three inch piece of curved rib was grafted in one end, to take root in the remnant of finger bone.

Even in the plaster cast, the amused patient could bring the thumb to it and anticipate the final result.

The Mahant was revered in the whole district. Every visitor listened to his glowing account. The story of the miracle that had given their holy man a new finger, reached Amritsar, then travelled down the line to Delhi. When the Mahant eventually returned to his shrine, it was to host a feast for all the hospital staff.

Though the riots of partition were almost forgotten, there was one spin-off that was not. The ready co-operation between the various missionary societies, which the troubles produced, continued. The committee that had been set up then remained in operation.

'You know how little I like committees,' Jonathan had said to Gunvor, the first time that he returned from Ludhiana, 'This is the exception. This one does a lot and talks little. We've pooled money and resources in equipment and staff, dividing out the urgent jobs amicably.'

There had been a home-spun medical school for women at the eastern end of the province, for a good many years. It was in the thick of the bloodshed, and soon became the joint responsibility of all the churches. Jonathan was asked to give a course in operative surgery; if he would arrange the timing, he could perhaps be the external examiner for the nurses as well. There would be anatomy and physiology for juniors and surgery for seniors.

'I'll have to watch you,' Gunvor warned him. 'Four days with a bevy of female admirers!'

His route ran down the Grand Trunk Road for fifty miles from Amritsar, to the predominantly Sikh town. This was the road that Kim had walked, talking to the rani in her purdah chariot. He set off at dusk after an afternoon in the theatre. The road would be relatively clear after dark, so he could make rapid progress. His headlights picked up shrouded figures in wayside hovels.

As he passed through isolated hamlets there were glimpses of interiors lit by oil-lamps; groups talking over open fire or charcoal brazier in the courtyard.

An American mission had pioneered in this area, before it had become British. It willingly handed over its property to enlarge the medical college, as it became a shared responsibility. It was to one of these American buildings that Jonathan was taken by the night sister, since he had called first at the hospital on arrival. She walked ahead of him along a verandah with a uniform line of doors. She threw open the last one, wishing him a good night's sleep. The overhead fan, turning slowly and complaining at every turn, was quite unnecessary; probably

194

intended to discourage mosquitos, he imagined as he switched off. It was well after midnight and he was asleep as soon as his head touched the pillow.

After breakfast, he went straight to the mortuary and inspected the corpse. When it had been transferred to the Anatomy Department, he worked out with the professor of surgery, what operations he should demonstrate. He liked this white-haired woman, a survivor from the early days of the teaching programme. She was quite unflappable he discovered. He had a hanging skeleton moved in, together with a few anatomical charts. It looked a very modest-sized room, but he understood that there were only ten women nearing their finals. In a year these young women would be the backbone of a dozen small hospitals. They saw themselves as possibly the only doctor in an emergency. Guntur was very pleased with the competence and reliability of Dr Masih, who had joined them at Stewartpur.

'She's ideal for the women's clinics. She can talk away intimately in Punjabi', he told Brunhilde.

Jonathan, expecting ten, was unprepared for a room crowded with at least thirty. Every girl in the clinical years must have decided that it was too good an opportunity to be missed. They were desperately keen to see every move in each operation, pressing as close as possible. He described the scene to Gunvor on his return.

'They pressed so close that I thought that I would be flattened on the corpse. I've always thought of Indian women as demure, but I've revised my opinion after this experience.' She was highly amused, picturing her courteous husband fending off Amazons.

By contrast, the examinations for nurses called forth his sympathy. The standard was high. Some of the school's earlier graduates were now working in the U.K., others were matrons or tutors in other parts of India. Most came from homes with conventional ideas on the place of women; they would be breaking the mould; they were desperate to succeed. He treated them gently and they responded well. They had obviously swotted hard.

He dined with the staff – all women. They were preparing for change. Dr Hildreth, the Principal, had been appointed by the new committee. Jonathan knew her as Mildred, the down-to-earth superintendent of a Zenana hospital thirty miles from Stewartpur.

'We hope that before long, the University of Delhi will accept us for the M.B.,B.S. course and provide a reasonable subsidy. Of course we will be co-ed.'

'That will be an upheaval!'

'We've made a start as you must have noted today. We opened two

195

wards for men some time ago; the outpatients is quite crowded with beards.'

One of the professors said:

'I don't particularly like those clinics. I shall be glad when the Board appoints a few men to the staff. Those greybeards undress me every time they look at me.'

'I can see that they'll soon be after you, Guntur, as physician to outpatients and Professor of Medicine.' Jonathan concluded his racy report on his return.

On one of his subsequent visits for a Board of Management, Jonathan met Joshua Mukherjee, the Vicar of Simla.

'You must come and visit us, the next time that you come to this end of the province. Eleanor came from Cambridge to teach in Bishop Heber's College; she loves to have visitors who can talk about England.'

He jumped at this opportunity to visit the old summer capital of the Raj. It was, of course the place in which his parents had met and married. The imperial grandeur had gone, though it was still a popular summer resort. St Michaels' was still a plum clerical appointment. Its vicarage was faintly musty, with its heavy old furnishings, but it was large and beautifully situated.

'It's quite a romantic visit for you, Joshua tells me,' said Eleanor Mukherjee.

'My mother says that my father proposed to her in the restaurant of Lowry's Hotel, after the Swiss manager had asked, "has the memsahib enjoyed her tea!" They had only met about ten days before!'

'Joshua took much longer to get round to it,' she laughed.

'I didn't know how your parents would react,' Joshua defended himself.

'I think they had a devout Bengali girl lined up for him. However they were quite sweet to me, though cautious at first.'

Jonathan wondered whether the absence of any children was deliberate. Mixed marriages posed many problems.

'Booth-Tucker conducted my parents' wedding here in Simla, and his wedding present was a trek to Ani.'

'My parents in Calcutta used to speak of the Major Tucker, who upset the Raj by wearing Indian clothes and preaching in the open-air. But if the Raj was outraged by his tactics, the Indian press took up his cause, lambasting the British for not treating a Christian as fairly as they did both Muslim and Hindu.'

'Ah', he jumped in again before Eleanor could forestall him, 'I'm interested in the bit about the honeymoon, for I was out at Ani last

196

month. It must be a rare chapter in church history, for the little corrugated iron church there was built with Salvation Army money!'

'How come?' Eleanor got in this time.

'When the Army closed its headquarters here in Simla, after the illness which took the Booth-Tuckers back to England, it was no longer possible to maintain the isolated station so near to Tibet. The fruit-farm was sold and the Christian community handed over to us, since we had the church and school at Rampur.'

'Is that the Rampur on the old Hindustan-Tibet road?'

'Yes. The Army had held meetings in the farm manager's house. Hence the donation for another building. It is still a stimulating church to visit. Many of the old people still sing Army choruses as they work in their terraced fields.'

'We still get Ani apples in the market here,' Eleanor added.

'How did you come to India?' Jonathan asked, turning to Eleanor and changing the subject. But a smiling Joshua was in before her.

'She was a confirmed school marm – real Zenana mission-type, when I rescued her.'

'Educating the daughters of most of the Indian clergy,' she came back at him.

'The church has played a big part in the education of both Indian and European alike, hasn't it? I was educated at Ambrose Jones in Naini Tal.'

'Good school.'

'True', Jonathan responded, 'tho' it couldn't rival an English grammar school. But the calibre of the staff made up for any other deficiency. It's setting on the top of a mountain could hardly be bettered. It proved a sound foundation for me.'

'The world's changing,' mused Eleanor. 'Discipline in the upbringing of children is waning, whilst old goals are no longer alluring. Most of my girls wanted to be teachers or nurses, now...' she fluttered a hand, Jonathan looked at this sixty-year-old churchwoman, seeing the eager girl of forty years earlier, firmly set on being as well qualified as she could be, to bring enlightenment to the down-trodden women of India.

They fell silent as they moved out onto the verandah, which commanded a view along the winding road to Narkanda and Rampur. As they drank their tea, Jonathan introduced another reason why he had accepted their invitation.

'Whilst I am here my mother would like me to visit the cemetery. It's a sad errand. My elder brother is buried here.'

'Tell us the story.' They spoke together in their surprise.

He told them of the young mother, bringing her first child to Simla with a fever that could not be diagnosed in their remote settlement. Eleanor accompanied him to the quiet graveyard. They stood looking at the small marble slab with the date 1911.

'Tell me more of the story,' Eleanor asked again.

'It's an age ago, isn't it, but I don't suppose my mother has forgotten that long journey from the jungle with a baby running high fever, or the kindness of the lady who offered her hospitality and stood by her at this graveside. She didn't speak of it and I doubt that many of our friends realise that Mary was a second child. In a rare moment of intimacy with my wife, she told her "I was already pregnant when I stood at the grave." She has never been back, though I believe that she will be happy that I have been here.'

He picked one or two wild flowers growing out of the side of the slab, putting them carefully in his notebook.

Later, Jane took the tissue paper from her son's letter and put the flowers on the stool beside her chair in Sheringham. She read the letter again. That love-child was the only one born in their first quarters in the Terai. She was back again with wild animals and the snakes and rats in the roof. She saw again Stephen's huge logs being dragged effortlessly by the borrowed elephant. The old Sansiah settler – husband of the child's ayah – was standing before her, asking that she trust him to carry the baby to his own hut, so that he could guard it through the night that the sahib was to be away on business. All her life she had been trusting people. A surprising number had returned her trust with a like confidence and love. Her tears were of joy not grief.

'You know Gunvor,' Jonathan said one evening, when he had finished supper and the discussion on the day's doings, 'I remember one of the surgeons that I worked for as a dresser in student days, saying "When you get to my age, you'll find the excitement of life-saving operations is of less importance, than the ability to make a correct diagnosis".'

'How old was he?'

'I don't know. He seemed to me to be looking for retirement and a comfortable armchair!'

'Are you getting middle-aged my love?'

'I do not understand what that means, but I do feel a growing interest in diagnosing the community's disease, and in thinking in terms of prevention rather than heroic intervention. Improvements in anaesthesia and of course the antibiotics have made such exciting surgery possible, that it is easy to become obsessed with it.'

'So are you warming to Guntur's proposals for a district-wide service promoting good health?'

'I suppose so, though I think this has been prompted by a discussion I had with the Minister of Health in Chandigarh recently. I was trying to get more of the rationed building materials we will need for a new operating suite and intensive care ward. He actually offered us a direct grant for community health. He was quite candid. "You missionaries have the confidence of the ordinary Punjabi. It makes it easier to put over new ideas." Then in the post there was a letter this morning from our own H.Q., describing a new department for development projects. Schemes of the kind the Health Minister wants, would be strongly supported by the overseas-aid funds all the Western nations have set aside.'

'You will never be able to settle for a smooth professional life, either as a surgeon or an officer, will you my love?'

'Is someone else feeling middle-aged?'

'I certainly yearn for a settled life near to our children sometimes.'

Jonathan waited, then returned to his theme.

'We could make a gentle start, by widening the scope of our weekly dispensary, that Guntur runs in the old town at Ranjitala.'

'Can I come?'

'Now that's a great idea. I'll discuss it with Guntur. It must be his baby.'

Morning sunlight fell in a narrow band, although the sun was already high in the heavens. Ranjitala was a walled city, with several wide gates but very narrow streets, so that a single bullock cart could cause a traffic jam. Somehow the twentieth century had still not arrived here. As in Amritsar, every trade had its quarter. Some you could tell on approach by their distinctive smell, or by the calls of the vendors. The metalworkers had musical distinction; the hammering of copper or tinplate, or the hiss of steam as hot metal was thrust into water in tempering.

It was all of a piece, from the ornamental arches of the gates, to the long lines of workshops and lockup retailers. There was a periodic courtyard of a richer merchant, but all was built centuries earlier in the tiny hard-baked Mogul bricks. They appealed strongly to Jonathan, who had bought a couple of lorry-loads from a ruined property, using them to build a circular wall for a raised flowerbed, at the approach to the outpatient hall. He found them to be so hard and dense in texture, that they could be shaped with a hacksaw. They were more like terracotta.

It was a challenge to drive an ambulance, built on the narrow lines of a jeep chassis, through these congested streets, rutted by centuries of bullock carts. They were impregnated with flour, spices, charcoal and vegetables; in fact anything that could fall off a heavily laden cart. If dung were not so valuable as a fuel, it would have added to the mixture.

Next to the dispensary shop, a house had been demolished; land left vacant, so they could park off the lane. They all shared the chore of carrying bags and cartons into the building, where Harnam Das had commenced to transfer his medicines to the shelves. Gunvor and Brunhilde with the help of Shanti, the fifty-year-old Punjabi nurse, began to reduce the waiting crowd to order. Each wanted to be the first in the queue, on one plea or another. Shanti's Punjabi must have been choice, for it raised gales of laughter.

From long experience Jonathan had learned that showmanship, drama – even sheer pantomime, could help to get new ideas across. Up went the colourful public health posters. Meanwhile the two wives, rigged up a Punch and Judy type booth, for the puppet show they had perfected for village audiences. Grandma was there and the young daughter, with domineering husband and crying baby. The crowd quickly recognised the types. They nudged or laughed outright as they recognised their neighbours, and more reluctantly, themselves. All the drama of a measles epidemic was portrayed with a dying child. They'd all had first hand experience of such tragedy. They were first hooked on the show; then their anger over the indifference of the 'authorities', the village panchayat or the municipal council, produced catcalls and shouted protest. They quietened down, for help was at hand. Along came the public health team; there was a loud gasp as the hypodermic needle went into one of the dolls.

Out of the corner of his eye Jonathan saw a khaki figure in the open doorway.

'Who do you think the police are after?' he asked Harnam Das, who silently eased his way through the enrapt audience to the policeman. Jonathan watched their animated discussion, then saw the khaki turban disappearing down the lane.

'He wanted to know what the "dil lagi bhat" was all about. He was intrigued by the "funny stuff"'.

Eventually Jonathan left Gunvor and Guntur to an exhausting session, with all the aches and pains that trouble every household. The nurses had their hands full, with a new enthusiasm for innoculations.

He wandered down the lane past the piled baskets of fruit and vegetables, the open, rolled edge gunny sacks of pulses, flour and cornmeal. There were baskets of nuts, dried fruits and sweetmeats. He came to a crossroads and turned left, into quite a different quarter. Though this was the goldsmith's area, it was no more smart than that he had just left. Other than a tatty cabinet or two, displaying cheap gew-gaws, the shops were indistinguishable from their neighbours. In a few one could look through an arch to a back office with an old-fashioned heavy safe.

'Namaste sahib', Mohan Lal greeted him; his hands together as in the Western picture of a child at prayer. He was sitting on a brightly coloured mattress, his back comfortably against a silk covered bolster – a spider waiting for flies. He patted the mattress beside him in invitation. Jonathan squatted and asked after the goldsmith's family and the state of the trade. They liked each other. Mohan Lal had painful recollections of his son's car accident. It was the doctor's skill and compassion that had turned sorrow into relief. Jonathan appreciated his craftsman's ability to turn designs, on grubby pieces of paper, into fine jewellery.

Salvationist women didn't wear jewellery, but from his pocket he took out his notepad and drew a design that had been long in his head 'I want you to make this for my mother.'

'Aisa?' He drew out a pendant on a gold chain from a cupboard behind him. He held it high as an example.

'In silver please, and I want a little stone at the centre.'

Mohan Lal got up and moved over to the shabby Chubb in the inner office. Jonathan followed him. As he watched the goldsmith's routine flourish of keys, he had a mental picture of a young Mohan Lal haggling for his first safe, at the Thieves' Bazaar on the outskirts of Lahore. He could see it being loaded onto a thela, a crude barrow, and trundled the sixty miles by two coolies in rags. Mohan Lal swung open the massive door, bringing Jonathan back to the present. Inside, the safe had been fitted by a local carpenter, to provide a nest of small drawers. There was a pause whilst the jeweller decided which drawer to open. In his hand he held a carefully folded square of tissue paper. He opened it and tipped out a pile of polished fragments of jade. He drew out a second packet, this time red carnelians. Jonathan turned the little piles over with a finger.

'Wohi', he pointed to an oval jade.

But Mohan Lal wasn't satisfied. For a mother, something more valuable was surely indicated. He opened yet another drawer. This time it was a sparkling heap of small diamonds with a few opals.

'These are better,' he said, 'and surely in gold?'

'You don't know my mother; she will love your workmanship, but would never wear anything really valuable.'

201

'What? Afraid of thieves? Surely not in Vulaiyat?' he queried unbelievingly. The word literally meant one's homeland, but under the Raj had come to mean Britain; an image of sound government, honest people and general wealth.

'No,' Jonathan replied,' she thinks of all the poor people in India who can't afford enough food.'

The merchant, rich despite his simple dhoti and well-worn waistcoat was crestfallen.

'I'll give you a donation for your poor patients,' he offered hopefully. 'Or better still,' as the rash thought surfaced, 'I'll pay for a new ward.' He paused as he thought of safeguards, 'If you will call it Mohan Lal Ward, and treat any poor man I send free.'

As they passed through the lofty Amritsar gate in bottom gear, and changed down as they moved into the broader road through the suburbs, the sun beat down on the new market gardens, enterprises of the erstwhile refugees. There were newer crops. Greenstuffs and onions were traditional, but now there were tomatoes as well as potatoes. Tastes were changing. Beyond the patchwork of smallholdings, was a copse of mature shisham trees, as well as the fringe of younger ones, grotesquely shaped from the depredations of the goatherds, pruning every leaf for their voracious animals.

Through the trees Jonathan could see the dome of a crumbling tomb, impressive no doubt, three centuries or more ago. Princes and saints were alike honoured in death.

'I've never been able to find out whose tomb that is. I know that the prophet whose vision of an amalgam of the best in Hinduism and Islam gave birth to Sikhism, came from somewhere around here.'

They reached the main road, turning right for home. This had been a standard military road, broad and flanked by shade trees. Now the verges were littered with twisted ironwork and waste from foundries. There were half a dozen iron chimneys, flames issuing at the base. Bearded men were pouring molten metal into a series of moulds; castings for standard items of farm machinery.

'When I see the way in which whole families, ousted from Pakistan, have made new lives here – and prospered,' said Guntur, 'I can't understand why the Palestinian problem is so intractable.'

It was June again and the hospital was full despite the heat.

The rains had started in the United Provinces to the east; Stewartpur looked daily for the burning sky to cloud over.

Jonathan was not surprised to feel jaded. In a few weeks now they would be able to drive up to Dharmsala for a break.

By the next day he realised it was more than the heat. He must be sickening for something.

'You've only drunk your tea,' Gunvor gave him a reproachful look, as she took his tray away, with an untouched bowl of fruit and cereal.

'Perhaps you had better ask Guntur to see me. I've certainly lost my appetite, which is quite something!' His smile did not disarm her.

'The sooner the better in my judgement. I'll just get Guntur before he's off to morning prayers.'

His friend came hurrying. Despite his customary smile and professional manner, he was anxious.

'You're not on any medication, are you Jonathan?'

'No. We are no longer on malarial suppressants, thank God. And to anticipate your next question, no, we haven't had any meals out.'

The doctor turned to Gunvor, leading her out of the room.

'Have you kept stool and urine?'

'In the loo.'

As he feared, the urine was dark and the stool pale. He returned to the patient and lifted an eyelid for a better view of the sclera. He thought that he detected yellowness. Jaundice was developing.

'I'll take a blood specimen for the lab, Jonathan, but I've little doubt that you are in for a bout of hepatitis.'

'We haven't had any cases have we?'

'No, but it's a long incubation period; you may have been in contact with a healthy carrier any time during the last six weeks. When we have the lab results, I'll inform headquarters. Even if it's only a mild attack, it may be several months before you get your energy back. I wouldn't be surprised if the Colonel suggested bringing your homeland furlough forward.'

Guntur agreed that it would be better for Jonathan to be nursed in his own bungalow, Gunvor and Brunhilde getting any nursing assistance they needed from time to time. The danger of infection was minimal and they knew the ropes.

His temperature rose and he became delirious. Gunvor sat with him, occasionally mopping his face with tepid water and a dash of her precious eau-de-cologne. He only had a sheet over him; a table fan was rotating from its corner pedestal, with a quiet hum. Despite this it remained enervatingly hot.

Gunvor at last admitted that she was tired, and accepted Brunhilde's offer to relieve her. There was a great mutual respect between them. Brunhilde would not forget those that had become her true friends, during those post-war agonies of Germany, not only the devastation and hunger, but the Nuremberg trials and national shame. Some of the first Salvationists she had met were Swedes. An impoverished International Headquarters had been only too happy to let Swedish money and goods, underpin the relief programme in stricken Europe. So there had been an easy rapport. Brunhilde never gushed, but she had a feminine charm that lent a quality to the common life of the small group of expatriates, who each loved his native land, but shared a deep love of their adopted home.

Brunhilde had never expressed an opinion on the Chief Medical Officer but she admired him and was glad to be part of his outfit. She watched his peaceful face. His eyes were closed and his features seemed older and frailer than yesterday. She could have kissed him. She had a sense that this was to be a mortal blow for him; she was already seeing the refinement of grace in a human face.

Gunvor had undressed and fallen asleep on her bed, with just the mosquito-net for privacy, but before sleep had come she too had glimpsed the possibility that Jonathan was drifting away from her. Her thoughts projected into dream. They were both in an orchestra producing divine music. They were both harps, it wasn't clear whether they were plucking the strings or being plucked by unseen hands. She couldn't remember whether any of the great composers had written a double harp concerto; perhaps Mozart had. It was inspiring music. They were definitely in the andante, or even adagio, movement and the solo instruments were weaving a haunting melody and counterpoint. It was as though they had different but complimentary interpretations of the same motif. The dream slowly faded, but not before she was certain that they were the harps, and God was plucking the strings. She awoke refreshed. The vision lingered. The harps were imperfect human instruments; the music was divine. She had no need to turn to God in prayer or to vocalise her needs. God knew that she wanted her husband restored to health.

Jonathan was too ill for many visitors, but they came day by day in droves. Most were erstwhile patients or their relatives, shy and anxious, for their doctor was a fixed star in their firmament. Nothing must be allowed to remove him. They came with little gifts of eggs or ghee or mangoes. Many brought garlands. To them they expressed a prayer, for they had been woven in a temple. Very soon the verandah rail was festooned with flowers. Gunvor had empathy with the simple village people; she was unprepared for the affection and concern of the more sophisticated folk from the mills. She watched one or two of them who had been admitted to the bedroom. They had no words as they gripped his hand. Here was one who had shown them affectionate care; one who knew them intimately.

His temperature was variable and he had moments of lucidity; he even asked for a drink. The mills' friends had ransacked Amritsar bazaar for the more exotic fruits that might tempt him. Instead, he begged Gunvor to eat the luscious alfonso mangoes. She had a better idea, and reduced them to a pulp and made him an iced drink. He smiled his appreciation.

The Colonel flew up from Delhi to Amritsar where Gunvor met him with the car. He had the administrative concern for the hospital and his most senior doctor, but he confided to Dr Mann,

'You only realise what a choice spirit you have with you, when it seems you may lose him.'

Jonathan was lucid when he arrived. The Colonel read the 13th chapter of Paul's letter to Corinth – from a new translation.

What we see now is like the dim image in a mirror; then
we shall see face to face.
What I know now is only partial; then it will be complete;
as complete as God's knowledge of me.

Jonathan managed an 'amen' to the Colonel's intimate prayer, and a smile as they parted.

Gunvor took hope as he asked for fruit and another jug of her lemonade. The remission was short-lived.

Brunhilde relieved her for the night. When the morning came he seemed so drowsy. He was unwilling to eat; by afternoon he was delirious. Gunvor sat holding his limp hand. He moved and there was a weak grip.

The minutes ticked away and as she watched him intensely, his eyes opened. There was an uncertainty in his gaze, which gradually faded and he smiled at her.

'I've been dreaming, or perhaps it was a trance. We were lecturing in America and a film director appeared at two of our lectures. He said he wanted to make a film on our lives and had his script-writer with him. He put me on the spot; he seemed to think that big money, was the way to my co-operation. If I would not take it, a massive grant for the hospital.' He was speaking very quietly and slowly, with long pauses. 'I didn't like him. He wanted to twist motives, make dramas where there were none. He was looking too for racial tensions.' Their eyes held for a moment and he smiled.

'I think he was visualising a sequel to "A Passage to India".

'You were a bit restless and then went very still, as though a nightmare had passed.

'It was as though sun had dispelled night. The director and his scriptwriter had gone. It was not only sunlight but music – glorious music. Everything had become suddenly clear. I no longer saw through a glass darkly.'

He had no more strength to describe how life's greys had become black and white, how opposites were held in harmony rather than conflict. Even his inadequacy had been swallowed up. She sensed his huge content as she stroked his face. He stirred and she leaned over him, and he raised a hand to run his fingers over her dear face in turn. She could just hear him say, 'All will be well.'

His eyes closed and he was very still. It was a long while before she realised that he was not breathing.

Glossary

aisa	thus	ji han	yes sir
angrezi	foreign	koi hai	expatriate
ajao chokra	come here boy	khad	hillside
baba log	children	khuss-khuss	straw packing
bagh	garden or orchard	I.M.S.	Indian Medical Service
bajri	fodder crop akin to maize	lakh	ten thousand
bhisti	water-carrier	maidan	parade ground
bhaja	hand-pumped portable organ	mali	gardener
		mujhe do	give me
bandobast	arrangement	mangta	do you want?
bibi	wife	pahari log	hill people
bidi	leaf-rolled cigarette	pukka	proper
		shifa khana	hospital
burra sahib	boss	sigari	charcoal brazier
cankah	limestone	tal	lake
chaprassi (peon)	messenger	tabla	earthenpot drum
chowkidar	nightwatchman	thik hai	O.K.
chup raho	be quiet	tonga	two wheeled carriage
desi	indigenous		
dhobi	washerman	thunder-box	commode
gaddi	shepherd	vakil	barrister
Ganesh	Hindu elephant god	V.T.C.	Vocational Training Centre
huzur	your honour		